Dedication

For the believers and unbelievers.

The Sorcerer's Tusk

Callumron Series Book Two

D. A. Cairns

Published by Rogue Phoenix Press, LLP
Copyright © 2023

ISBN: 978-1-62420-720-4

Credits
Cover Artist: Alana Cairns
Editor: Sherry Derr-Wille

Chapter One

Ande Bienvenu was furious. Disappointed as well, and surprised in a pathetic self-loathing kind of way. Why? She'd happily spouted her misandrist diatribes whenever given half the chance. Even a quarter of a chance or less. Men were trouble, nothing but a source of agitation and distress. It had only taken one rotten failed relationship for her to figure it out and take a subsequent vow against any further intimate involvement with penis-owning humans. Everywhere she went, worked, and socialized, Ande kept her guard up. Her instinct was honed as sharp as her sarcastic wit. The pleasure she derived from the put-downs, the knock-downs, and the take-downs of men who made any effort to breach her fortress was the single most satisfying thing in her life. Why had she allowed Callum Steele to crawl under her skin?

When staring at the phone failed to bring her sister back online, Ande stood and wandered over to the window of her hotel room at Mercure Istanbul Bomonti. Life was oblivious to her pain, ignorant of her confusion, and she accepted that. Ande was a single woman, a tiny part of an enormous tapestry which mattered to a few more miniscule threads, but was invisible to most of the rest.

She turned to admire the rug hanging on the wall above the bed. It was beautiful: a classic Anatolian pile-woven rug. One of countless other works of art produced for centuries in this ancient city which had embraced modernity without sacrificing her traditional soul. Heavily influenced by the arrival of Islam in the latter half of the eleventh century, the ornaments and patterns mirrored the cultural diversity and political history of the whole region. Thousands of years of civilization expressed with wool pile on a wool warp and weft. Undeniably beautiful.

Her phone rang, interrupting her thoughts. 'Yes?' She listened with her eyes still fixed on the rug. 'Okay. Thank you. I understand.' Ande tossed her phone on the bed and continued her study of the ornate wall hanging. The scarab beetle motif was unmistakable, but many of the other shapes and patterns were mysterious. Perhaps she could sign up for a quick course in Anatolian rug semiotics while she was here.

A section of the woven beetle frame detached and scattered across to the other side of the rug. Ande blinked, stared, then moved closer to see what it was. Of course, it was a bug, but what kind of bug. Certainly not a scorpion. She shuddered suddenly at the memory. In a flash Pitch would be able to tell exactly at what member of the most populous species on the planet she was looking. She wondered if he was still in town, considered calling him, then remembered how upset she was after the phone call with her sister, Adama. She was in no mood for pleasant entomological chit-chat. The call with her sister, like nearly every other occasion they spoke, had been frustrating and galling.

Adama—the beautiful queen. Born in Australia, with exotic looks and a name to match as the only indications of her Congolese heritage, Adama was the baby of the family. The spoiled little brat, inwardly disdainful of her origins, was too determined to be Australian. Worst of all she was a hopeless romantic. Why had Ande called Adama to share her heart? Because her elder sister Fimi had not been available. Adama didn't get it, didn't offer even a glimmer of sympathy, let alone compassion. Ande should have waited for her older sister, because now she lacked the emotional energy to go through it all again with Fimi, even if she could reach her. She didn't have time now. Her taxi would be downstairs waiting to take her on the twenty-minute drive to the airport to pick Callum up. She could use that time for awkward small talk with the driver, or to work out what she was going to say to Callum. Why did she offer to pick him up?

She'd cut him off completely since Mae Sai: blocked his number, blocked him on Facebook. She'd been so hurt by Callum's heartless disregard for her feelings, she had determined in an instant to never speak with him again. If need be, she'd quit her job to avoid having to see his face or hear his voice. Yet here she was again, running around these shrinking circular paths towards the inevitable gut-wrenching question in the eye of the hurricane. Why did she care? How had Callum sharked through the net protecting her beach? How did he get in?

The elevator reached the bottom floor, disgorging its occupants into the foyer which hummed with movement and conversation. Ande strode towards the exit, her heels clipping on the polished tiles, moving quickly, despite her reluctance to go, she ignored a call from the reception desk.

'Miss Bienvenu! Miss Bienvenu!'

With a cigarette hanging from the corner of his mouth, a driver with a mandatory thick black moustache and three days growth, looked at Ande and nodded. 'Miss Bienvenu?'

'That's me,' said Ande as she reached the car and opened the rear passenger door. 'Lose the cigarette mate!'

The driver raised a bushy eyebrow then turned and wandered over to a colleague, commencing an animated conversation. Ande climbed into the cab and stared at him. When he finished his cigarette he flicked it into the gutter, before returning to the cab, and falling into the driver's seat with a grunt.

'I hope you aren't going to charge me for your indulgence.'

He started the engine, and said, 'Airport, yes?'

'Yes. International.'

Ande was thrown back against her seat, as the driver tore away from the curb to enter the crawl of traffic. She'd read that Istanbul was the most congested city in the world with average speeds of five kilometres per hour. Surely Google maps had lied when it forecast a twenty-minute drive to the airport. Ande had been warned not to hire a car, which she thought was a ridiculous idea anyway, and even the taxis were, in the minds of many, a massive waste of money. Yet here she was. Considering The Doghouse was picking up the tab, and she was not eager to get to her destination, she decided to relax and enjoy the privacy and relative silence of a private vehicle steered by an uncommunicative driver. Ande had things to figure out. She needed to pull herself together. Callum's travel dates were in The Doghouse calendar, so the day before his scheduled departure from Dubai, she messaged him, offering to come and pick him up. Why? It was an unnecessary addition of salt to the wound of Ande's ill-considered kindness. Callum's curt response gave her no indication of how he felt about seeing her again. He'd already apologized a hundred times before she blocked him, so what else could he say? Knowing Callum, he would say sorry again. They'd probably be the very first words to leave his mouth.

Something crept along her calf. She flinched and screamed, reaching down to slash her open palm to remove the creature which had taken liberty with her bare leg. The driver turned his head, momentarily.

'Beetle,' he said.

'Whatever!' snapped Ande. She searched quickly in the vicinity of where the bug might have crash-landed. 'What's it doing in here? And was that a horn on its head?'

Silence from the driver prompted her to call Pitch. Ande was not sure whether the driver was flat out rude or just didn't understand English.

'Ande,' said Pitch, 'what a lovely surprise. How are you?'

'Beetle with a horn.'

'Huh?'

'Are there beetles with horns in Turkey?'

'*Anaplophora glabbripennis.*'

Despite her heightened aggravation, Ande laughed. 'You're amazing, Pitch.'

'It's an invasive species: a newly introduced xylophagous species which attacks both deciduous and coniferous trees and has been rightly named a pest. It's a major issue here. Probably the biggest talking point at the conference. What to do about the rapid spread of this new species. Well, not new, but new to the country. Relatively new, anyway.'

'Stop it, Pitch. You just blew up my new word decoder in the first sentence. I was doomed from then. You kill me, really. Does it have a normal name?'

'A normal name? That's a little offensive to us scientists.'

'Okay,' conceded Ande, settling into the rhythm of banter. 'Does it have a common name?'

'Asian long-horned beetle. Why do you ask? Pray tell. After all this time without so much as a *how are you Pitch* or *I miss you Pitch*, why a sudden call about *Anaplophora glabbripennis*?'

'I just had one crawling on my leg.'

'Unless you haven't shaved your legs for several months or you've contracted Treeman Syndrome, that seems highly unlikely.'

'Why?'

'They usually stay in the trees where they are born.

6

Where are you?'

'In a taxi on my way to AVM airport.'

'There you go then,' said Pitch. 'Even less likely. What would an Asian long-horned beetle be doing in a taxi, let alone skulking up the leg of a young woman?'

After carefully examining the seat and not finding the offending insect, Ande decided to drop the subject. There was a pause in the conversation which Ande eventually filled. 'While I have you…'

'Yes?'

'I'm going to meet Callum.'

'And how do you feel about that? You haven't spoken to each other for a while, right?'

'Yes. Not since Mae Sai when I helped him back up to his room after the shenanigans with that crazy woman.' Ande stopped talking. She was reliving the incident again, but she didn't want to. She'd already done it to death. Being remarkably sensitive for a middle-aged male entomologist, Pitch waited on the other end of the line, allowing her time.

A kaleidoscope of colours filled her eyes: a sudden explosion of tears.

'Ande?' said Pitch. 'Are you okay?'

'No, Pitch,' said Ande, snuffling the words out. 'I'm not, but I will be.'

'You're crying. I'm sorry I upset you.'

Ande tried to staunch the flow of sorrow and frustration by wiping and pressing her eyes with the heels of her hands. 'Damn it. I'm not even angry with Callum anymore,' she said. 'It's me, Pitch. Ridiculous,

7

hypersensitive, melodramatic me. Why'd I let him get under my skin? Why did I do that? For this pathetic schoolgirl blubbering? What's the point?'

'Take it easy, Ande,' said Pitch, seemingly unmoved either by the volume of her outburst or its content. 'You obviously have strong feelings for Callum. Otherwise, we wouldn't be having this conversation and your face wouldn't be resembling a waterfall.'

'It's not that bad,' protested Ande, suppressing laughter. Pitch was so good at disarming tension. From some it might have seemed like an insult at worst, or just plain insensitive, but Pitch had both the tone and the timing to pull it off. She took the phone away from her ear and sniffed a few times, before making another attempt at mopping her tears. Satisfied she was sufficiently composed, she brought the phone to her ear once more. 'Thanks, Pitch.'

'You'll see his ugly face soon. Are you ready for that? What are you going to say?'

It was a great question. Ande hadn't given it any thought. She wasn't the type to rehearse big moments. She shot from her hip if inspired to do so, but if she didn't have anything to say, she would simply keep her mouth closed. 'I'm not going to say anything,' she said. 'Let's see what he has to say for himself.'

'You're anticipating something which will give you some ammunition to give him a gobful. Right?'

'I don't know what gobful means, but yes, I'm expecting him to say something.'

Pitch laughed. 'Of course, he'll say something.

He'll be polite. He can't help himself, but what if he doesn't say anything? You know what I mean?'

'What if he wants to pretend like Mae Sai never happened?'

'He could go that way,' said Pitch.

Ande recalled Callum's persistent and childish denial of all the coincidences in his life since he left Australia for Thailand. All those fours kept popping up everywhere, but Callum didn't want to talk about. Didn't want to explore possibilities. He was stuck inside his little rationalistic box. Whatever had caused his uncharacteristic behaviour with what's-her-name was probably something else Callum was quite prepared to ignore. *Deny. Deny. Deny. Forget about that. That's ancient history.* An offence from two minutes ago was still ancient history. This line of thinking riled Ande.

'He's good at denial,' she answered finally. 'You're right. There's every chance that's exactly how he'll play it.'

'And you'll accept that?'

'We'll see.'

'Let me know if you see that *Anaplophora glabbripennis* again, won't you?

'Catch you later, Pitch.'

The creep through Istanbul became a slow painful one as they hit the outskirts of the airport precinct. It was more like a commando crawl through mud under barbed wire. Ande checked the clock frequently. The driver honked his horn just as often, and occasionally threw in a barrage of nasty sounding words. In this belligerently impatient fashion, they eventually arrived at the terminal whereupon an argument erupted between Ande and the driver: the latter insisting that Ande had kept him waiting and he should be compensated for his time. Naturally, it was not expressed anywhere near as succinctly as that. The debate escalated speedily until an airport security guard marched over to intervene, telling the driver to get moving or else. Ande understood little of the brief conversation between them, but only needed to look at the guard's face and see his hand hovering over his holstered pistol to figure out what 'or else' meant.

Ande and the guard watched the driver pull away. Her expression of gratitude to the guard was met with a stony-faced grunt. Ande smiled politely, then entered the arrivals hall. Checking the boards, she located Callum's flight and noted it had landed already. Friends and family filled the available space, buzzing with expectation to greet their arriving loved ones. Ande decided few passengers had passed through Customs and Immigration yet, so she found a place to stand and wait without being obliged to move every thirty seconds. She began to speak to herself quietly, in her head. It was a pep talk she deemed necessary given her hands were shaking a little and she did not feel as solid on her feet as she would have liked. She needed to toughen up. She needed to show nothing beyond the appropriate level of professional pleasure at seeing a colleague. If he was going to pretend nothing happened, then she would match his dogged indifference to the past. She could do it.

She spotted Callum after he had seen her. She'd

been looking in the other direction. She cursed. Now he had another advantage. She revved up the self-talk. *Compose yourself, Ande. Be cool. Be cooler than cool. Be aloof. No emotion, girl. You can do it.*

He was waving at her now. She waved back, pushing out the faintest of smiles which he either didn't notice or pretended not to. He increased his pace, momentarily disappearing, lost in a mob of exiting passengers who were being swamped with displays of affection. Ande strained to see him, but not overly. *Easy,* she cautioned herself. *Don't be bobbing all around the place looking for him, like he's something precious, someone special. He's not.*

Quite suddenly, in the middle of Ande's internal babbling, Callum appeared in front of her and said 'Hi.' Ande responded by doing a completely inexplicable thing. She hugged him. Really hugged him. During the hug, forgetting all about how cool she was going to be, she whispered a greeting into his ear.

Chapter Two

Ron had never heard that simple greeting delivered in such fashion and was intrigued. Ande should have been as mad as hell with Callum. Instead, she had not only embraced him, but also welcomed him with a very intimate whisper. Ron shuddered. What had he gotten himself mixed up in? He had never been to Istanbul before, but he assumed he would be able to find a similar establishment to Mae Sai's Four Club, where he could lead Callum and help him back on track. He was, after all, here to help the pitiful man.

Callum and Ande, with Ron riding on Callum's shoulder, drifted along with the human tide as it floated out of the arrivals hall, dispersing through the exits to the car park or to vehicles illegally stopped, like leaves blown by the wind into the gutter. Guards roamed the curb, glaring and threatening. People seemed unimpressed by the warnings as though they were playing a role in a familiar scene, or as though a sense of entitlement overrode any concerns about actual danger. The trio headed for the taxi stand, but before they reached the confused muddle which might have been a queue, a shadow caught Ron's eye. 'Back soon, buddy,' he said to

Callum as he leapt from Callum's shoulder onto the path and scurried away towards the source of his fascination.

'Hey', said Ron. 'You. Wait a second.'

It was fast, agile, and evidently uninterested in conversation, flickering as it weaved through people, poles, and benches. Perhaps it was a trick of light which made it appear as though it was here but not here. Parts of its body sparkled then disappeared before re-emerging from darkness. Ron felt dizzy looking at it. Focusing on his pursuit, not wanting to lose sight of this creature, he called out a second time, then a third, as the interplay of light and shadow wrought havoc with his eyes.

'I just want to talk.'

Maybe it couldn't talk. Maybe it didn't want to. Whichever was true, Ron stopped. Giving up the chase was disappointing, but he reasoned, as he watched the distance between himself and the creature increase, it was hopeless. For now, anyway. His eyes watered from the effort of trying to discern what he was looking at. The strange little beast might merely have been going about its business: furtive and shy, shocked at being noticed. Or it might have deliberately captured Ron's attention, to lead him somewhere, or simply to lead him away from Callum. Damn!

Ron raced back to the taxi rank to find it empty. There were neither more passengers waiting in the queue nor cabs waiting to ferry them to their various destinations. All gone. This was a busy international airport. Like heavy raindrops splashing on the ground, planes landed regularly, dispersing their loads of suitcases and people.

Usually, the human tide flowed unabated, yet Ron was looking at a dry riverbed. A drought. Where had everyone gone? He searched the vicinity. There were airport officials in all the right places, but no passengers. The security guard at the taxi rank stood silently, still, staring at something or maybe nothing while his counterparts, distributed along the pick-up zone were likewise present but somehow disconnected. There was also a complete absence of celestial beings. Ron could not detect even the faintest trace of any angels or demons.

Inside the terminal, café operators sat, wistfully perusing the dearth of potential customers, while other airport staff walked purposefully backwards and forwards without stopping, speaking, or doing anything other than walking. Perplexed, Ron squatted beside an ATM to think. What was going on here?

'It's clever, isn't it?'

Startled by the voice right beside him, in his ear, in fact, Ron leapt to the side, turned to see who had spoken to him.

'What do you think?' it said in a seductive feminine voice.

Questions swarmed in Ron's mind, but he held his tongue, not consciously ignoring her request for approval, but overwhelmed by what he saw. Her body was serpentine: narrow, smooth, and muscular, as it wound along the floor behind her. The scales shimmered the full spectrum of colours. A meter of this torso was elevated, erect, and her head was an octopus. Her tentacles swayed, moving independently, providing a gentle ride for countless creatures just like the one Ron had followed earlier.

'You have bugs all over your tentacles,' said Ron, to break the silence. 'And your head.'

'Thank you for noticing.'

Her appearance was so magnetic it was impossible not to stare, but as he did, Ron experienced the same discomfort as he had done when trying to keep an eye on the single bug. Now there were many of them. Ron feared the unpleasant and intoxicating light show might bring on an epileptic fit.

'You're welcome,' replied Ron without meaning to speak.

In amongst the flickering squall of insects, Ron saw many eyes. He began to count them.

'Eight,' she said.

'Huh?'

'I have eight eyes. I'll save you the trouble of trying to count them.'

'That's handy.'

The magnificent creature might have smiled, but Ron could not see her mouth. Did she have one? Were her words audible? Or was he hearing them inside his mind, rather than through his ears? He thought of Callum for a nanosecond, then attempted to settle himself from the angst.

'I'm sure you have a thousand questions,' she said. 'And I'd love to answer them, and if there's anything else I can do for you…' She moved closer, breathed the words: 'Just let me know, sugar.'

Ron inched away from her, cringing at her blatant suggestiveness.

'It's so nice to have company. Someone to talk to. Someone to show this to.' A few of her tentacles floated up as she spun her head from left to right, all the way around. Some of the bugs fell off as a result, like carriages breaking loose from an out-of-control amusement park ride. 'To share this with. What's your name?'

'Ron,' he replied. 'Nice to meet you.' Nice to meet you? Where did that come from?

'Walk with me, Ron,' she said as she began to snake her way down through the arrivals hall.

'Ah, don't you mean slither with me?' said Ron. He laughed to make sure she knew he was joking.

Surprisingly she got it. 'Indeed, honey.' Her laugh was sincere yet restrained. 'Slither with me, if you can.'

As he walked beside her, he looked over his shoulder and marvelled at her sleek body, all five meters of it. Had to be at least five meters. What the hell was she? And what was going on here?

Chapter Three

The muscles in Callum's stomach were drawn tight as a drum. Every word which raised its hand for permission to join a sentence lost its nerve and shrunk back to the murky depths of his confusion. He was thrilled when Ande called to offer him a lift and had spent almost the whole trip rehearsing his forty-seventh apology. So miserable about how they had parted, and so desperate to reconcile, Callum even offered lame-sounding prayers to a God who he didn't quite believe in. The warm enthusiasm of her greeting had never entered his reckoning. Every scenario he played out in his mind was based on her lingering rage. Even though she had reached out to him, he half expected her to use the opportunity to berate him again. Callum knew Ande well enough to know that forgiveness was, if not foreign to her, at least a long and difficult road.

As the taxi edged its way back to the city centre, the scene in the backseat was comical. They rode in silence, alternatively, staring out of the window, then straight ahead. When Callum was sure Ande wouldn't see him, he glanced at her. In a laughable game of brinkmanship, she used the same tactic. Who would speak first?

When Ande screamed and slashed at her leg, the stand-off between them was pushed off the cliff into an abyss of insignificance.

'What?'

'Beetle!'

'What?'

'Beetle! Beetle!' said Ande, now squashed against the door as she searched the shadowy back seat for signs of the insect. 'There was one on my leg as we came in. I called Pitch and he said it was an Asian long-horned beetle. That's not what he said at first of course. You know him. He had to show off by telling me the scientific name first, but then I told him to speak English and he laughed.'

She shuffled left across the seat towards him, eyes wide, fearful and searching, until a sudden shift, positioned her half on Callum's lap.

'He said no way there are Asian long-horned beetles riding in taxi cabs,' she continued, sliding further onto Callum's lap.

Callum gulped but remained perfectly still. Any more movement might have caused an embarrassing reaction. Fortunately, she soon bounced off, returning to her seat.

'They can't just disappear,' she said, still looking around feverishly.

'It's pretty dark back here,' said Callum after clearing the awkward dryness from his throat. 'And beetles are pretty small, so…'

'Damn it, Callum.'

She was looking right at him now: a sledgehammer through the ice. Until then, it was as though he was invisible. First, her reticence to speak or even look at him, which was probably due to the discomfort caused by her greeting, and second, when she freaked out over the presence of a beetle on her leg. Even when she landed on him, she hadn't noticed him. Callum might as well have not been there, but now she was fully focused on him. This was the Ande he knew: a blazing, high rise pendulum of emotion. He gulped again, tried to hold her gaze, attempting to say something with his eyes because he couldn't trust his voice.

'You always want to explain everything away, don't you?' said Ande. 'After all we've been through. All we've seen. You're still stuck in your stupid irrational logic.' She never once averted her eyes from his, not for a second. 'I'm telling you I've had two beetles on me, in two different taxis, and they both disappeared. And there aren't even supposed to be any of them here. Not here. Not in the city. Maybe in the bush. On trees. That's where they live, Callum. That's what Pitch told me.'

In the midst of Ande's ranting, Callum decided to deflect her anger by actively listening to her. It was a long shot which might land him in deeper trouble, but he thought it worth the risk. 'What else did Pitch say about these beetles?'

'They're a pest. An invasive species which Pitch and his bug-loving buddies chatted about at length at the conference.'

'That's right,' said Callum, satisfied he was sailing

into calmer waters. 'I remember Pitch saying he was also coming to Turkey. What's the chance of all of three of us ending up in the same country again after our Thailand adventures?'

Ande regarded him suspiciously. He saw her shoulders slump a little, noticed the muscle in her neck slackening. She looked away. Finally.

'Quite a coincidence,' she said. 'If you believe in that sort of thing.'

Emboldened, Callum pressed on. 'Do you know his schedule? It'd be great to catch up with him.'

After a long, excruciating pause, Ande replied in a dispassionate tone. 'Yes, it would be.'

The taxi driver swore as the cab stopped suddenly, throwing Ande and Callum forward. The driver poked his head out of the window and bellowed at the car in front. Evidently, not pleased with the outcome, he withdrew his head, pushed the door open and scrambled out onto the road, heading for the driver of the other car, who Callum could see was also out of his vehicle. Callum wanted to look away but couldn't.

'I swear these drivers are all insane,' said Ande. 'I don't feel safe at all here.'

Their driver managed to shirtfront his new enemy onto the bonnet of the car where he popped a few short jabs into his nose, before releasing the man. Enraged further by the violence done to him and ignoring the river of blood flowing from his nose, he scrambled to his feet, fighting back bravely. Their driver was much stronger though, too strong, absorbing two gut punches before delivering one heavy blow to the man's kidney region which dropped him instantly.

'I don't know how that helps us go any faster,' said Ande, her voice detached, indifferent. 'Now we are stuck behind a driverless vehicle.'

Callum watched as their driver yelled some more at the man before wrenching him up off the road and shoving him back behind the wheel of his car. He slammed the door and stormed back to his taxi.

'I wonder what he said.'

'Probably suggested he drive more carefully and keep his seatbelt fastened,' quipped Ande.

Despite the tension, Callum laughed. Ande looked at him and laughed as well.

'This doesn't change anything, Callum,' she said. 'I'm still mad at you.' She paused, waiting for Callum to answer, but changed her mind. 'I might forgive you one day if you're lucky.'

'I hope so,' said Callum.

'I said maybe.' She glared at him again. 'And only if you're lucky.'

When she smiled, Callum felt like crying, but he restrained himself. He wasn't sure how he felt about luck anymore. Prior to Thailand, before he miraculously survived a plane crash, preceding his encounter with Ron, then the giant scorpion and the demon hordes, in his old life, luck of course was a thing. 'Time and chance happen to all' was a piece of biblical wisdom from Solomon, but no less true for those who didn't believe in God or the supernatural realm. Life itself was a product of an accident, a random gathering of atoms crashing into each other to spawn existence. Everything happened by a natural process. Chemistry 101. Organic molecules forming out of nothing and organizing themselves into larger bio molecular structures which in turn became living organisms. At least that was how Callum understood it. He wasn't a scientist. However, he knew enough to be able to easily reject the arguments of supernaturalists about creation. The world was a beautiful place, mind-blowingly diverse, but it was not produced from the mind of a heavenly creator by the utterance of mere words. Intelligent design? Bunkum. Luck was an acceptable norm. A given. Everyone believed in luck. Even those who said they didn't. For Callum though, the issue had become clouded since Thailand.

The taxi was moving again as the driver manoeuvred around the vehicle in front, making sure, on passing that he again expressed, with extreme articulation, his feelings to the driver who caused the problem.

'Are you hungry?' asked Ande.

Lost in a tumult of confusing emotions, Callum merely grunted. 'Yeah.'

'If we're lucky we'll make it back to the hotel in time for breakfast.'

Chapter Four

'Oh, how my manners have deserted me,' she said. 'It's been so long since I had company. My apologies.'

She stopped suddenly, and Ron found his hand in the wet embrace of one of her tentacles.

'Patricia Courtney-Walsh. It's a great pleasure to meet you.'

Ron's arm rose and fell rhythmically until Patricia was satisfied with her display of cordiality. Not a novice when it came to weird and wonderful things, to the unspeakable and terrifying, to grotesque characters, and inexplicable phenomenon, Ron was nevertheless amazed- and amused. Reflecting on his choice of words, delightful struck him as more apt, yet he felt to use such a word would emasculate him. He had meant to express surprise and amusement, but in a comical way. Faced with such a delectable amalgam of human, serpentine, and octopus- like features, Ron felt Patricia Courtney-Walsh was a decidedly ill-fitting title.

Patricia slithered on with Ron skipping beside her, occasionally forced to swerve or leap out of the path of a careless swishing tentacle. 'Everyone has a story, Ron,' she said. 'Would you like to hear mine?'

The question implied an opt out which Ron was certain did not exist. He was also becoming more certain that Patricia possessed telepathic ability. He had been wondering how this strangely feminine ectoplasmic creature ended up with such a drab human name. Before he could give his consent, Patricia began.

'I was born in Barbados in—'

'Could I have the abridged version, please, Patricia?' said Ron, cutting her off. 'I have business elsewhere.'

The poke in the ear from one of her tentacles caused an unpleasant flashback to his time as Sludgeslick's prisoner in Mae Sai, although it was a pretty cool trick to be able to produce useful shapes from a flabby, amorphous body. Considering Patricia's stunning form and Sludgeslick's horrid-looking but remarkably efficient body, Ron felt a tinge of jealousy. He was nimble and fast, but otherwise not at all imposing. At times that had worked to his advantage, but now he felt like a naughty schoolboy walking the halls of the school while the almighty principal lectured him on his behaviour.

'Here we are,' she said, as though she hadn't poked Ron or been about to regale him with her life story. She turned aside and disappeared through a wall. Ron followed her. 'Welcome to my private place.'

Ron didn't immediately look around as one would normally do in similar circumstances. He was troubled by a new thought, one which prophesied warnings about lonely people, who having finally been rescued from their isolation, at least in part, by the arrival of an unexpected guest, would not readily give up their new friend. Patricia forced his hand once more.

'What do you think?'

It was a very cramped space: an underground burrow with sufficient room for Patricia's coils and tentacles, but not much else. Stuffed into one of those relatively tiny vacancies, Ron wondered what to say. Patricia might not have been especially interested in Ron, as such. More likely it was the concept of 'other', ably embodied by Ron, with which she was interacting. It was pretty one-sided. Ron learned quickly he should play along, but to what end. To save his life? To make his latest incarceration as pleasant as possible? As a delaying tactic, to buy time until he could figure out how to get away? He could have fled at any point, but morbid fascination had trapped him. And now? He decided to run. The wall had other ideas.

'Ron, my darling,' said Patricia. 'What on earth are you trying to do?'

'Run away.'

He'd just walked through the wall, but now was unable to exit. Apparently, Patricia had locked it. As far as Ron could discern the outward signs of emotional injury, Patricia looked hurt. There might even have been a glint of a tear in two or three of her eyes. She turned her head, in a dramatically feminine expression of embarrassment, no doubt designed to make Ron feel like an insensitive and ungracious jerk. So what? He held his tongue.

Chapter Five

'As I said before, I talked to Pitch while I was on the way to the airport to pick you up.' After these words, Ande immediately averted her eyes and sipped her coffee.

Callum allowed it, but he was losing patience. The tinkle of spoons in cups and on saucers provided a harmonic backdrop to the other sounds of breakfast. The air was sticky, stirred ineffectually by ornate overhead fans. He looked around, observing the unobtrusive service amidst the buffet hustle and closely co-located tables. He looked at the tablecloth admiring the beetle motifs stitched into the double folded cotton edges. They reminded him of Pitch, but he didn't want to talk about Pitch.

'Have you been to Istanbul before?'

'Give it a rest, Ande,' said Callum. 'I'm getting a little tired of this dance.'

A glass fell to the floor, smashing both itself and the ambient sounds of the dining room. Sentences were chopped off. Heads turned. Necks strained. Callum knew that Ande would seek further refuge inside the disturbance, but he was determined to push her into the conversation they had to have. The talk which had been circling their relationship like buzzards around a corpse.

The sooner the issue was out in the open and resolved, the sooner they could resume normal communications. All this awkwardness was not only irritating but also exhausting. Second guessing himself had become second-nature to Callum with respect to Ande. In recent times he had been gifted a good deal of clarity, despite the bizarre circumstances. Although he was still coming to grips with that, he was at least heading in a particular direction. Ron had been a gold mine of information and even though the angel had not yet returned, Callum was certain he would. Ande, on the other hand, epitomized uncertainty.

'Oops,' said Ande. 'Remember that time in the office when your coffee mug launched itself off the desk?'

'Ande,' said Callum. 'Can I ask you a question?'

She looked away again as though expecting an old friend to show up.

'Ande?'

In the back of the taxi, it had been easy to avoid eye contact, not really noticeable, but since they walked into the dining room, it was as obvious as a shag on a rock. Ande either looked at him suspiciously and furtively, or not at all. Callum felt uncomfortable too, but they needed to talk about what happened. No good could possibly come from continuing to sweep it under the rug. The rug? The rug under the table was bubbling. There was something underneath it, moving erratically. It caught Callum's attention. He leaned down to investigate, but just as his fingers reached the surface of the rug, the movement stopped. Whatever was under there had not only ceased its motion but also disappeared completely. Not satisfied,

Callum lifted the edge of the rug and had a thorough look.

'Callum?' said Ande. 'Is something wrong?'

Carefully bringing his head up from under the table, Callum simply smiled. The cause of his amusement was twofold; he realized he had grown so accustomed to weird happenings that he was not at all bothered by this one, and secondly, he was now the one injecting, perhaps inventing distractions. After pressing Ande for so long, he was the one doing the dodging. It was not without good reason, of course, but still he knew how it might seem.

'I thought there was something under the rug, but I guess I only imagined it.'

'Maybe you didn't.' Ande smiled. 'You've experienced more than your fair share of weird occurrences. Some imagined. Most not, right?'

Callum smiled 'I've become a sort of beacon for the odd and eerie, haven't I?'

Silence followed: the familiar pattern of intermittence which now characterized all their conversations.

'Callum,' said Ande. 'I know what you want to talk about it and why, and I agree it's probably a pretty good idea, but the thing is…'

'We've got to go, Ande.'

Callum stood, bumping the table, spilling her coffee. He moved to her side and grabbed her hand.

'What?'

'Let's go,' said Callum. 'No time to explain.'

'I thought we were going to talk about the elephant in the room.'

'Something bigger than an elephant is going to be here in a moment. Quick. Come on!'

He was already rushing towards the exit of the dining room when a wave of sound erupted. Screams of horror and a high-pitched scratching, clicking sound. He felt things crunching under his feet. Ande did too, stopping to stare at the floor. Callum jerked her from the paralysis.

'Callum,' she called to his back. 'What's happening?'

They reached the open door where Callum stopped suddenly and turned back to survey the dining room.

People were running everywhere, crashing into each other and colliding with furniture as the clicking, scratching sound intensified and chaos descended. An old man fell, his stick extending from the floor like a periscope. A portly woman tripped over him, stumbling to collapse against a young couple who were running in the opposite direction. Once down on the floor, no one could rise. Trapped under foot, trampled. A little girl flew through the air, her blonde ponytail trailing behind her. There was a random hat. A shoe. More shoes. Rising and falling. Anger. Cursing. There was nothing comprehensible in the cacophony. Nothing recognizable in the scrum of panic-bedevilled bodies.

Callum looked down, concentrating on the stampeding horde on the floor. The people being tossed like clothes in a washing machine camouflaged the cause of the whirlwind. Beetles. Millions of beetles. Billions maybe. Harmless little beetles, but so many of them and the noise was deafening. Frightening.

'Callum,' said Ande, pulling his hand as she pointed at the seething, teeming mass of insects on the floor between the boots and backsides. 'Beetles.'

The door closed without warning, pushing Callum and Ande out onto the footpath. Callum tried to pull it open, but it was stuck. He yanked on the handle again and again, to no avail.

Inside, the people continued to bubble and broil within the sickening human insect soup which Callum now saw was thickening. He moved to the street front, looked in through the floor to ceiling window. The level of beetles was rising. He guessed there were now a couple of centimetres thick on the floor where they hadn't been crushed, or where they had space to lay, one upon another. He watched in despair as the beetle tide rose, subduing the human resistance, slowly devouring it in an unhurried feast.

Callum became aware of Ande's hand gripping his forearm. 'Callum?'

There might have been a question hiding in her fear, but the terror robbed her of words. Callum had seen worse, much worse. He was curiously horrified, but largely unmoved. Questions formed a jostling queue in his mind, impatiently waiting for his attention. The rationalist riff-raff elements had long been exiled from his brain, giving way to no less acute, but significantly more open-minded Sherlockism. This was a supernatural event with a supernatural cause, and clearly fate had brought him to this point in time with the express desire for him to solve the case. He was having an epiphany of purpose.

'Callum?' said Ande, still squeezing his arm. 'What's happening? What are we going to do?'

'Do?' said Callum in a quizzical tone as if the idea of some mitigating action had never occurred to him. 'There is nothing to do. We can't do anything about that.'

'But Callum!'

The victorious beetles begun to disperse, scuttling away from the battle scene, draining out through every available egress. Within minutes, the cafe exodus was complete and all that remained were partially consumed corpses: countless tiny wounds covering every exposed centimetre of human flesh. Approaching sirens wailed in the distance as onlookers massed at the café window like iron filings to a magnet.

'Let's go, Ande,' said Callum. He pried her fingers off his arm and relocated them inside his hand. 'The show's over.'

'The show, Callum?' Ande stopped suddenly. 'The show? How can you be so heartless? The people. Those people…'

Callum gently pulled her away from the mob, squeezing through the ghoulish rubberneckers. Whispers ran through them like fire. Half-truths. Speculation. Meaningless ignorant words.

'We can't do anything,' said Callum slowly spacing out the words for emphasis. 'We should be thankful we got out when we did. If I hadn't felt that one beetle squirming under my foot, if we hadn't been stuck in an extremely awkward stop-start conversation which afforded me the opportunity to actually pay attention to something besides you, which is what I should have been paying attention to. Well, I could go on about the 'ifs' forever, couldn't I?'

The brief pause Callum offered was left empty by Ande.

'But what good does it do,' he continued, 'to wonder endlessly about possibilities? It's time to remove the emotion and investigate. That's what we need to do.'

Ande stopped again, jerking Callum's arm. They were some distance from the café now and had crossed the street. Before Ande could speak, a police car sped past; its siren drowning out any chance of being heard. A brilliant flash of light illuminated the street, more powerful than sunlight. It was followed by an explosion.

'What the hell?'

'That was from back near the café,' said Callum. 'We should go back and check it out.'

'Wait, Callum,' said Ande. 'You realize we are hotel reviewers, right? Not some sort of paranormal investigation team.'

'Maybe we should be,' said Callum. 'Maybe, this is another sign that…'

'That what?' she said, incredulous. 'That we should change professions? What are you talking about? Where is all this coming from?'

Callum sighed. 'It's all coming from somewhere, Ande. I can't deny what's been happening.' He rubbed his chin and the side of his face. 'Things have changed.'

Evidently sensitive to the importance of Callum's words, Ande began to walk, still holding his hand. He allowed it without thinking. It seemed natural. An act of comfort for her. He wouldn't reject her at this point, nor would he draw any inferences about what this meant for their relationship. The much-needed and almost delivered conversation lingered in the subtext. Pretending it meant nothing and trying to simply move on was how Ande was dealing with it, at least superficially. Callum was no genius when it came to the capricious mystery of women, but he knew enough to know there was always something else. There was always more to the story. Always more beneath the surface. He was prepared to go there, to dive deep, to face the issue, but his good intentions were redundant in light of Ande's reluctance. Refusal. She was undoubtedly still hurting, but for whatever reason she was unwilling to discuss it.

After five minutes of walking along Sokak 4, they reached St Sophia's Square, which among other points of interest, was home to Hagia Sophia Museum. As there was no rush to be anywhere, Callum suggested they enter and have a look around. It might prove a nice distraction. Still shaken, Ande seemed unconvinced, but after some cajoling, including making mention of the world-famous mosaics made of gold, silver, glass, terracotta, and stone, she relented, and they climbed the staircase.

'Some of the mosaics here are more than six hundred years old,' said Callum.

'Nice to know you still have your hotel reviewer's hat on despite leanings in another peculiar direction.'

'It isn't at all peculiar when you think about it, Ande.'

Normally very keen on architecture, but currently distracted, Ande ignored the impressive features of the ancient museum which had a rich history dating back to its first incarnation in 537 AD, when it first opened as a place of worship.

At the ticket booth, Callum handed over two hundred lira, not yet able to shake off the discomfort or intense curiosity about what happened at the café. Ande was entrenched in her silence despite the occasional characteristic outburst. They weren't holding hands anymore, but walked in step, neither one of them lagging or pushing the pace. It was as though they had walked together in unison for years. Feeling each step, enjoying each moment. Callum's relationship with Ande was a bewildering knotted mass of ragged strands. Not for the first time, Callum realized his affection for Ande was as far from collegial and cordial as the moon was from the earth. Never mind Mars and Venus. The gods of war and love respectively, forever destined to be unequally yoked: both strange bedfellows and obvious companions.

Ron entered Callum's thoughts now. Where was he? He could have answered some of Callum's questions about the bloody beetle stampede. He would have shared Callum's enthusiasm to probe its origin and cause. He would have talked incessantly, filling all the empty spaces with a marvellous mixture of wit and stupidity. He would have only held Callum's hand if he intended some devilish trick to embarrass him, like on the plane to Istanbul during which Ron caused a hilarious face-palming epidemic. Ron inevitably took his jokes too far, but Callum had come to see them as harmless attempts to provide excitement in the dull troughs between their adventures. Callum would have enjoyed Ron's company. Not confusing. Not uncomfortable. Not like Ande who stirred his feelings to the extent he felt like a load of laundry in a washing machine. As ridiculous as it sounded, Ron was safe.

Where was that cheeky little demon?

Chapter Six

'I'm sorry to cause offence, Patty,' said Ron. 'But you've sort of got me trapped here like a prisoner.'

Some of Patricia's eyes opened wide. 'You're a guest. Not a prisoner.'

Ron was through wasting time. Every so often he found himself in dire circumstances, potentially life-threatening, with no obvious escape and no saviour likely to arrive in the nick of time. At these times he clothed himself in bravado, expressing a devil-may-care attitude to his foes, and a fatalistic attitude to his situation. This was another of those occasions.

'The word *guest* implies one has some freedom in relation to accepting or declining invitations, and having accepted, to then choose one's own time of leaving.'

'Who is one?' Patricia giggled as Ron face-palmed himself. 'What are you doing, Ron?'

'I want to leave,' said Ron. 'I have things to do, and I am just not enjoying your company.'

Again, a wounded look appeared on Patricia's head and certain parts of her body. Her tentacles changed colour, dimming to grey from vibrant green. Even the bugs noticed the change of temper, as they largely deserted their tentacle fields for safer hiding places. 'Ron, why are you being so cruel?'

'Look,' said Ron. 'If there is some other reason, a valid reason for you incarcerating me then please inform me. Otherwise, I'm leaving.'

'Incarcerating? Whatever do you mean, Ron?'

'I mean keeping me here against my will. I want to go, but you won't let me. Incarcerated. Imprisoned. Locked up! Get it?'

Patricia held her ground, facing away from Ron: randomly twitching tentacles, the only sign of her irritation. Ron waited to see if she would say anything. He reasoned she was exerting as much self-control as she could muster. As she seemed naturally unpredictable, Ron knew she was the kind of creature who only exuded charm until such time as she was slighted in any way. Becoming an enemy of Patricia was probably as easy as falling out of a tree. She possessed coiled, potential anger, which the discerning soul detected and avoided arousing. If you burned her, she would smoulder with vengeance for the rest of her waking days and all the way to the far end of eternity.

Finally, she turned her eyes upon him, all eight of them. Ron experienced another cold shiver of dread. 'Can I tell you something, Ron?'

'Tell me I'm free to go and wish me well.'

A tentacle appeared around Ron's neck, quickly winding around the length of his body. He squirmed in resistance but quickly succumbed to her superior strength. Soon, he struggled for breath, wheezing out a few words.

'Something else then?'

'Listen carefully, motor mouth,' said Patricia. 'This could have gone one of two ways.' She relaxed her grip on Ron slightly. 'You chose the hard, unpleasant way. The way that made me angry. The way that led to pain. The way that prevented us from ever being friends. The way that guaranteed animosity between us. The way…'

Taking advantage of some extra oxygen in his lungs, courtesy of less tension around his chest, Ron interrupted Patricia. 'Okay. Okay. You made your point. You brought me here against my will hoping I would be pleased and grab the opportunity with both hands. Hoping that you and I would become besties and live happily ever after. Hoping…'

This time Ron was unable to finish, for as fast as he spoke, his words only served to further anger Patricia, who demonstrated her displeasure by squeezing Ron's mid-section harder.

'I'm not going to kill you, Ron, but I can hold you like this indefinitely. Tighter. Looser. Tighter. Looser. Really tight.' She presented a serpentine grin.

Ron was trying to find his happy place, to enable him to endure Patricia's monologue and worse, the actions demonstrating her words. He was thinking about Callum and about the awakening. The angel. Ande. Sludgeslick. He recalled the events in Mae Sai. Ande. Before that, and before that and further back. The poltergeist unit, the academy, school, Mum, and Dad. Mum and Dad? What?

A violent expulsion of air. Falling. The floor. The pain. Gasping.

'Oops,' said Patricia. 'Perhaps I got a little carried away there.'

On his hands and knees, Ron clutched at his throat, massaging it. His chest too, bruised and aching, received some attention as Ron tried to find his voice and his brain in the midst of the fog of near suffocation. He couldn't recall ever being as close to death as that. Instinctively, he realized he had only survived because of good luck rather than good torture management on Patricia's part.

'It's all because of the Book of the End, you know,' said Patricia. 'It was foretold, and who can foresee what will come of ancient foretellings?'

Hoping to hell that Patricia's question was rhetorical, Ron concentrated on getting his breathing back to normal. Having missed the early warnings of her deranged and derelict state of mind, dismissing them as idiosyncrasies, Ron now experienced the full weight of this creature's madness. On a whim, a churlish tantrum, Patricia had nearly killed him, and now she was babbling about some prophecy from the Book of the End. He needed to stall her further; needed some more time to plan his escape. Although it was true Patricia was insane, she was not stupid, and she had a significant physical advantage over him. Considerable care would be required to avoid injury or death.

'Are you familiar with the Book of the End?' she said. 'Of course, you are. We all know it inside and out. We must. It's drilled so deeply into our minds we can never be free of it. Never escape its brooding sophistication. Its ghoulish descriptions of spectacular abominations.'

To pass the time, while Patricia engaged in her theatrics, Ron strolled through the pages of the Book of the End in his mind. He had learned many years after, his mind having been soaked in devilish propaganda, that the Book of the End was essentially the same book which concluded the collected works of divinity called the Bible. Written by John while on exile on the island of Patmos, the Book of Revelations formed the spine of the Book of the End, but it had suffered substantial revision. It was easy enough to remove a religious truth and replace it with another one. The key to the success of such blasphemy was directly linked to the magnetism of the leader.

Joseph Smith convinced many men and women to ignore the fact that he was a proven liar and swindler who was prone to using violence to make his point, and accept that he had received a new revelation from God. The Latter-Day Saints were simply a cohort of demons assigned to Joseph Smith who only needed to continue to incrementally blow arrogance inside his burgeoning hubris to create a powerful modern prophet.

'You know that most of the book was authored by a follower of Jesus Christ,' said Ron.

He was desperate to get involved in this discussion but was still uncertain of Patricia's mood. He couldn't risk igniting her rage again until he was ready to run or fight to the death. He smiled to himself. If he wanted to, he could start a fight to the death now. It wouldn't last long though, and it would certainly be Ron himself who lost. Aside from the fact she was wrong about the Book of the End and growing more erroneous with every word, she was sounding increasingly calm. Why was she talking about the Book of the End anyway? Where was this dreary monologue headed? Soon, he would be ready to take Patricia on. In the meantime, he had to decide whether to remain silent, which was incredibly difficult for Ron, or dive into the conversation.

Patricia moved away from him, appearing to lose interest in Ron although still talking as though she required an audience or imagined such adoration. 'That image of the sword coming out of Jesus' mouth is terrifying. Don't you think?' she said. 'For years I was fearful of that sword. Scared of truth, scared of the bearer of that sword and that fool's ramblings about victory and glory amid the ghastly visions, and yet it isn't true at all. Here we are, right? The Prince of the Powers of the Air has dominion. We do what we like. We do his bidding, and he bids us do whatever he likes, and we bid others do as he bids us and others to do like what we do.'

'Knock it off,' said Ron, finally unable to bear anymore of Patricia's nonsense. It seemed he was doomed to run from the malevolent clutch of one conceited gasbag to another. Surely, the other side weren't so full of themselves. Ron thought of the angel he had met in Callum's hotel room on the night of his awakening. There had been a dignified simplicity and sincerity in the way he spoke. Ron had not yet met anyone in the kingdom of darkness who spoke with such powerful humility. Ron realized Patricia was still speaking. 'I said knock it off.'

Patricia stopped and whirled certain parts of her

body in Ron's direction. With pieces flying and spinning all over the place it was hard to tell in which direction she was travelling. The sight of bug-laden tentacles, eyes and flaccid skin folds presented a confusing and disorienting image. While Ron was trying to ascertain whether he was in danger, an eye appeared immediately before his own. This eye probed his, deeply investigating, searching for something. Ron endured the examination in frozen suspense.

'I don't know what to do with you, Ron,' she said. 'I was told to keep you here. To keep you away from Callum, but that was the extent of the instruction. I thought I might be able to extract some advantage for myself while carrying out my orders. I hoped to ingratiate myself with Slerfgerg, and at the same time amuse myself with the company of a pet. But now…'

'But now,' said Ron, nodding at Patricia's unsurprising disclosure. Of course, Slerfgerg was behind this. 'You are going to let me go, and if anyone asks, I'll say I got away using my extremely impressive repertoire of escapology skills.'

'That wouldn't do at all,' said Patricia.

'No?'

'No.' She backed away from Ron once more, withdrawing her ocular detective. 'I would be blamed for letting you go. I would be punished for my failure. Surely, you can understand that I couldn't do that. And who would believe that you overpowered me? Or even outwitted me?' She laughed. 'It's preposterous, Ron. Preposterous! Look at you.'

'Did Slerfgerg say anything else about me?'

For a moment, the hordes of insects on Patricia's body ceased all movement, but just for a moment. Ron studied Patricia searching for any weakness, any stray word, any opening through which he could enter her fortress and disarm her. He certainly couldn't run. She was right about that.

'Slerfgerg?' said Patricia in a strange, wistful tone. 'I hardly know him.'

A fleeting change, a darkening in the hue of the skin around her eyes told Ron she was lying. She had blushed. Not only did Patricia know Slerfgerg, but she knew him very, very well. Ron's mind raced off down the track which led to unpleasant images and concomitant feelings of nausea. A few flashing pictures of Patricia and Slerfgerg in intimate positions caused a disturbing pulsing in his veins, and bile to rise in the back of this throat.

'What did you do to fall so far out of his favour?'

'I could ask you the same question,' said Patricia.

'Yes, you could.'

The pieces were slotting together nicely now in Ron's mind. Slerfgerg was looking to take Ron out, but unlike before when an assortment of inept minions had been given the task, Slerfgerg was now bringing in some heavy artillery. Thwarted by circumstances in Thailand, Slerfgerg had needed to bide his time and wait for another opportunity. There were still many unanswered questions of course. The biggest, the glaring riddle, was why Slerfgerg was after him. It was way too much trouble to go to to simply reprimand him for impertinence. He hadn't done anything wrong as far as he knew, other than be an irritating personality. Patricia would reveal some of these answers if he played his cards right.

'Well?'

'Yes,' said Ron.

'Don't be so dense.'

'Given the situation and how aggrieved I feel at the way you have treated me, you can appreciate me not being terribly interested in exchanging information with you, though I admit to being curious about a few things.'

'Okay, Ron,' said Patricia, relaxing a little, withdrawing her bulk to give him some more room. 'I can play along. I'm feeling generous and I can't see any harm in it.'

'I'm going to tell you everything I know and you're going to tell me everything you know about me and Slerfgerg, and then you're going to release me.'

Ron didn't see the tentacle sliding towards him from the right until it was coiled around his waist, then his chest, then his throat. He was back on the precipice of death once more.

'I don't know how you concluded from my words that I was willing to enter some sort of deal with you,' said Patricia, suddenly releasing her grip on Ron. 'I don't think there is any possibility of that happening. We are not equals, not in any way. You do not have any bargaining power. You'll tell me what I want to know, or I'll hurt you.'

Ron managed a smile. 'I see.'

Chapter Seven

Under a radiant full moon, Pitch waxed lyrical about his favourite subject while Callum and Ande sampled Turkish culinary delights between sips of Okuzgozu, exchanging occasional glances in a shared reaction to Pitch's enthusiasm. When Pitch paused for a sip of the wine himself, Callum seized the opportunity.

'Terrific wine, isn't it, mate?'

'I can taste the cherries and raspberries,' said Ande.

'Oh, and the mint,' added Callum. 'Delightful.'

'Okay, you two,' said Pitch. 'I know beetles aren't the most interesting topic in the world, but seriously. Aren't you even a little bit amazed by what I'm telling you?' He emptied his glass and took the bottle from Ande's outstretched hand. 'Thank you.'

'What I'm more interested in,' said Callum, 'is the particular group of beetles in the café at the hotel this morning.'

'The ones that appeared *en masse* and *ex nusquam*?' said Pitch.

Ande nearly choked on a mouthful of lamb.

'The very same,' said Callum despite not knowing

what Pitch had said.

Pitch smiled, and called Callum's attempted bluff. '*Ex nusquam*. Out of nowhere.'

Having recovered her composure, Ande cleared her throat and sipped from her glass.

'Let's talk beetles then,' said Pitch.

'Do beetles swarm?' said Callum. 'Is what we saw today typical beetle behaviour? I've never seen that before. Is it normal?'

'There are over 350,000 species of beetle so it's a little hard to generalize in some areas, and I confess to not knowing everything there is to know about beetles.'

'You're too modest, mate, I'm sure.'

'What about that one?' Ande pointed to a one-centimetre-long specimen inching its way across the table from beneath Callum's plate.

'Looks like a juvenile stag beetle.'

Ande shuddered involuntarily. 'I feel like there are bugs everywhere.'

'There are,' said Pitch.

Callum watched the beetle crawling until it hit the saltshaker, then resuming after a period of contemplating the problem, attempting to go over, before finally deciding it was preferable to go around the obstacle. The beetles which invaded the café earlier evidently recognized no such impediments. Was it their numbers? The sheer, seething mass of twitching carapaces which produced such monstrous behaviour? It had been an attack, but for what purpose? It would be best to take Pitch to the scene of the crime and let him investigate something tangible, presuming there was some physical evidence of the event remaining. 'Let's go to the café. I want you to have a look.'

In response to Callum standing as he delivered the suggestion, Pitch said, 'Can we finish dinner first?'

Callum stayed standing, projecting urgency.

'Sit down, Callum,' said Ande. She handed him his glass of Okuzgozu. 'Chill.'

'They've probably cleaned up all the evidence anyway,' said Callum, reluctantly taking his seat.

Ande winced. 'I hope so.'

Lowering his glass, Pitch redirected the conversation. 'You were asking about the swarming activity of beetles?'

Poking the beetle on the table with his index finger, Callum said, 'Yes.'

'Some do. Swarming leaf beetles become active in large numbers following the first storms of the spring to summer season. Especially in North Queensland. They're quite destructive, as are a number of herbivorous beetle species. Plague soldier beetles form huge mating swarms but then disperse quickly afterwards. European chafer beetles too. Now I think about it, I think most of them swarm during their mating seasons. The sexual riot goes on for a day or two and then all the females go to ground or into trees to lay eggs.

'Okay,' said Callum. 'I'm going to go out on a limb and say that swarming is a normal mating season activity.'

'Let's go with that,' said Pitch.

'The problem is that the swarm we witnessed this morning seemed more about food than sex. Locusts are infamous for their feeding swarms. Bees swarm,' said Callum. He paused, scratching his chin. 'Or is that just a collective noun for bees?'

Pitch smiled. 'It's both. What you saw might well have been a one-off event, but it sounds like…like something very unnatural. Mainly because of where it occurred. Urban areas are not typically overrun by bugs. Heavy human populations tend to not play nicely with insects. Bees and butterflies? Okay, but the others, even beetles? We're not huge fans of bugs, are we?'

'There's another one,' said Ande.

'And another,' added Callum. 'Where the hell do they all suddenly come from?'

Ande stood. Callum stood, Pitch did likewise. Chairs, pushed backwards with force, crashed to the floor. Beetles assembled, conglomerated on the table. Some of the female patrons screamed when they saw what was happening at the other table; screaming louder when the swarm was replicated on their tables.

'It's happening again, Callum,' said Ande, grabbing hold of his arm and squeezing it, pulling him closer to her. She trembled.

Pitch stared at the shimmering, clicking mass of insects on the table. 'Remarkable.'

It was not a frightening situation. Callum had reacted out of instinct, without feeling any fear. There was no threat, nothing to suggest they would be harmed in any way, yet his heart beat faster as images of this morning's deadly swarm invaded his mind. Ande was afraid. Perhaps it was contagious.

'This is a mating swarm, right, Pitch?' said Callum, resisting Ande's attempt to pull him further away from the table which was blanketed by black, brown, and orange bugs.

'Can you smell that?' said Pitch, overlooking Callum's question in favour of something more interesting.

Callum paused, sniffing the air theatrically, gesturing in the fashion taught to him by his high school teacher. A method to ensure that none of the particular gas being 'studied' entered the respiratory system via the nostrils. A wafting movement provided enough sensory input without putting the inhaler at any risk. 'No.'

'Me neither. So, they aren't Carabids.'

'What are they doing?' said Ande. 'It looks like a war.'

'Of course,' said Pitch, stepping close to the table and reaching out his hand.

'Pitch!' said Ande. 'No!'

'It's fine, Ande,' he replied, holding the beetle between his thumb and forefinger. 'Relax. These are bombardier beetles, different kinds, but all bombardier beetles, I'm sure, and I can see they are squirting each other, fighting. I don't know why, though.'

'Squirting?' said Callum. 'You mean urinating?'

'No,' said Pitch, squatting now at the edge of the table to gain a better view of the action. He put the beetle in his hand down in the middle of the melee. Suddenly, he snapped his head back, lost balance and collapsed on his backside. Laughing, he removed his glasses and examined them. 'Remarkable.'

'I'm glad you're finding all of this so fascinating, mate, but can you please explain what the hell is going on?'

Pitch cleaned his glasses and refitted them to his face before resuming his crouching position at the rim of the elevated battlefield. He began filming the scene on his phone, providing commentary: 'Bombardier beetles have this really cool defence system. They're using it on each other now, even though they are not predators. They don't seem to recognize members of their own species. It's not unusual, of course, for bombardiers to hang out with other beetles when not hunting.'

'Of course,' said Callum.

'Basically, they have a cannon at the tip of their abdomens with which they squirt—quite accurately, too, by the way—their enemies. The popping sound you can hear, the one you might not have realized was popping, is the sound of their cannons firing a hot noxious chemical spray. The spray is produced from a reaction between two chemical compounds hydroquinone and hydrogen peroxide.'

'I have a number of questions, Pitch.'

'Shoot,' he said. 'Or squirt if you prefer.'

'You're hilarious.'

'Can you two clowns please quit the joking?' said Ande. 'I don't see anything funny here at all. Our dinner was just rudely interrupted by a bunch of fully armed angry beetles.'

As the trio viewed the action, the screams abated,

and likewise the gasps and other expressions of discomfort and horror. The insects were not interested in the humans, so the latter simply watched the novel spectacle with a mixture of amusement and bemusement. Soon, the riot itself ebbed as the dead and wounded plummeted to the floor, leading to the slow, yet inevitable abandonment of the war zone.

Pitch continued to film until the last of the living insects had disappeared. 'Your questions, Callum?'

'What would cause what we have just seen?'

'Ah,' said Pitch, attending now to his phone, watching the footage he had captured. 'That would require considerable speculation on my part. I've never seen anything like it. In a restaurant of all places. I could write a paper on this.'

'Never mind the paper, mate,' said Callum. 'Start speculating.'

With their table now free of insects, Pitch and Callum resumed their seats. Pitch turned his phone off and placed it face down on table, pushing aside some tiny corpses to make space.

'You're just going to carry on as though nothing happened?' said Ande. 'You can't eat off those plates. Or drink from those glasses. You can't do that. We should go.'

'We should ask the waiter to clear the table, bring us fresh glasses and another bottle of Okuzgoza,' said Callum. 'What say you, Pitch?'

'Capital idea, old man.'

'For God's sake,' said Ande. 'Are you two

insane?'

Callum and Pitch exchanged glances, but it was Callum who answered, despite knowing it was a rhetorical question. 'I don't think so, Ande.' He smiled. 'Something amazing just happened and I reckon we should talk about it.'

'Why?'

'Why not?' said Pitch.

'Why not indeed,' added Callum.

Ande's hands darted to her hips, and she added a furious stamp of her right foot to her show of disapproval. 'I'm leaving.'

Without commenting, both men watched Ande walk away before resuming their conversation. Callum smiled. He knew Ande well enough to know she often overreacted but did not carry the torch of angst for long. She might even re-join them once she'd shaken off the creeping jitters brought on by the beetle gate crashers. For now, Callum was much more interested in this new phenomenon. Like a tadpole which grows into a frog and upon leaving the water discovers the world looks different, Callum was much more aware of the other parallel world in which he wandered since his awakening in Mae Sai. Whatever suite of possible explanations he had assembled for a particular mystery, supernatural causation had now come firmly into the frame.

'Scorpions,' said Pitch, leaning back away as a team of waiters fussed over the table like seagulls competing for food scraps.

'Scorpions,' repeated Callum. 'And now beetles.

Makes you glad to be an entomologist, doesn't it?'

Soon the table was cleared, and fresh glasses appeared which were quickly filled with Okuzgozu. The bottle was then positioned on the table for easy access should refills be required, which they certainly would be. Pitch picked up his glass, lifting it and tilting it towards Callum. 'Cheers!'

'Cheers!' said Callum, reciprocating the gesture, tapping his glass against Pitch's. 'I almost feel like this is what I do now.'

'What do you mean? Drink local wine and talk about insects and arachnids?'

Callum emptied his glass, then refilled it. He offered a top-up to Pitch, who nodded, holding out his glass. 'Do you believe in coincidence, Pitch?'

'Sure. Happens all the time.'

'What does it mean? What's it for?'

'Just the universe being a smartarse.'

'People say things like that a lot,' said Callum. 'But they don't believe it, do they? You know, the universe is telling me something. The universe is smiling on me. The universe this, the universe that, as though the universe is a person.'

'Classic anthropomorphism.'

'Exactly,' said Callum. 'The universe is not a person. It can't do anything. It just is, and any interaction between people and the universe has to be natural and impersonal, right?'

'Of course. But people say all sorts of things they don't mean. Just parroting expressions they heard from somewhere else without giving them any thought. No examination of their value. Just words.'

'Words for what purpose? To fill holes in the conversation? To deflect? To avoid?' Callum stared at his glass of wine. 'Why do we waste time with meaningless words?'

Pitch smiled. 'That is a question perhaps best left to hash-smoking philosophers in Amsterdam.'

'Okay.'

'We, on the other hand, have more pressing matters to address. More urgent mysteries to solve.'

'Right,' said Callum without conviction, still staring at his glass. His thoughts were running around an open field, waving their hands. Aside from the immediate problem, there were Ande and Ron and a rising tide of dissatisfaction with which to deal. Callum had not been so naïve as to think his life would simply return to normal after Mae Sai, but if he was honest, he had fooled himself into thinking he was still in control. He kept being thrown into bizarre situations in which he was faced with things he could barely accept as real let alone comprehend. Ron kept him grounded. He was becoming increasingly dependent on him, but where was he now?

Chapter Eight

Once more Ron emerged from a thick soup of asphyxia, blinking furiously, gagging, retching, trying to reconnect to reality. Patricia had lost interest in him whilst unconscious but now he was awake, she spun her collection of twirlable body parts to inject herself into the entire emptiness of space around him. This again denied him any opportunity to think. Ron was fast on his mental feet, but being robbed of oxygen was not conducive to problem-solving or any sort of thinking. He needed a little break, to figure out how to get away from Patricia, but like a cat playing with a lizard, she only allowed him time to catch his breath, before hurting him: striking, tossing, squeezing. It was beginning to feel like a hopeless situation.

'Welcome back,' she said in a voice oozing malice. 'Ready to talk now? Civilly and informatively.' She smiled a bizarre approximation of courtesy. 'Can you do that, Ron?'

Fearing a third attack on his respiratory system would prove fatal, Ron panicked, gushed the only suitable answer. 'Yes, ma'am,' he said. 'Anything to please you. Anything. What can I give you? What can I tell you? Only please, please don't choke me again. I...please. Please. What is your pleasure?'

'You're a terrible actor,' said Patricia, scowling at her wretched prisoner. 'Suddenly a snivelling sycophant willing to do or say whatever necessary to avoid a little pain and discomfort.' Her largest eye leapt to Ron's face. 'Very, very unconvincing.'

Ron resisted recoiling from her, enduring the interrogatory glare whilst mulling over her saying his near death by suffocation amounted to nothing more than a little pain and discomfort. He clenched his fists, swallowed hard several times, ordering his eyes to remain locked onto hers: defiant. He was outmuscled, and neither speed nor agility would save him. Investigating his inventory of tricks brought no hope. Like that fat slug demon in Mae Sai, Lutevo, Patricia seemed to be especially sensitive to falsehood, so he would not be able to lie his way out. He had but one card to play.

It was not the weapon of choice for servants of the Father of Lies, but employed judiciously it could be effective. Theoretically, anyway. Ron had never tried it. He'd only heard of others using it. He'd scoffed at those pusillanimous creatures, driven by fear to use this weapon, almost believed himself to be above such weakness. However, desperate times not only called for desperate measures but necessitated the exile of pride.

'I will tell you everything you want to know,' said Ron. 'Everything I know. Whatever may be of interest to you.'

'The truth?' said Patricia, suspicion dripping from

her lips. 'Are you really going to tell me the truth?'

Ron nodded. 'I need to find a human called Callum. He is supposed to be with me, or I'm supposed to be with him. We're supposed to be together.' Callum detested the snivelling tone in his voice, but ploughed on. 'He might need me. He might be in trouble.'

Patricia laughed. Loudly. So loudly the sound hit Ron in concussive waves, beating him further into the corner. 'Ridiculous,' she said when she recovered her composure. 'You can't be concerned with the welfare of a skin bag. Why would you be?'

Ron had not expected Patricia's reaction. The claustrophobia was augmented by Patricia's derision, which was thick in the air, leeching into Ron's bloodstream in painful gasps. He might be permanently damaged. A whirlwind of raging indignation erupted in his heart, strengthening his will, his desire to not only live, surviving this creature's capricious wrath, but to unload a wicked and unforgettable revenge on her. The vanity of such impotent anger only added fuel to the fire. He would fight her until his very last breath.

'There are bigger things going on, Patricia. Bigger than you realize. I don't know exactly why I was assigned to Callum. In fact, I suspect it was a spiteful and misguided attempt to set me up for a potentially fatal failure.'

'Who assigned you?'

'Our mutual friend, Slerfgerg.'

'Slerfgerg?' Patricia, pondered, paced a little, as much as a serpentine creature can pace. 'Of course.'

Not wishing to aggravate her, Ron allowed the

implications of this new information to run around in her mind. Interestingly, and pleasingly, he could tell it was new information. Slerfgerg had ordered Patricia to capture and detain Ron for an undisclosed purpose. Patricia's reaction was an unexpected victory for Ron, although he didn't know exactly why. Out of necessity, Ron was learning to read Patricia very quickly. He had surprised her, which meant that Slerfgerg had not told her anything about Ron's original mission, nor who had given him the assignment in the first place. Slerfgerg might or might not have told Patricia some elements of truth to underpin the genuineness of his orders. Not that he would have needed to do that. Underlings didn't have any right to question commands. They were generally told as much or as little as the commanding officer deigned fit for the accomplishment of the mission. Ron knew that, so he was still in miry, murky water figuring out what it all meant. Slerfgerg could have just as easily misinformed Patricia. Maybe Ron could trick Patricia into revealing everything she knew even as he spilled his guts to her.

'He wants to know what happened in Mae Sai.' Patricia had stopped moving around, evidently finding a calm place from which to again exert her authority. 'Don't tell me he could have just asked you himself. You've gone rogue, Ron. You are not reporting to Slerfgerg or anyone else for that matter. You're making it up as you go along. Slerfgerg believes something happened in Mae Sai which caused you to abandon your oath of allegiance to the forces of darkness.'

Ron snatched one of Patricia's tentacles as it

wafted past his face and bit it, clamping down with every ounce of strength in his jaw.

Patricia howled, flinging Ron from one side of the room to the other where the impact with the wall ejaculated the air from his lungs inside a final desperate grunt. He looked up to see her staring at him. Not touching him. Not strangling him, not choking him. Just boring holes in his head with every one of her eyes.

'I'm not having fun anymore, Ron,' she said. 'You hurt me. And not just my tentacle. My feelings, Ron. I've been very patient and kind with you. I'm not usually like that.'

There seemed no other possible course for Ron to pursue, so he bit Patricia again. This time chomping harder and deeper, compressing his anger into the force of his jaws. He knew he'd soon be flying across the room again. To prepare, he purged the air from his lungs, but instead of the rush of wind by his ears, he experienced rising pressure in them and in his lungs as Patricia wrapped another tentacle around him. She didn't make a sound, nothing at all. He'd hurt her worse than the first bite, but whatever pain she felt was swallowed or buried inside her formidable wrath. Her face showed the strain of her struggle for self-control.

'Talk to me about Mae Sai before I kill you.'

It was an empty threat. Patricia appeared to lack self-control, but her tantrums were clearly calculated. She could have quite easily killed him several times, but she always managed to stop one step, one second short of the final blow.

Ron squirmed in her grasp, twisting his head, bending his neck as best he could, trying desperately to sink his teeth into her again. He couldn't reach though.

'Ron, this is pointless,' she said. 'Just tell me what I want to know, and I'll let you go.'

Panting from the exertion, Ron relaxed in Patricia's vice grip. He would bite her again as soon as he had the opportunity, but he would need to talk to her, to distract her. 'There was some trouble in Mae Sai, but it really had nothing to do with me or Callum. A couple of old warlords, Lutevo and Concupiscence, were squabbling over territory and that coincided with the return of Harut, who came to free his brother. Then there was this giant scorpion which attacked everyone, and we survived somehow to get on a plane and come here to Turkey. Sadly, I haven't made it out of the airport yet, but I'm sure when I do, I'll find it to be a wonderful country filled with all manner of delightful sins and abominations. I'm really looking forward to it. If I make it that is. I am going to make it, right?'

Drowning in Ron's verbal diarrhea, Patricia relaxed her grip and Ron pounced. This time, she shrieked in pain, and flung Ron into the ceiling where his head cracked the plaster, showering them both in white powder. Although delirious from the collision, Ron still had enough wit to recognize an opportunity. The ceiling. He glanced at the flaky plaster coating him, whilst keeping an eye on Patricia. He only had milliseconds to act, maybe less. Maybe a nanosecond before she attacked again. Why had the ceiling succumbed to the force of his body? Every other time Patricia had pitched him against the walls, he had made no impression at all. It was like the bathroom brawl with the angel in Mae Sai. For some reason his body had been too corporeal to pass through the walls, but not solid and real enough to crash through them. He broke some stuff though. The television. A mirror. Why could he not get through these walls? And why could he now damage the ceiling? Ron looked up.

As Patricia's tentacled grasp snatched at thin air, Ron propelled himself to the ceiling, to the exact place where his head had left an impression. This time when his head hit the ceiling, he smashed straight through it, into a dark open space of infinite dimension. He was flying. Free. Overcome with unspeakable joy and relief, he almost thanked God. Where could he be though? Such a vacuum. Where was he?

Then he opened his eyes.

A small blue and white bird flapped furiously, hovering in front of Ron's face. 'I see,' he said.

'Tweet. Tweet,' said the bird, before flying away as though having delivered an important message, it needed to hurry off to deliver the next one.

'Caw! Caw!' said a much larger black bird as it passed Ron, cocking its glossy head slightly, in a lazy, half-interested manner.

Ron realized he was still moving through the air, but with much reduced alacrity. In fact, he was decelerating at a remarkable rate. Enough to force him to extend his wings and begin to use them for their intended purpose as opposed to merely displaying them every now and then as wicked ornaments. With his wings fully extended, Ron quickly broke his descent, managing to hover with the same energetic flapping displayed by the blue and white bird. He had escaped. It was true. Having escaped Patricia and her erratic sadism, Ron was literally as free as a bird. Although there were many questions to be answered about his bizarre and torturous experience since arriving in Turkey, Ron had only one thought on his mind. Callum.

Chapter Nine

The call was inevitable. A part of Callum expected it every waking hour. When he was busy enough to have the luxury of peace within the comforting boundary of a specific task or set of tasks, he could almost forget about the call. Almost. Like a flock of black kites circling the sky above a bushfire waiting for the angry flames to flush out the little beasts on which they could gorge themselves, so did Callum live with the dread anticipation of the call.

'He's gone.'

His mother's voice was a grief-soaked whisper, barely audible down the line. Lost for words, Callum swallowed hard, tried to be strong. 'Mum.'

'When I woke up this morning,' she said. 'Your father didn't.'

A rush of air filled Callum's ear. 'What do you mean, Mum?' said Callum as if he didn't know exactly what she meant. 'What happened?'

'He was fine when he came home from the hospital last night, and we—'

'From the hospital? Why was he in hospital?'

'Oh Callum,' she replied, causing Callum to instantly regret raising his voice. He bit his tongue, trying to chew an apology from it.

'Sorry, Mum. What happened?'

Her voice strengthened as she spoke. 'He'd been having trouble breathing. More than usual, and the doctor had said that if this happened, we should come in. Your dad didn't want to, of course. He was the worst patient in the world. Impatient. Proud. Argumentative. Ungrateful. It was like he took his illness as a personal assault on his dignity. He could never accept the reality, so every trip to the hospital was like another defeat for his ego. Another win for the cancer. Anyway…'

Callum thought his mum sounded like herself now, as though she had blossomed inside the safety of a factual recount.

'They managed to stabilize him after draining his lungs a little, but there was so much cancer there, it was like he only had half a lung. Still, you know, he seemed a little better and he didn't want to stay. Neither did the doctors think he needed to, so we went home. After dinner I helped him shower and put him to bed. Then I lay down beside him as he fell asleep. I had this feeling…'

'Oh Mum,' said Callum as she crumbled, sobbing quietly. He could hardly speak himself as he pictured his parents lying in bed together, side by side: affectionate, little kisses and touches, bidding each other goodnight for the last time. Except they didn't know it was the final time they would conduct this beautiful ritual which they had practiced every night of their thirty-two-year marriage.

Finally recovering her composure, she continued. 'I had this feeling that I was going to lose him. He was so deflated. So sick of being sick. So ashamed of being such a burden. The stupid man. I loved every moment I had with him, even when I didn't like it. Oh, that doesn't make sense.'

'It doesn't have to make sense, Mum,' said Callum. 'It's okay.'

'In the morning, I couldn't rouse him, so I called an ambulance. They said he was in a coma and I knew that was it. I knew he wouldn't wake up. God was finally going to end his suffering and take him home.'

These words of faith now meant something to Callum. He felt a stirring in his spirit where previously such sentiment would have amused him. A section of himself, a long-hidden component now responded to his mother's expression of faith. He couldn't only hear the conviction in her voice, but he could feel it. His spine tingled. 'Thank God,' he mumbled, uncertain of whether this was appropriate.

'He's at rest now,' she said overlooking Callum's response, which in other circumstances might have been impossible for her to ignore. 'But Callum, I...'

'I know, Mum. I know,' he said, even though he had no idea. Thirty-two years of marriage. Their love was older than he was. Callum was clueless. He felt the gaping wound, the hole left by the evacuation of his father from this world to the next. He loved the man. Knowing he hadn't seen his father for months or spoken to him for a little while—he couldn't remember how long, which meant that it was too long—brought regret to the door of Callum's heart. He heard it, asking to be let into the wake.

'At the hospital,' continued his mum, 'they confirmed the comatose state and said it was only a matter of time. They couldn't say exactly how long, but if I wanted to call family members to come and say good-bye, I should do that, so I did, but you were so far away in Turkey you couldn't have come back in time, so I waited. I'm sorry.'

'It's okay, Mum,' said Callum although a flicker of unjustified anger was present. He could have been, should have been given the opportunity to get back to say goodbye. He tried to think now what his last words to his father had been. Had they been kind words? Happy words? Encouraging words? He couldn't remember.

'We'd agreed beforehand that no extraordinary measures were to be taken to save him. That's why he was so reluctant to go to the hospital even though it was necessary. He felt he should have been allowed to die in peace at home. But things are rarely that simple. In the end he got his wish. He just went to sleep and never woke…' She began to cry again.

Callum almost asked about the funeral. He nearly mentioned it might be hard for him to get back if it was too soon. He was close to forgetting this moment had nothing to do with him.

'I'll be there in a couple of days if I can get a ticket. I should be able to.'

'You're a good boy, Callum. I love you.'

Pouring her special brand of grace all over his shameful selfishness, his regret, his sorrow, his feelings of uselessness, made Callum weep. He somehow managed to say, 'I love you too, Mum. I'll see you soon,' before he hung up, lay down and allowed himself a good cry.

Hearing a knock on the door of his room, Callum lifted his head. Wanting to force it away by ignoring it failed when Ande's voice rode the persistent rapping. 'Callum? Callum! Open the door. Callum!' As he rose from his bed, numb from the news of his father's death, Ande kept speaking through the closed door. 'We have more bugs downstairs. Heaps more, Callum. It's crazy. You gotta see this.'

Callum opened the door on Ande, just as she was about to open her mouth for another burst. He'd always been told he shouldn't play poker.

'Callum?' Her voice was softer. She reached for him, but when she touched his arm, he felt nothing. 'Callum. What's wrong?'

Raising his head to face her, he said. 'It's my dad.' She touched his arm.

'He's dead,' he said softly. 'He died.'

The embrace was so natural, so needed, so nice, Callum felt urgent tears welling again. After some time, he pulled away, looked at Ande. 'Thanks. What about these bugs?'

Ande shook her head. 'Forget that. It's not important now.'

He didn't want to cry any more, didn't want the hot face, the shortness of breath or the blurry vision. 'Come on,' he said. 'Let's go and have a look.'

Chapter Ten

The scene confronting Ron when he arrived at Callum's hotel breached the breadth and clarity of his vocabulary. The floor of the lobby was carpeted with a seething, stuttering, clicking mass. Crawling insects of uncountable volume were everywhere he turned. Ron wasn't afraid of anything corporeal, let alone little insects, but he found the tangled mass gathering inconvenient. Fascinating, but a monumental nuisance, nonetheless. He was tired of flying so would have to walk through the insectoid sea to get to the counter or the lift and make his way to Callum. Ron climbed onto a nearby table to gain a little elevation, as he considered what to do.

People were perched on tables, chairs, and other bits of incidental furniture, attempting to avoid the plague. Although their faces were a mixture of fear, disgust, and wonder, Ron couldn't see any harm being done by the insects. Patrons wishing to come in through the lobby doors from the street could not because passage was blocked by onlookers while the hotel guests already inside were not able to go anywhere. They were trapped.

Ron was surprised the much larger humans weren't simply stomping their way to wherever they needed to go.

Although, a broiling mass, the bugs seemed not to be aggressive. Even if they were, surely, they were harmless anyway. The reaction of the people fit with what Ron knew of human nature but stood in stark contrast to the logic of the situation.

As he studied the rolling wave of tiny, segmented bodies, Ron noticed some of them weren't actually very small. Although still dwarfed by people, and by Ron, but some of them were nearly the size of a child's hand. The surface of the sea suddenly appealed to Ron as an adventure, so he stepped over the table, and with great dexterity and impressive balance he light-footed his way across the lobby to the service counter.

'Excuse me,' he said to the concierge.

Ron repeated himself, forgetting he was invisible, added a theatrical throat clearing sound to gain the attention of the young man. When that failed, he slapped the man's cheek. The man remained entirely fixated on the six-legged freak show. Ron studied his hand, frowning, before realization determined it should be struck, palm first against his forehead. 'I can only do that with Callum,' he said to himself as he flopped to the counter, deflated, suddenly missing his human friend more than he should have. 'Ah,' he said. 'Woe is me.'

In the midst of this unbecoming display of self-pity, Ron's eyes lighted upon the hotel's guest registry which was open on the computer. For a moment, just a fraction of a second, he thought he might be lucky enough to see Callum's name without needing to work out how to scroll down the page. Tired from the escape from Patricia, he couldn't summon enough demonic magic to interact with the real world. 'I'm not a ghost,' he said, again to an audience of one. 'This shouldn't be a thing. It's not a thing for demons not to be able to impact objects. I couldn't go through walls, until I found that weakness on the ceiling at the station otherwise known as Patricia's Palace of Perniciousness.'

Ron smiled. Not bad. Palace of Perniciousness. 'But wait,' he said, turning dramatically to face the concierge who remained completely oblivious of Ron's presence beside him. 'Wait a minute.' He studied the ocean of creepy crawlies. 'I walked on them. Not through them.' Ron grabbed the concierge's magnificent green coat and pulled it, trying to pull the wearer of the coat towards him. 'I walked on them. I walked on those bugs.'

With still no reaction from the concierge, Ron sat cross-legged on the counter, adopting a posture suited to his present need for wisdom seeking. He continued to study the insects. Deeply pondering, attempting to force himself inside their minds to discover their true nature. This was not normal behaviour he was witnessing. It didn't feel right. It felt like someone was causing this, orchestrating it. He hopped off the counter onto the surface of the bug sea, then carefully selected an insect. He picked it up and stared into its eyes, although initially he had some trouble finding its eyes. 'What's this all about then?' he said aloud to the bug.

Ron put the bug between his teeth and bit lightly to test the strength of the carapace. It popped apart, squirting a bitter liquid into Ron's mouth. Delicious. What was it

D. A. Cairns

exactly? A familiar scent, twice experienced, filled his head flooding the anatomical highways and byways, resurrecting memory. Of course, sulphur. 'So, this little fellow has some demon juice in him, and I presume the others do as well.' Ron picked up another bug and flicked it into his mouth, before chewing it, savouring the pleasing taste. The only other question was why? Okay, there were many other questions, but that was a big one.

'Any questions?' said a familiar voice. Ron turned quickly towards its source, seeing Ande and Callum standing in an open lift, staring out at the apocalyptic scene.

'Eureka!' said Ron.

'If we stand here much longer, the lift will fill up and we'll suffocate, right?' said Callum.

'Yup.'

Ron listened carefully as he approached the lift. Callum hadn't seen him yet and Ande couldn't. He didn't want to startle Callum by virtually materializing in his face, although he couldn't immediately figure out why not. Previously, he wouldn't have hesitated. Ron shook his head. It must be the aftereffects of his time with Patricia. He hoped that was all it was, and that said effects would wear off. He was beginning to miss his malevolent and mischievous self.

'Shut the door then,' said Callum. 'Back up we go.'

The elevator doors squeezed against the mass of bugs, pushing them up, out and in, crushing bodies effortlessly.

Just before the doors closed, Ron heard Callum

71

say, 'Shouldn't the doors have become stuck. I mean, you only have to—'

Ron stared at the closed door, glanced up to watch the numbers above the elevator entrance light up as the lift ascended. Callum was right, of course. The doors should not have been able to close. He'd seen people stop the heavy automatic doors with nothing more than a touch. How did the doors pulverize that many solid things conglomerated? The answer lay in the insects' otherworldly origins. Ron kept his eye on the numbers, noting the lift stopped on the tenth floor. He scooped a handful of the bugs from near his feet and poured them into his mouth, crunching away with a certain satisfied sagacity. The answer to the question why could only be answered after the who was revealed. For it was the who which knew the why. Ron chuckled, before remembering he had a mouthful of bugs. This made him gag a little, but that also seemed quite a humorous thing in the circumstances.

'Perhaps I can be of assistance?'

A demon had appeared in Ron's peripheral vision during his self-amusement. He turned to face it. That it was a *she* had not immediately occurred to him based on the voice. Ron might have naturally assumed all demons who presented themselves unannounced were male, but he didn't know why that would be the case. Before him was a female of slender build, a little taller than Ron. He admired her muscles as he searched her arm for the rank scars.

'You won't find them,' she said.

'Find what,' said Ron disingenuously.

'What you're looking for. I had them removed,' she said, eyeing Ron in an uncomfortably familiar manner. 'Well, it, I should say.'

'It?'

'I had it removed.' She waited for the penny to drop. 'I only had one scar.' Further pushing the envelope of propriety, she touched his arm. Turning him slightly so she could see his scars. After studying them very briefly, for in fact there was not much to study, she removed her hand. 'I am Alix. With an 'I'.'

Ron rubbed his arm where Alix had touched him, trying to erase the tingling feeling she'd caused. 'Hi Alix with an 'I'. I'm Ron with an 'o'.'

Alix smiled, condescension dripping from her thin lips. 'These are mine,' she said, casting her arms wide in a triumphant arc. 'My pets. Do you like them?'

Without meaning to, Ron looked around and nodded, thus feeding Alix's no doubt veracious pride. He reeled himself in, recognizing a clever seductress at work. 'Must be hell to clean up after them.' Her laughter seemed genuine, which Ron found very confusing. 'And the food bill?' he continued. 'A nightmare, right?' The second comment evidently crossed some invisible boundary because the humour drained from her face, overtaken by resurgent disdain. Her pride reeked.

She looked at Ron who returned her studious gaze, patiently waiting for her to speak. Ron knew full well she would be a talker, a skilful boaster, a delighter in lofty speech which she poured down on those beneath her.

'What are you doing here?' she said.

The question was surprising. 'I'm visiting someone.'

'Visiting?' she said, moving closer to Ron. She sniffed his neck, then stared at him.

He was already bored with Alix's performance, so he decided to change the subject, to move onto the front foot. 'Do you often bring your pets out to create disturbances like this?'

Alix turned her back on him. 'When the need arises.'

Ron couldn't have cared less. Her rudeness and cryptic responses were enough to send him in the other direction. He walked towards the elevator, enjoying the rise and fall of the insect-infested floor. He watched the illuminating numbers above the doors, descending. He waited. When the door opened, it revealed more gasping astonishment from the occupants of the lift who quickly decided to return. During the frantic, repetitious button-pushing, Ron stepped inside.

The people he was sharing the lift with, a man and a woman wearing a red dress with silky auburn hair, were only travelling as far as the eighth floor. Ron would need the stairs from there.

'What are we going to do?' said the woman, clutching the man's arm.

He answered with a clipped accent which matched his moustache. 'Contact the hotel manager to find out what the devil is going on.'

What the devil indeed, thought Ron as the elevator

ascended.

'Then stay in our room until the matter is sorted out.'

The understatement made Ron smile. However, none of this was his business. His business was Callum. He'd been gone too long, and clearly something was wrong. Something had happened. In the brief moment he'd seen Callum in the lift and heard his voice, he could tell, things weren't right. Ron had become so accustomed to Callum, his idiosyncrasies, and nuances of behaviour that even the slightest change screamed for his attention. *Notice this. It's a sign.* There were many signs. Numerous portents. One had only to observe and consider.

'That was terribly rude of you,' said Alix.

'I thought I'd been dismissed, your majesty.' He watched a tiny vein in her neck announce itself.

'There's no need to be so antagonistic.'

'There's no need to be so full of yourself.'

At this, Alix smiled, the sincere expression Ron had seen earlier. Why were females so…so all over the place? It was so much easier to deal with the male soldiers sent to kill him with their fists and their feet. Patricia's tentacles, as well as her mouth, like Alix's were very unpredictable. The switching between good cop and bad cop, the flipping in and out of controlled decorum was unnerving. He had thought himself rid of another capricious demon when he walked away from her in the lobby.

'Ron,' she said, once more touching him as though they were lovers, as though she was uncertain still of his affections for her and was afraid to give herself fully to him. 'I'm sorry. Please forgive me.'

She's sorry? What kind of demon says sorry? Shaking free of her amorous hand, Ron looked her directly in the face. 'I'm busy. I don't have time for stupid games. I don't care who you are or what you are doing here.'

'I don't have time for games either,' said Alix before slapping Ron's face, then disappearing.

His cheek stung for a few minutes, but Ron was more bewildered than hurt. There were some bugs on the floor of the lift. Bits and pieces of the slain, those hammered by the weight of the doors. Among the detritus were survivors, tottering and skittering around. Hungry, Ron picked up a few choice-looking living specimens and popped them into this mouth. As he chewed, he caressed his cheek which still burned with a weird residual prickle.

The elevator stopped. Following a tuneful ding, Ron glanced up to see the number eight illuminated as the doors slid open. The man and woman who had travelled the rest of the way to their floor in awkward silence exited the lift and turned right, scurrying down the hall towards their room. Ron stepped out, searched for the stairs, saw the sign, and headed for it. When he opened the door to the stair well, Alix was there.

'Bloody hell!' said Ron.

'What an interesting expression,' replied Alix.

Ignoring her completely, Ron stepped around her and proceeded up the stairs, taking them two at a time to put as much distance between him and Alix as possible. At the first landing, Alix appeared before him again. 'Can we talk, Ron? Ron?'

The next flight was gobbled up three steps at a time. When Ron reached the door at the second landing, he exited the stairwell without slowing down. In the hall he turned left and galloped past doors with descending numbers: ten-o-nine, ten-o-eight, ten-o-seven, ten-o-six... He stopped, suddenly aware he didn't know Callum's room number. Turning to check if Alix had followed him up the stairs and out onto the tenth floor, even though that wasn't her style, Ron gathered his thoughts and quieted himself. Although he didn't feel afraid of Alix, in fact she seemed quite innocuous, he was irritated, because she was interfering with his thinking in a way which he couldn't quite define. He reflected again on his behaviour post-Patricia. She'd obviously messed him up more than he at first realized. Alix could have been swatted like a pesky fly or exterminated like all her creepy little insect pets deserved to be, but Ron had avoided her. He'd allowed her to get under his skin. Her touch was magical.

'I'm trapped in a shmaltzy romance narrative,' said Ron as he slumped to the floor, banging the back of his head repeatedly against the wall.

Chapter Eleven

It seemed like the only sensible thing to do. With grief weighing heavily on his shoulders, paralysing Callum's heart, he knew he could either surrender to morbid inertia, or keep moving. He had to find something else to think about, to focus on.

After their brief visit to the madness of the insect infested hotel lobby, Ande insisted he do nothing. She expected nothing, she said. She understood. She embraced him again, naturally and warmly, as though they hugged each other multiple times every day and had done so for many years. She tried to get him back to bed, offering him a beer or something stronger if he preferred, but he declined, insisting he needed to do, rather than be. He needed action and distraction. 'Besides,' he said, 'it's not like I didn't know this day was coming.'

Ande shook her head, not understanding. Wanting to comfort him, her face betrayed rejection, as if she took offence at him for knocking back her offer of solace.

'Come on,' he said. 'let's get back down there and get into it?'

'Get into it?' Ande cocked her head. 'We were just there, but we decided to come back, and I really don't think now is a good time to be getting into anything, do you?'

'Yes, I do. I changed my mind. I want to go.'

With many persuasive words, Callum finally convinced her, insisting also as they walked back down the hall to the elevator that Ande fill him in. 'What have you been doing? Have you learned anything new?'

Ande didn't answer immediately, perhaps wondering whether it was wise to indulge Callum in this way, pretending he hadn't just received such terrible news about his father's death.

'I've been doing some research on insects and mythology,' she said. 'After I left you and Pitch admiring them at the restaurant.'

Callum noted the long pauses at the end of each of her sentences as though she was waiting for him to change the subject at any moment, or to confess he really couldn't deal with the bug crisis right now. That he needed to cry or get ridiculously drunk or something. 'We weren't exactly admiring them, Ande,' he said. 'It was more like professional curiosity.'

'Anyway, do you want to know what I found out?'

When they reached the elevator Callum pressed the down button. The door opened immediately, which they didn't think anything of. They also failed to notice a heavy sprinkling of crushed beetles on the floor of the lift. Nothing new there.

'Do tell,' said Callum. 'What did you find out?'

'The Sarikaleci tribe is one of the oldest tribes in Turkey,' said Ande, as though this was a statement of earth-shattering importance. 'They have a story about a sorcerer with the head of a rhinoceros beetle.'

'What?'

'They have a story about—'

'I heard what you said, but...' Callum couldn't find any words, so he simply waited for Ande to continue.

'To cut a long story short,' she said.

'Very unlike you.'

Ande frowned with an accompanying akimbo stance which Callum had always found very cute. He didn't want her to be cute right now, though. That wasn't good for him or for her. She was clearly still hating on him for what happened in Mae Sai, and he had just lost his father. Not to mention the fact they were in the middle of another bizarre, otherworldly experience, hot on the heels of the giant scorpions and demon wars in Thailand. It was too much. Callum did not want Ande to be cute, or compassionate, or funny or gracious. If she was going to continue to be herself then he might well lose his mind, or do something very, very drastic.

'There is an important anniversary of what the Sarikaleci call the First Incident of the Sorcerer's Tusk.'

'Were there subsequent incidents?'

'Please stop interrupting me.'

Ding! The elevator announced its arrival at the lobby and the door slid open to reveal a scene which once upon a time would have shocked Callum but was now becoming so commonplace as to barely interrupt the conversation. Barely.

'Here we go again,' he said, as he gestured for

Ande to step out of the elevator, onto any clear patch of carpet she might be able to find. That was not going to be easy. The overall scene was one of relative calm given the swarming invasion which filled the lobby. People seemed to be regarding the insects as curiosities rather than objects of fear, which was different from how they had reacted at the café where they'd had breakfast earlier in the day. Perhaps that would change once they began to feel the twitchy irritation of multiple nibbling mandibles.

'This doesn't look as bad as the last one. It seems relatively safe,' said Callum. 'Should we find somewhere to sit so you can finish the story?'

'Are you sure it's okay?'

'Probably.'

'That's not very reassuring,' said Ande. She searched the room briefly before, turning and pointing at reception. 'High ground?'

Callum ignored the crunch of exoskeletons under his feet as they walked to the reception desk and hoisted themselves up onto it, right beside the concierge with the fear coloured face.

'Don't worry, mate,' said Callum. 'They look pretty harmless.'

The concierge gave Callum a look of horrified misunderstanding.

'Leave him alone, Callum,' said Ande. 'You're not helping.'

Everything seemed too strange. People were moving but only very slowly, inching towards unspecified destinations. The flight instinct was evidently retarded but not completely disabled by the fawn instinct. 'They're like deer caught in the headlights, aren't they?'

'Don't you mean rabbits?'

Callum looked at her, saw her cheeky smile and cursed her again for being so irresistible. 'No, Ande I mean deer.'

'Oh dear.'

He couldn't help himself then, laughter exploding from deep in his chest. 'Stop it!'

Ande winked, flashed Callum with a bright smile, before continuing. 'The First Incident of the Sorcerer's Tusk was followed by a second and third incident, but only the first one is commemorated because it was the first.'

'Obviously.'

Ande crossed her legs casually. 'This year marks the five hundredth anniversary of the First Incident.'

'The five hundredth?' exclaimed Callum. 'Damn!'

They continued to watch the glittering sea of bugs roil around the reception floor: the overall level neither higher nor lower. The sight had the same mesmerizing effect as fire. Every now and then, strange shapes materialized within the mass, impossibly real images of creatures other than beetles. Callum imagined he saw a bull's head, broad and fiercely countenanced. There was also a rhinoceros, a mangy dog, and a few scorpions. Distracted by the visual riot, and by a lingering grief which surged and abated like the tide, Callum left the obvious question unasked until Ande strode into his silence.

'The five hundredth is a biggie because the Sarikaleci prophets say the ancient sorcerer will rise from the depths of hell and release six plagues from within his tusk. Callum, are you listening to me? I worked really hard on this research, and learned my stuff in order to present it to you…what's the word? Efficiently, that's it efficiently, because I know you like that.'

Callum turned his head to face Ande, studied the elegant chiselling of her cheek bones. 'Succinct is a better word. What about the sorcerer?'

Ande turned to meet Callum's eye. It might have been sheer fantasy, but he could have sworn there was a brilliant smile in her eyes, something appreciative and deep. Something revealing. Something very Ande, playful and enigmatic. 'You missed the bit about the plagues coming out of the sorcerer's tusk, right? I thought *that* was an absolute killer. Rising from the dead, well, that's been done before, hasn't it?'

'Sure,' said Callum. 'A whole bunch of Greek gods, Osiris, and the phoenix, of course.'

'Of course,' said Ande. 'In Africa it's normal for people to believe in voodoo spirits, people who come back to life in physical form.'

'Zombies,' said Callum. 'And don't forget the most famous alleged resurrection, definitely not a zombie: Jesus.'

Ignoring the Jesus comment, Ande continued. 'Ready for the big reveal, the connection? The first plague…' She paused, escalating the drama, swung her arms wide, palms up. 'Behold.'

It was not inconceivable. It should have been, but it wasn't beyond the realms of possibility now that they were witnessing, first-hand, a plague of insects which had spewed from the tusk of a resurrected Sarikaleci sorcerer. There were many things which Callum was beginning to take for granted and many others which, although experienced for the first time, he could easily accommodate in his radically transformed worldview. He knew Ande was still clinging to logical answers, to the rationalism which had sustained Callum for so many years. Although Ande's was a conscious denial of the supernatural world, her turning her back on something which was integral to her culture, the belief system which underpinned Callum's walk in the world, was far less intentional. It did, however, form solid ground on which he could confidently walk. *Did* being the operative word, as it was meaningless now. Defeated, disassembled, torn down by what? By Ron initially, and later that angel whom he had not seen since, but whom Callum sensed was never far away.

'What other possible explanation could there be for this?' said Ande.

'You don't believe that myth, Ande. I can hear it in your voice. Why is it hard for you to accept a supernatural explanation?'

'It isn't hard at all. Remember my background, and I told you about my sister, Adama,' said Ande. 'It's not that I don't believe it or can't believe it. I can. I do, but I, I guess I don't want to.'

Here was confirmation of what Callum suspected. 'Why? Why not just go with it?'

'Sometimes,' said Ande, very slowly and

thoughtfully, 'when you replace the kitchen, you have to replace the bathroom as well.'

That seemed way too philosophically dense for Callum to penetrate, but perhaps she was hinting at the rejection of her culture which he suspected. Feeling that words might desecrate something sacred at that moment, Callum continued staring at the boiling bug infestation at his feet, searching for the bull or any of the other fantastic creatures he had seen. His mind was swampy, his thoughts thick and lumpy. This was all becoming too much. Magically and mercifully, Ande changed the subject without attempting to explain her metaphor or require Callum to.

'Are you going to go home for your dad's funeral? You're going, right? You have to go.'

'I spoke to my brother earlier,' said Callum, avoiding the question.

'I didn't know you had a brother,' said Ande. 'Younger or older?'

'Younger. His name's Darren. We aren't very close. Too different I suppose. He's always been a bit loose.'

Ande frowned. 'Loose? You mean morally loose?'

'No. Just loose, you know?'

'No.'

'Forget it. I love him, and I miss him, and even though it's for a shitty reason, I'm looking forward to seeing both him and Mum again. It's been a while. My fault, but it's been a while.'

'Families are bloody complicated, aren't they?'

In another one of those moments Callum would remember forever, he and Ande looked into each other's eyes and their minds melted into one: all their hopes, experiences, dreams, everything said and unsaid, blended smoothly into a deep simpatico. An instant in time, but at the current rate of occurrence, these shared moments would soon be great enough in number to fill an album: snapshots of intimacy, of deep connection. A relationship like no other he'd ever experienced.

'I'm leaving Monday morning,' said Callum. 'I couldn't get an earlier flight. The funeral's not until Wednesday so it'll be fine. At least I won't be a complete write-off when I arrive. Not like when I did a day trip to W.A. for my grandmother's funeral.'

'Monday morning's perfect,' said Ande.

'Perfect because?'

'I thought we could attend Mass at Istanbul's oldest and most famous Roman Catholic church. It's a must see for tourists and I haven't been to Mass for years.'

'I've never been to Mass,' said Callum, feeling strangely elated and queasy at the same time. He hadn't been to church since he was a boy, since when his parents stopped forcing him to go and resigned themselves to a prayer vigil of indeterminate length for their lost son. He'd never really felt an antagonism towards the faith of his parents, but he likewise had never taken it as his own, and everyone knew that God had no grandchildren.

'Like I said,' said Ande. 'Perfect.'

'I think we should go now,' said Callum, pointing at the sudden swell in insect numbers. 'It's about to get crazy again.'

'To church?'

'To anywhere but here.'

Chapter Twelve

Pitch was oblivious to Callum and Ande's latest misadventure. Oblivious to everything in fact except for the huge rhinoceros beetle posturing aggressively not more than thirty centimetres from his wonderstruck face. Just one glorious *Oryctes rhinocerous*. One marvel of nature to capture his entire attention, rendering him immune to discomfort, to the heat, to the disapproving stares of curious onlookers. A giant beetle so far from its natural habitat. What was it doing here?

Owing to its length and a preponderance of wannabe polymaths, the conference had been a tremendous disappointment. Potentially stimulating and exciting, next-level beetle mania, it had proved to be a yawn fest. Pitch kept tuning out and drifting away in his mind: back home to his wife and his comfortable bed, then to his secret lover and her sweetly dangerous embrace. Back to familiarity. He even longed for the companionship of his new buddies, Ande and Callum, lingering in thoughts of them and the role he might have to play in them eventually getting together, which was how he saw their future. Not that he was any sort of matchmaker, but Callum had seemingly taken a shine to him, and was quite willing to confide in him when he needed to vocalize the emotional turmoil in his mind. That was fine by Pitch. Callum was a little like the son he wished he'd had instead of the one he ended up with. No. That was unkind. Pitch had been telling himself for years to be grateful instead of resentful, but it was the hardest, most exhausting fight of his life. There were days when he wanted to quit and just be the man most expected him to be. He was forever letting people down, so why keep trying? Especially with his son. Although he tried his best, the man who still acted like a boy, his son, threw everything back in his face. Rude, disrespectful, wilfully stubborn to his own detriment. 'Of course, mate,' Pitch's friends would say, 'if that's how he treats you, you can piss him off. Tell him to get out and make his own way. It's his choice to be an arsehole'.

Like his pig-headed son, the mighty rhinoceros beetle defiantly stood its ground in the face of a massive threat, its horn gleaming, proud and erect. It was amusing to consider how the beetle overrated its defences. Pitch was in no danger at all, and if it weren't for the fact that he was a respecter of insectoid space, he simply would have picked up this magnificent specimen to remind it how vulnerable it actually was. Luckily for the beetle, Pitch was not a predator. He was a fan, almost worshipping it as he lay prostrate on the rough ground, angling his head to gain the perfect view.

They might have stayed locked in this stalemate indefinitely, but Pitch became aware of a stinging sensation spreading slowly up his leg from his foot. As he twisted himself to examine it, the beetle seized the opportunity to escape. The effect of the sting was exactly like the drowning of the senses in alcohol. You drink for a while without feeling the effects, which encourages further consumption, then wham. Thirty minutes to an hour later, it hits you. Your head is instantly spinning, your words blend into an incomprehensible slurry and your fingers and toes start floating away from your hands and feet. Although it happened quickly, Pitch had been around the block enough times to know what was going on. The problem, the source of the panic he felt, was the fact he hadn't been drinking. This left poison as the only possible cause of what was happening to him. *Oryctes rhinoceros*! Damn bug. Despite the toxic fog and the shutters being dropped on his peripheral vision, his entomologist brain still functioned well enough to sort through the facts. Rhinoceros beetles were not venomous to humans, nor did they hunt or even hang out in packs, which ruled out the possibility that the specimen in front of his face had merely been a distraction for his mate to attack Pitch from behind.

Yet something had scratched him or stung him, and he was rapidly falling into unconsciousness. He might have lifted his hand, desperately trying to attract attention. He might have called out for help. He couldn't be sure. Darkness swallowed him.

Inside the prison of coma, Pitch woke as though from a deep sleep. Eventually, he blinked his way to clearer vision and became aware thereby of his new surroundings. Night had fallen and he was in a stone amphitheatre, it must have been a temple as it was lit by flaming torches and yes, there was an altar in the centre of this sideways diorama. People were gathered there. They were chanting lowly and slowly, swaying on their knees. A robed figure appeared from within the altar. Pitch couldn't see a face because it was buried inside the dark cave created by an elaborate hood. Looking more closely, he could see beetles crawling all over the dirt floor, covering the spaces between the worshippers. The altar too was decorated with the now familiar sight of six-legged creatures of all shapes and sizes.

Numb and disconnected, Pitch ran his hands over his body, confirming its presence. From his side view, he shifted and rolled to an awkward sitting position: his view of the scene now in correct perspective. He knew he was in a coma, that what he was witnessing was a vision produced by the poison which had been injected into his body, clearly a hallucinogenic. This was a dream state, not real. He knew that yet he also sensed there was something of significance here. There was purpose, a message for him to take away to he knew not where. Maybe, he…Pitch rebuked that thought. Surrendering to negativity would trap him. It was exactly like depression. One had to fight through the gloomy molasses, shake off the demons, beat the black dog. He shouldn't have been able to think so clearly, but as he could, he was determined to pay attention.

The robed figure stood erect, motionless, bathing in the adulation. When it raised its hands, Pitch half expected to see hexapods, but normal hands appeared from the depths of the folds of the robe. Certainly, the hands of an ancient being, but human, nonetheless. Pitch was unsure whether he was relieved or disappointed. With the lifting of hands, the chanting ebbed away, melting into murmurs before silence engulfed them all. It turned its shrouded head slowly surveying the amphitheatre, but when facing Pitch, it stopped. He had felt confident until then that his presence had been undetected.

The withered hands reached slowly to the sides of the hood, moving upwards and backwards to push the folds of the robe away to reveal itself. Pitch held his breath, although expecting nothing less than an equally withered face. Perhaps with eyes of fire a piercing glare directed at him and him alone. Pitch's anticipation was rewarded with a time worn visage of indeterminate gender. There was however one difference. In the middle of the forehead was a black spot which grew as Pitch watched. The creature was staring at him. Pitch stared back mainly because he was unable to look away. From the black spot, a node emerged and extended. First outwards, then upwards, spreading wider at its base but tapering to a point. Pitch recognized its shape, and in it the real source of horror. The protuberance bore a precise resemblance to that found on the rhinoceros beetle. The very same creature which had sent him in to the murky recesses of this trance. *Oryctes rhinocerous!* A sorcerer with a tusk.

Chapter Thirteen

Callum noticed them sitting in one of the front rows of St. Mary's of Sakizagac. The ancient cathedral in the old part of the city of Istanbul was an impressive architectural work complete with all the trappings he'd expected to see, from the life size wooden carving of Christ on the Cross to the massive wall of stained glass behind the altar.

Callum took everything in as he entered, but nothing seemed untoward—he had no other expectations of what an old Catholic church should look like—except for the couple kneeling near the front pew. It was not immediately clear to Callum why their presence should arrest his attention, but they looked somehow out of place.

Accompanied by the angelic sounds of an acapella choir, Callum walked slowly down the nave, pausing only to allow Ande to stop and bow before crossing herself in the universal display of affiliation with the Roman Catholic church. He followed her into a pew and sat on the hard bench as she knelt on the polished wooden kneeler. Callum glanced around the expansive interior, taking in the passion fresco presented around the three sides of the building, high on the walls above the congregation. Soon, his eyes fell upon the strange couple again, and there they remained.

'Welcome to St Mary's Cathedral on this twenty-second Sunday in ordinary time. Our priest tonight is Bishop Emeritus Eugene. Please stand to welcome the procession.'

Callum focused on the odd couple, hoping God wasn't offended by them being the object of his attention. She was skinny, bedraggled, gaunt. She sat one row back from the front pew of the cathedral. Her hair, frightened of posture and alarming of colour, was short and frizzy, perhaps the victim of one too many perms. Cut short off her shoulder, it might once have been straight or curly, blonde or brunette. It was unclear now. She was underdressed for anything other than the beach in a pair of tight denim cut-offs and a spaghetti-strapped singlet top. The thin straps of her bra stretched across her bony shoulders. She knelt, as the procession entered, probably praying for the mercy of Mother Mary.

He was tall, gangly, dishevelled. He sat in the row behind her, positioned further towards the centre aisle down which came the procession. His glasses large, bold, and thick of lens, presented a fishbowl view of his surroundings which might have matched his uneasy relationship with himself. He wore an unfashionable and oversized polo shirt which was draped across his hunched shoulders, hanging down over navy-blue workpants. It looked like he cut his own hair.

Callum couldn't put his finger on exactly what it was about these two that identified them as a couple, but he felt it, intuited it somehow. When the man moved discreetly, seating himself beside her, though not close enough to touch or even hold hands comfortably, Callum's suspicions were confirmed. Together at last, albeit in a clandestine fashion, the couple's thinness was exaggerated by their proximity. They were stick people.

Callum shifted his attention to the words of the hymn being projected high on the walls either side of the altar space. Neither one was comfortable to look at; a little too much to the right, the other too much to the left, both a little high, even when standing, to view without raising his head slightly. The twenty-second Sunday in ordinary time? Callum figured ordinary time referred to the time between special church times. Easter and Christmas were the obvious ones, but there were others. He might ask Ande about that later. Or not.

Giving up on the hymn, which had an awkward cadence and an unachievable pitch, Callum watched the procession pass on his right, down the nave towards the altar. A man carrying a mace led them, followed by a woman holding a large Bible aloft as though ready to release it into the air. Lastly, the priest, Father Eugene, resplendent in his robes of divinity. Callum was not entirely at ease with the trappings of Roman Catholicism. The setting on a pedestal of some men over others, the designation of them as the mediators between God and man, the adoration of dead saints and the deification of Mary, the mother of Jesus Christ. Callum was unsure what these things had to do with God, but he wasn't familiar enough with the Bible to refute any of these practices on solid theological grounds.

The skinny woman stood quickly, turning to nod to the priest as he neared, all the time unaware of Callum's eyes on her. Her equally scrawny partner also nodded as the priest walked past, then quickly turned his eyes toward the crucified Christ hanging from the wall. Following his religious glance at the cross, the man's gaze thereafter lingered too long on the woman beside him.

On reaching the steps of the altar, which numbered seven, the procession rearranged itself to form a line across the altar space, bowed, then climbed the steps to assume their positions for the beginning of mass. Callum now noticed the fish symbol, and alpha and omega symbols on the front of the altar. Thus engaged, he couldn't help but also notice when the omega symbol become distorted then reformed into a recognizable shape. An insect.

Callum nudged Ande, but she was in the middle of crossing herself so didn't notice. The beetle crawled away from the face of the altar, leaving an empty space. Callum sat, after everyone else, and only after Ande tugged his shirt. Sitting awkwardly on the hard pew, he glanced at her, muttered embarrassed thanks.

'You look a bit lost, Callum,' she said.

'The last time I was in a Catholic Church was for a baptism of some cousin I didn't know. I didn't know what the heck was going on other than that I was uncomfortable in the fancy clothes my mum made me wear.'

'Relax,' said Ande. 'The roof won't fall in.' She turned away, focusing on a woman with short, bright blue hair who was reading from the Bible.

A man walked down the centre aisle, beating his chest, hard enough for the thump to resound. His hair was wild and grey, unbrushed, uncut, and he must have shopped in the same store as Callum's stick couple. Seemingly oblivious to everyone else in the church or to what was happening, the man continued down the aisle, turning heads as he passed, until he reached the foot of the lectern where he paused, perhaps waiting to be acknowledged. The priest ignored him, so he turned, then half staggered to the front pew. He sat momentarily, before rising to return to the lectern. Callum watched with interest; his heart rate elevated slightly. This vagrant was certainly deranged, perhaps even dangerous. Would any of the faithful intervene? Would they eject this man or accept him as Jesus undoubtedly would have? Churches, in his limited experience, were filled with holy people who thought themselves a much higher grade of human. Callum winced. That was harsh. He didn't know anyone in this room apart from Ande and she, although at least a lapsed Catholic, at best a secret one, was not at all proud in the sense Callum was thinking about. This new state of second-guessing himself was unknown territory. Certain thoughts triggered almost instant pushback-type thoughts. Self-rebukes. This was his recently refurbished conscience in operation, and it was quite irritating.

Callum looked at Ande, realized her attention was elsewhere, and turned his eyes to the altar.

Everyone started singing in a foreign language. The words were on the wall, but Callum was no longer interested in singing, especially when he didn't know what the words meant. They were probably okay, but who was to know? Callum didn't know. He didn't know why he was fixated on the spindly Claytons couple in the front row when the church was filled with people from all over the world. Most were dressed to shame the poor, but all genuflected, and murmured their way through the mass, no doubt undisturbed by ridiculous and irrelevant thoughts like the ones Callum was entertaining. Free too, were they from distractions, effortlessly, re-positioning their crawling, climbing infants, hushing, and staying older children. Hands raised in unison to mumble the Our Father.

Another beetle caught Callum's eye.

It rested on the lens of the data projector and was hence magnified many more times, so many in fact as to be at risk of blasphemy in this holy place. It appeared first as a part of the letter *u*, but then morphed into an *I* before inching its way along the full length of the sentence and finally out of sight. Callum supposed it was normal to a certain extent, for there to be bugs everywhere; they were after all easily the most ubiquitous species on the planet, but given recent experiences, it was impossible for him not to perceive a potential threat in every insectoid appearance.

He began to search the cathedral more earnestly, more keenly seeking evidence of demonic activity. Ron was not here naturally. Despite his very *truth and light* leanings, hanging out in a church was asking too much of the little devil. Still, he would have been useful. Callum's spiritual senses were much more finely tuned since his awakening in Mae Sai, but his endeavours usually felt more like groping in darkness, driven by vague discomfit of mind, rather than effective spiritual discernment. There was something wrong here, though. There was trouble brewing in St. Mary's, but none of the details presented themselves.

The collection plate was passed along the rows of the faithful. Callum watched, saw sneaky hands ducking in and out, he heard coins, a few coins, spied the ephemeral glimmer of light on metallic edges. When the plate reached him, he meant to pass it on quickly, but instead laid it beside him and fished in his pocket for some loose change. Aware Ande was watching him, he released everything in his grip to the dominion of the church, which was another thing he didn't quite understand. Firstly, why people had to give money to the church, and secondly why he felt compelled to do it now. Passing the plate on, he and Ande exchanged looks. She smiled. He smiled back, hopefully. She turned away. This was all so weird and unnerving.

After the collection, Callum found a pair of beetles on the floor, preparing to traverse the mountain of his right foot. As he watched them, a few more joined the party. He allowed the intrusion, and soon the hikers had conquered the mountain and moved on.

It was time for the Eucharist. A young couple selected by someone who had the right to do such things—a deacon or elder or some such—carried the elements down the nave where they were greeted by the priest. He spoke with each of them briefly, smiling and nodding before blessing them and sending them on their way.

Callum felt suddenly and surprisingly jealous, wanting that honour for himself. To be picked out. To receive a blessing directly from a man of God, one of the Lord's chosen. What the hell was he talking about? A bizarre seduction had stolen his rationalism. To be fair, it had been eroding continuously, bleeding to death since Mae Sai, but now he was falling into a foreign liturgy. It was too much. He was used to the dissonance which began with the awakening, the sense that he was connected yet simultaneously more disconnected. Callum had grown accustomed to this strange tension, but as he sat in St. Mary's surrounded by pious and religious Roman Catholics, this felt like the next level.

And then it struck him, the thought, a forgotten desire, a buried dream, his longing to see his awakening angel once more. Since that night, and the dramatic rescue, Callum had been on his own. No. That wasn't exactly true. He'd never seen the angel or heard his voice, but he certainly felt his presence. Sometimes. Mostly it was hard to separate reality from super reality. The veil might have been torn from his eyes, but it had not been a clean break from decades of wilful blindness. His vision remained blurry, aside from the odd miraculous moment of clarity.

'Are you going forward for communion?'

Ande's question surprised him. 'I'm not Catholic.'

She smiled. 'I'm pretty sure God's okay with that.'

Another remarkable response, although Callum knew he should certainly have stopped being surprised by anything Ande did or said by now. He nodded, before turning to check for oncoming traffic down the nave. Stepping out into the aisle felt brave. It was also a timely diversion from the rising mixed tide of apprehension and excitement he felt thinking about what might happen. He followed the person in front of him, concentrating on maintaining a respectful distance and attempting to see what people in front of him were doing. Would he be expected to say anything when he met the priest? Thank you, at least. Another few paces closer. Ande was behind him, but he wasn't sure if that provided comfort or increased his anxiety.

He felt a bug under his foot but did not look down. He wondered if the crunch of the tiny exoskeleton was as loud to everyone else as it was to him. A few paces closer. He swallowed, wiped his palms on his pants. Only one person ahead of him now. Step. Crunch. *Don't look*. Step. Crunch.

'The body of Christ, broken for you. Take and eat,' said the priest, as Callum arrived to receive the sacrament.

Callum's fingers began to close around the wafer before it reached his palm. 'Thank you, Father.' That didn't even sound like his voice. He stepped to the side of the priest, faced the altar, and bowed slightly, as he had seen others do, before whispering a thank you, then placing the wafer in his mouth. This was a very quick process, but he still had time to look at the face of the altar from where he had seen the first beetle emerge. There were others gathering, swirling at the base in an appalling emulation of sacrificial blood. Callum blinked, turned away and returned via a circuitous route back to his seat.

Ande joined him, tapping his elbow from behind. 'Hey,' she said. 'That wasn't so bad, was it?'

'Ande,' replied Callum without slowing down or turning his head.

'Yes?'

'We've got a bug problem here.'

'You've got to be kidding,' she said, almost gasping. 'Here? Are you sure?'

'I wasn't until I went forward and saw a swarm around the base of the altar.'

'Are they anywhere else?'

When they reached their pew, Ande and Callum sat down quickly; oblivious to the music and the marching saints, they discussed the situation seriously. 'I've seen them here and there, but there's going to be another swarm for sure. I can feel it.'

'What do you mean you can feel it?' said Ande.

'I can feel something.'

'Ditto my previous question,' said Ande, unwilling to accept Callum's words on face value.

'Look,' he said, lifting the soul of his shoe to show Ande the remnants of the insects he'd squashed.

'Eww.'

'I'm just warning you to keep your eyes open, okay?'

'Okay. Mass is nearly over, so hopefully, if you're right with this mysterious feeling of yours, hopefully we'll all be gone before anything major goes down.'

'Can you knock off the American cop routine?'

'It was an accident.'

Callum turned away, not because he was upset with Ande's frivolity, but because he was desperate to prevent a disaster if he could. There was nothing obvious to cause alarm now. No justification for him to order an evacuation, or to even suggest that members of the flock get on their bikes. What would he say anyway? 'Please leave quickly because a six-legged apocalypse is about to happen?' He didn't mind making a fool of himself so long as it achieved a purpose other than his own embarrassment, but he couldn't bring himself to take the action he feared was necessary.

'Callum?'

'Does it feel colder to you now?' said Callum. 'Suddenly colder.'

'No,' she answered. 'And no, I haven't seen any flickering lights either.'

Ignoring the jibe, Callum ran his gaze across the front of the church, sweeping from left to right then up on to the wall, over the expanse of ornamental glass to the other wall, then down the side wall, in and out of the painted passion scenes. Christ carrying his cross through the streets of Jerusalem. Christ arriving at Golgotha, the place of skulls. All the while, Callum was looking for bugs, but he saw none. Despite the evidence of his eyes, he still felt an urgent sense of foreboding.

'Did I miss something?' said Callum, as the priest invited the mostly kneeling congregation to stand and join the final prayer.

Ande was blocking him again.

'The peace of the Lord be with you all,' said Father

Eugene.

'And with your spirit,' answered the people.

'The mass is ended. Go in peace and live the gospel.'

The choir launched into another lip-twisting, tonsil-bending hymn as the papal procession reformed at the base of the seven stone steps. Callum looked at their feet, then at the steps. Were they darker than when he first entered the cathedral? An invisible marker was blacking out the risers, one by one. The members of the procession turned and moved off down the nave towards the back of the church in the correct order and at precisely the right pace. Callum's eyes were fixed on the steps: the black steps. Wriggling, writhing, seething. The first scream came from the skeletal woman who finally grabbed her man, as though she had been waiting all her life for a reason to do so. He embraced her, naturally, as though he too had been dreaming of just such a moment for every minute of every hour he had sat by her side in the cathedral.

More screams followed. The procession stopped. People fled, scrambling to the ends of the pews and towards the nearest exits as fast as their feet could carry them. The bugs had burst the banks, exploding from the steps in seismic gushes, spewing beetles in all directions.

Ande grabbed a firm hold of Callum's arm and pressed her face into his chest. Something made Callum look up to the high ceiling where he briefly witnessed a blackening; a thickening cloud from which suddenly proceeded an enormous load of insects dumped onto the bodies and heads of those faithful who had not been able to escape. The weight of insects forced people to the floor, and while on their way there they collided into each other and against the hard pews as more groans and screams filled the cavernous cathedral. The floors, pews and other furnishings were blanketed with ticking, clicking, creepy crawlies.

'I've got to do something,' said Callum.

'What?' replied Ande. 'No Callum. What do you mean?'

'There's something in here that can stop this carnage instantly. Someone maybe. I can find it. And kill it.'

He brushed off as many bugs as he could, then freed his feet which had been buried. He stamped furiously, enjoying the efficient expression of anger which ended the lives of so many of the invaders. He could never kill them all though. He knew that. Where was the source? Someone was driving this slaughter, directing the carriers of carnage. Although this thought had not occurred to him previously, he was sure of it now. This was not random.

'Callum? Are you mad?'

'Get out of here, Ande.' When she didn't move, he repeated his command. 'Get out of here. Now! Move it!'

Fear was paralysing most of those who were trapped into surrender. Even though the insects were thick on the ground, they weren't strong or dangerous really. People were so overcome by hysteria they forgot the instinct to simply brush the bugs off and rush out the nearest door. Panic caused them to forget to help each other, to forget to care, to forget to see. It was a blinding, binding terror.

'It's her again,' said a familiar voice.

'Ron! Where the devil have you been? It's who?'

'It's safe now. The Mass is over.'

'Speaking of Mass…' Callum waved his hands around.

'It's her again. It's Alix,' said Ron firmly.

'What?' said Callum. 'Who's Alix?'

'She's causing this, like she caused the one at the hotel. She calls them her pets.'

'We've got to find her, then.'

'I already did.'

'Let's go,' said Callum. 'If we stop her, we can stop this, right?'

'Right,' said Ron. 'Stay here and let me get on with it.'

'I have to do something,' insisted Callum.

Ron was on the verge of launching towards his mission. 'You know what to do, Callum?' His frown caused Ron to spell it out for him. 'Call in the big guns,' he said, pointing to the ceiling. In a flash he propelled himself towards the stained-glass array at the front of the cathedral. Callum watched him rip through the air, and smash right through the window. This action acted like a massive fire extinguisher on the blazing firestorm of bugs. They disappeared in an instant.

Chapter Fourteen

Ron succeeded in not only hitting Alix and taking her completely by surprise, but also in making sure where he grabbed her was the safest for him to avoid her lashing out. He'd learned a lot from their first encounter at the hotel. She'd made a mess of him there, forcing him to hide like a frightened child from a monster even though she'd done nothing to him physically, apart from one touch. Alix, in fact, had nothing on Ron, except perhaps bigger balls, yet she'd disturbed him, caused unexpected and unwelcome feelings. None of it sat right with Ron. He'd stewed on the implications of that first meeting, wondering if he would have an opportunity for revenge, to fill her with her own brash impudence and make her choke on it. Every second of that encounter had been replayed in his mind, as he worked through what had gone wrong and how he would make it right next time. Her weakness, he determined, as with most upstart megalomaniacs, was herself. Her pride.

The initial move needed to be a two-in-one action, to knock the wind from her lungs, then pin her arms behind her back. So much could go wrong if his timing was out. If he failed to slide from the blow to the solar plexus, onto her back and lock her muscle cannons, she could hurt him. Fortunately, Ron had been correct to back his skill, and efficient in his execution of the manoeuvre.

Momentum carried the two demons higher in the air, rocketing upwards further away from St Mary's. Alix wrestled with him as air refilled her lungs, resisting, twisting, but he held firm as they soared into the sky. Ignoring the pain Alix's struggling in his arms was causing him, Ron held tight, focusing all his strength into his arms, willing his back and shoulders to support him in overwhelming Alix and subduing her. For as long as it would take, Ron was prepared. While others, namely Callum, might see Ron as a hero, this battle with Alix was personal. He'd also not been completely honest with Callum about his intentions. He had other plans for Alix besides terminating her existence, but those delicious grapes would die on the vine if he couldn't defeat her.

'Stop fighting me, Alix,' he said. 'You know I'm stronger than you.'

'You can't hold on forever.'

'You don't want to test that theory.'

'I do if it means eventual freedom.'

Sensing a lessening of Alix's resistance, Ron adjusted his grip slightly and moved from behind her to beside her. This had the effect of helping slow them down, but it also surprised her.

'What are you doing?' she said.

'Never mind,' said Ron.

Alix immediately began to struggle again, but Ron tightened his grip and she quickly tired. Her defiance nothing more than a short burst of weakened rage. 'That's better,' said Ron. 'We should probably talk about your freedom.'

They had almost come to a stop mid-air, which meant they would fall soon.

'Freedom's an illusion, you know,' said Alix.

'We're about to fall back to earth and you want to philosophize. You're nuts, right?'

Ron approximated a smile. 'Here's what's going to happen. I'm going to take us down and we are going to talk about the future, and how that future will not involve you wreaking havoc and wiping out innocents with your voracious and bountiful pets.'

Alix laughed, as Ron guided their descent. 'Who the hell are you to tell me what to do?'

'Who the hell are you to ask me who the hell am I?' replied Ron, mimicking Alix's outraged tone.

This time, Alix's laugh appeared less angry, less haughty, less like I'm laughing-now-but-I'm-going-to-kill-you-as-soon-as-I-can. 'Ron,' she said. 'You're killing me.'

'Not my intention at all, my dear.'

'My dear?' said Alix as they landed on a patch of grass beside a large Mediterranean Cypress. 'I do not understand you at all, Ron. Twice now you've spoiled my fun, and this time with violence, Ron. Such violence. What am I to make of it?'

'Make it of it what you will,' said Ron flippantly as he sat, generating his best, warmest smile which was not easy for a demon.

Alix frowned, pouted, got to her feet, then brushed grass off her backside.

'Can I help with that?' asked Ron.

'What is your problem?'

Standing suddenly, Ron skipped closer to Alix who recoiled instinctively, although the defiant hurt expression never left her face. 'That's the same as saying *what's wrong with you?*'

'And what's wrong with that?'

Ron turned and began to walk away from Alix while holding out his hand in a friendly gesture with which he surprised himself. 'Walk with me,' he said, 'and I'll explain some basic communication techniques to you.' Was that kindness he heard in his own voice? Couldn't be. Must be someone else's voice. Kindness? He was acting as though he liked Alix. Maybe more than liked. Maybe something unthinkable. He wasn't even sure it was possible for demons to fall in love. It was an oxymoron, wasn't it? Demon love? What did the Christians say about love coming from God because God was, in fact, love? Love personified. He stopped and spat viciously on the ground before him.

'Whoa there, fella,' said Alix who had taken his hand and was happily following him. 'What was that for? And give me a heads-up next time so I can grab an umbrella.'

'Rose-coloured glass caught in my throat. You know how it is?'

They kept walking back towards the cathedral in silence, holding hands. Ron was intoxicated by the victory, and the intimacy. 'If you want to have a successful conversation,' he said, 'you don't start by asking the person what's wrong with them.'

'Why?'

'It puts them offside straight away. Makes them defensive.'

Alix stopped walking, jerking Ron to a halt in the process. 'You're the strangest demon I've ever met.' She tried to pull her hand free of his, and Ron found it was with great reluctance that he eventually released his grip on her clammy hand. 'It's kind of what we do, you know?' She studied his face, waiting for the penny to drop.

Ron knew what she meant, but he didn't care. He was different, and transforming daily almost by the hour into a new and unforeseen, once impossible to conceive, version of himself. Alix clearly felt some affection for Ron or else she would not have endured his romantic behaviour. Either that, or she was so stunned by his inexplicably non-demonic conduct she didn't know what to do about it. Holding Alix's gaze confidently, aware she was making a pathetic attempt to read his thoughts, he allowed a third possibility to come into play. Alix might well be setting him up. It was time to answer her, and by speaking to her, clarify what was going on in his own mind.

'The thing is I might be moving in another direction.'

He didn't know he was going to kiss Alix. He just did it. And it wasn't a quick one either.

'What the hell?' she said, before wiping the back

of her hand across her mouth and spitting at his feet. 'What is *wrong* with you?'

Ron sighed and was about to correct his ashen sweetheart again, but she snuffed out any verbal response by smothering him with a powerful and violent kiss of her own. Ron threw his arms around her as she bit his lip and poked her tongue deep inside his mouth. With so many new and intense emotions swamping him, Ron thought he might simply explode on the spot, or burst into flames. When they finally parted, it was with heaving chests, shaking legs, and very big, diabolic grins.

'Whoa there,' they said in unison.

'We need to talk,' said Ron.

'We need to *walk*,' said Alix. 'I have nothing to say.'

'I have so much to say. We need to—'

'Walk!' she insisted, grabbing his hand, leading him this time towards the cathedral.

St. Mary's was now awash with emergency service personnel, flitting in and out amongst the flashing lights atop their vehicles. All the lights in the cathedral were on. Ron and Alix had a good view of the exterior, the surrounds, and as they neared, they could see the hole in the rose-coloured glass wall through which Ron had propelled himself and Alix. It was so difficult not to talk that he felt sick, pregnant with words. Parts of Ron which he didn't know existed were now being exposed. It was more than unsettling, but it did give him an insight into what Callum had been, and was still, going through with his worldview transition. Ron had never been able to shake the memory of the angel's offer for him to cross over to the light. The absurdity and potency of such an offer had been eating him up ever since. At times, truthfully most of the time, he could beat those unnerving thoughts and feelings away, but his best method for doing so was to talk incessantly. Normally, that wasn't a problem. Even with that psycho Patricia who could easily have killed him, he had still barely been able to restrain his tongue.

Alix was a completely different bucket of prawns. She was now in control of him. He knew it. Was that a good thing or bad thing? How could he figure that out if he couldn't talk about it? He needed to verbalize his concerns, to spread the pieces of the puzzle out on a table, and swish them around with his fingers, searching for matching shapes and colours. Colours. They stopped walking and looked up at the stained-glass wall.

Even with an ugly hole smashed through the middle of it, it was still a magnificent sight. Would there be anything beautiful in this world if people didn't believe in God? He would have loved to be able to discuss it with Alix, but knew it was yet another entirely inappropriate thought which was best confined within the recesses of his mind.

They walked on, around the left-hand side of the cathedral where Ron could see a huddle of people. Hoping to find Callum, he held off on any further conversation with Alix, resisting his powerful and natural urge to talk. In an abnormal display of passivity, Alix followed him. The small crowd emitted indistinct whispers of words which meant nothing to Ron. He finally spotted Callum standing with Ande, but also noticed a scrawny female nearby. Standing alone and aloof, she appeared to have an admirer, an equally thin and unkempt male who reached for her with furtive glances. As Ron and Alix entered the group he could smell them, all of them.

'Not pleasant,' said Alix, crinkling her nose.

'You read my mind,' replied Ron.

Alix laughed. 'Yes, I'm a telepathic genius.'

'Ron!' Callum stepped through and around some people, pushing to get to him. 'Where have you been? Where did you go? What's that doing here?' With this last question Callum pointed at Alix while Ron felt her grip on his hand tighten.

'Take it easy, baby.'

'Did you just call her "baby"?'

'Don't call me baby, sugarplum,' said Alix.

Ron laughed, then realized it wasn't the right time. Callum was angry. 'Sorry, Callum. Take it easy. Alix and I have had a chat, and—'

'And what? You're besties now? Lovers?'

'What's he on?' said Alix.

Ande pulled Callum's arm, moving to stand in front of him. 'Who are you talking to?'

Callum was about to answer Ande when Ron interrupted. 'How could we be lovers, Callum? You know I'm a demon, right?'

'You know you're holding her hand and she's kinda standing in your shade.'

'What?' Ron was struggling to keep up with Callum's outburst or understand the point of it, or its cause. 'Standing in my shade? What does that mean?'

'And you called her *baby*,' continued Callum, building his case brick by brick.

'Are you okay?' said Ron. 'You seem upset.'

'Callum, are you okay?' said Ande, placing her hand on his shoulder. 'Why are you talking to yourself?'

Callum shrugged her and looked her direct in the face. 'I'm not talking to myself. I'm—'

'Callum!' cried Ron. 'Take a breath. Calm down. We can talk about everything when you lose your girlfriend.'

'She's not my girlfriend.'

'Who's not your girlfriend?' Ande waited. No one said anything. 'Who is this not girlfriend of yours?'

Callum looked at Ron and nodded. 'Later, Casanova.'

Ron raised his free hand, made a dramatic slashing gesture, albeit in front of his trademark grin. 'Roger that Romeo.'

As he and Alix walked away, Ron heard Ande pressing Callum for answers while he did his best to deflect her curiosity. Clearly, Callum was upset about the beetles in the cathedral and the fact Ron had waltzed back to the scene of the event, all cosy with the perpetrator of said disaster. That was reasonable. *Okay, Callum. I get it. Not a good look.* Ron would have to straighten out a few things with him, but he couldn't do that until he had picked Alix's brains. The problem with that was that every time he thought about finding out whatever useful information he could, all that came to mind was how he could jump her bones. The chemistry was off the chart. Fire and ice. Ice and fire. This was going to be more of a volcanic eruption than a relationship. A guaranteed supernatural disaster.

Having just passed the skinny guy, lovesick protector of scarecrow woman, Ron realized what it was about them that had caught his attention. He stopped and stared at them.

'What are you looking at, Ron?' asked Alix.

Ron ignored her, stared hard at the man first, then the woman. He waited, changing the angle of his view ever so slightly, to capture different slivers of slight. It didn't take long, until he found the right perspective and saw who they were. Or more correctly saw what they were.

Chapter Fifteen

'I think we're being followed,' said Callum.

'And you're putting your arm around me because...'

'Sorry, Ande,' he said, releasing her quickly. 'Instinct.'

'Chauvinistic insti—'

'Sshh!' said Callum, placing his index finger first on his lips, then on Ande's. 'Listen!' he whispered harshly.

They'd stopped walking now and were looking back into the shadows which assembled randomly along the street, peeking from corners, spilling carelessly into the light. The decision to walk back to the hotel after St. Mary's had been mutual, although Callum originally suggested it with a casual reference to fresh air. He spoke as though the cathedral had merely been a little stuffy. He was still trying to make sense of what happened himself, so their conversation to this point had been off-topic. Evidently, they were now masters of avoiding issues. Callum had even made a ridiculous attempt to discuss architecture, a subject about which he knew nothing.

'I can't hear anything,' said Ande. 'Or see anyone or anything moving at all.'

'Exactly,' said Callum, with a note of Holmesian triumph. 'We're still in Istanbul, right? We haven't been mysteriously transported to Caringbah on a Monday night?'

'Caringbah?' Ande screwed up her face. 'What on earth?'

'Not important,' said Callum, gently taking Ande's elbow and turning her in the direction they had been walking. She didn't resist him, but was probably fighting a strong urge to make some smart comment. 'I'm just saying,' he said, 'it's unusually quiet for a big city. It's not late and even if it was, we're only a few blocks from the biggest cathedral in town. Where'd everyone go?'

If Ande was unnerved, she didn't show it. Callum knew she was as good at not showing her true feelings sometimes, as she was at letting them paint the walls. He suspected there was always something lurking beneath the person she showed him but doubted she would ever open up to him again following Mae Sai. Any chance for them to move on, to either continue a much less awkward version of their relationship, or to change gears, if that's what he wanted-what she wanted as well, of course any chance hung on their ability to deal with Mae Sai. So far, they'd done a terrible job.

'We aren't completely alone,' said Ande suddenly after a few minutes of silent walking.

'Huh?'

Ande pointed at the footpath. 'See?'

Callum crouched, strained his eyes to see more clearly in the shapeless darkness.

'See,' said Ande. 'Another one of our little beetle friends.'

'Oh,' said Callum. 'We're calling them friends now, are we?'

Ande ignored the comment, although Callum could have sworn that he saw the ghost of a smile on her face.

'Just a coincidence I'm sure,' said Callum. 'I mean beetles are as common as anything. Beetles, bugs. Insects are the most populous species on the planet.'

'Really, Callum?' Ande stood and looked down at him, arms akimbo, a trademark and intimidating pose of hers. 'You're really going to keep playing the coincidence card? After all we've seen. You must be the world champion of denial, right? The world champion!'

She walked away and Callum would have followed except something caught his eye, making him take a few involuntary steps in the opposite direction. What first appeared amorphous, suddenly took shape before his eyes: a couple walking, but not just any couple. The skinny odd couple from St. Mary's. It wasn't seeing them which caused Callum's heart to beat faster though, despite having only just expressed his amazement there were no other people around. Nor was it a concern the couple were known to him. The alarm was raised by their sudden appearance. Where did they come from? There'd been nobody in sight until they popped out, emerging from the darkness as though using it to conceal themselves. From the substance of those murky shadows, they formed wraith like appearances.

'Ande!' shout-whispered Callum without taking his eyes off the two people walking towards him. They were still some way off. 'Ande!'

'What?'

Callum jumped. 'What the hell?'

'You know your whisper is really loud, right?'

'Can you see them?'

Ande looked in the direction Callum was pointing, and the latter immediately felt the crush of the former's grip on his arm. She whispered into Callum's ear. 'Where did they come from?'

'I don't know,' said Callum. 'It's that weird non-couple from St. Mary's.'

'You know them?'

Ande pressed in tighter to Callum, the simple act infusing him with a manly feeling. He felt protective, then heard the leonine tone in his voice. 'I don't know them exactly, but I noticed them there. I was curious about them.' Ande tugged at his arm, trying to reverse him but he was unmoved, immovable. 'Let's introduce ourselves.' Liking his behaviour, Callum busied himself with congratulations topped by a slice of self-analysis as the couple approached, still wafting in and out of solidity, or so it seemed.

'I think we should go,' said Ande, jerking on his arm again with the same result. 'I don't like the look of them much. At all really.'

'It's okay,' said Callum. 'We'll just say G'day and make small talk, maybe walk a ways together.'

'Callum, I really—'

The two ghostly figures were right in front of Callum and Ande before Ande could finish her sentence. Although Callum was unnerved by their alacrity, he was still not at all convinced they were dangerous. Surely if they could appear and disappear, mingling their atoms with the hues of the night, if they could cover distances effortlessly and instantly, if they could do all that, then violence was inevitable. If they intended it. They might just as well have been Caspar types, despite their appearance. In any case, Callum was quite prepared to stand his ground. Running away now would not only be an exercise in futility but would also cost him points with Ande, who Callum believed was probably, hopelessly impressed with his heroically courageous performance.

'Hello, Callum,' said the scrawny man, extending his hand.

Ande was now behind Callum, squeezing his arm more tightly. He could hear her heart smashing against the inside of her chest.

Callum took the man's hand, surprised by its solidity and warmth. 'G'day. You know my name.'

'I know your name.'

This situation should have been overwhelmingly tense. Instead, it was merely awkward; like meeting a stranger at a party, wanting to be friendly if only to help pass the time and relieve discomfit but not quite knowing how to go about it. Idle banter was not usually difficult for Callum but given the man and his companion were not human, it was more challenging than usual to know where to take the conversation. Not human, but not angels; at least nothing like the angel who had visited him for his awakening. Not human, but neither were they demons; nothing like any of the demons he had encountered in Thailand. What were they then? There was only one way to find out.

'Who are you?' said Callum. 'And what are you?'

'My name,' said the man, 'is Corpulent.'

Callum laughed out loud. Ande pulled on his arm again. 'Callum, please. Let's go.'

'And I,' said Corpulent's companion, 'am Elephantine.'

Callum's attempt at a compliment was destroyed by his laughter, this time dissolving into a fit. Ande struggled to maintain her grip on his arm while Corpulent and Elephantine stood still, stony faced and silent. Callum composed himself. 'Really, great to meet you. Are you demons?' It sounded absurd in his ears, but with a sigh, Callum continued. 'You don't look like any of the demons I've met before, but I realize there are many of you, so I probably have very limited experience.'

'Callum!' said Ande, with one last heave on his elbow to get him to move.

'You're no doubt aware of the irony of your name?' Callum raised his right eyebrow. 'You're not an Aussie demon, are you? A Down Under Devil? We do that a lot in Australia. Use ironic nicknames. You know, the unusually tall bloke gets called Shorty. That kind of thing.'

Corpulent looked at Elephantine, who mirrored his enigmatic expression. He took a step forward. Callum responded with a step back. Despite Callum's initial concerns which he'd successfully masked with bravado, he began to feel a tickle of apprehension. True, had Corpulent and Elephantine meant him and Ande any harm, it probably would have happened already. True, there was nothing at all threatening or aggressive about their behaviour. It was certainly weird, unsettlingly odd in fact, but Callum still did not feel they were in danger. Yet, his heart was beating fast, and a rabid thirst bothered his throat. He licked his lips, held his ground, and took hold of Ande's hand. She accepted this comfort.

Elephantine stepped closer to them, but this time Callum didn't move. As he studied her face, she reached to her forehead, beginning a slow scratching motion against her skin. It sounded a little like sandpaper. She stopped, then twisted the nails of her thumb and forefinger deep into the skin. Callum was losing sensation in his hand courtesy of Ande's ever tightening grip as they watched in horrified silence. Elephantine removed her finger and thumb to reveal a hole from which no blood flowed. In place of the expected rush of claret, came a beetle, quickly followed by another.

Ande screamed. Callum gasped. Elephantine moved her lips into the approximation of a smile. Corpulent, who had also observed the demonstration, albeit completely without reaction, commenced a replication of his partner's actions with his own fingers and his own forehead. The result of this surgery was more beetles.

Enough was enough. Callum spun around and bolted away, yanking Ande along beside him; at least initially. He soon out-strode her and was forced to stop and wait when the previously terminal connection between their hands was broken by the strength and speed of his flight to safety. He realized then that Corpulent and Elephantine had made no attempt to follow them. At a distance of a hundred meters they remained.

'Are you okay, Ande?'

'No,' she said, staring at him. 'What the hell? No, I'm not all right.'

'Yeah. What the hell?' echoed Callum. 'How could you see them?'

'With my eyes, of course. What were they?'

Turning away from the stationary strangers with holes in their heads, from which beetles flowed, Callum and Ande walked on, only to be confronted by the couple they had left behind.

'We have a message,' said Corpulent.

'Let me guess,' said Callum. 'Something to do with beetles?'

'Leave Istanbul immediately.'

At this announcement, Ande did something very unexpected. She lashed out with her foot, aiming a well-directed side kick into Corpulent's stomach who collapsed backwards in a gangly heap. Callum looked at Ande. 'Nice. I didn't know you could do that.'

'Me neither.' She winked at him.

Corpulent remained on the footpath, tangled like broken spaghetti, while Elephantine looked on. After finishing a survey of her partner in terror, she turned to face Callum and Ande. 'We have a message. Leave—'

With another perfectly targeted kick, Ande cut off Elephantine's words, sending her tumbling onto what used to be Corpulent. There was no movement from either figure, no reassembly, no puff of smoke, no sounds of reconfiguration.

'Damn!' said Callum. 'That was very effective. Why didn't you do that before?'

Ande stood, staring at the ruins of her victims, shaking her head. 'What now? Wait!' She walked towards the fallen figures, no longer recognizable even as the counterfeit humans they had been. 'Check this out Callum.'

He followed, joining her to kneel within arm's length of what was now coming to life. Tiny trinkets of clicking noises, mingled with scratching and, it couldn't be scratching and sighing. 'Can you hear that?'

'Sounds like bugs,' said Ande. 'Lots of them.'

They watched as the pieces of Corpulent and Elephantine transformed into beetles of all shapes and sizes which appeared to merge from within the detritus and from within each other. Each beetle was born or formed, then gave birth to another and so on until the mound of fake flesh was a swarming pile of insects. Spindly legs, shiny carapaces, horns, and antennae, colourful, mesmerizing.

'Remind you of anything?' asked Callum.

'I'm guessing we're not in any more danger than we were before this,' said Ande, avoiding the question whilst gesturing at the beetle. 'So...'

'So, what do you think about the warning they gave

us? Do you think we should take it seriously?'

Ande looked at Callum, searching his eyes, making him feel violated. She had a terrifying intensity about her which fortunately she seldom used, not on him anyway. It was both frightening and exciting at the same time. Callum's feelings for Ande were becoming increasingly complex and given what they had already been through together, that was really saying something. With the immediate danger over, Callum wasn't sure now how to be with her. If he moved too far in a direction which displeased her, he would probably end up sprawled on the road courtesy of that wicked sidekick. When she finally spoke, an irrepressible burst of air escaped his lips.

'I think we need to get to the bottom of this beetle business.'

Callum laughed in admiration as well as amusement. 'Excellent alliteration.'

'What?'

'Never mind,' said Callum, unwilling to give Ande a grammar lesson. 'I'm really pleased you think so because I couldn't agree more. We're going to need help though.'

'Pitch?'

Callum nodded. 'Exactly the man we need for the job, but there's someone else we need too. Someone who's a little better equipped and probably a lot better beetle informed.'

Ande laughed. 'Good one, Callum. Beetle informed. That's funny.'

'Is that what I said?' He smiled, considering not just his inadvertent pun, but also how he was going to introduce Ande to his invisible friend.

Chapter Sixteen

'I have demons under me, you know,' said Alix.

'How unfortunate for them,' replied Ron. 'Or fortunate, depending on how they feel about it. I think I'd probably enjoy it.'

Alix scowled.

Being at the airport brought back some unpleasant memories for Ron, so he was trying to keep it light with her. Despite her indignation at Ron's jests about her party tricks, Alix was not able to keep the smile off her face. He could see her valiant attempts to beat him down, to focus his thinking and the conversation, and he admired her for it. However, Alix was out of her league. Having already proved herself almost his physical equal, she was endeavouring—without being subtle about it, to outwit him in the intellectual arena. Never one to blow his own trumpet, Ron had to concede that he was pretty damn good, and Alix would most likely fail. He liked her determination though.

'You would be enjoying that in your dreams, I suppose,' she quipped.

'You know what they say about dreams, my sweetness.'

'Don't call me that!'

Callum was checking in, shuffling forward in the corral, a blank expression on his face. After providing an entertaining recount of his run in with Corpulent and Elephantine at the hotel while he packed for his trip, he'd fallen into a reflective melancholy. Quiet on the way to the airport, he resisted Ande's attempts to cheer or comfort him. Ande was still in the dark about Ron. Ron wondered why Callum hadn't told her, when clearly, he and Ande were close. Naturally, Ande could not see or hear Ron because she hadn't awakened, but he did think it reasonable that at least Callum should reveal his existence to her. It was a little hurtful if he thought about it.

'When's your friend going to snap out of it?' asked Alix.

'You know his father died, right?'

'And?'

Ron stared at Alix for a few moments, considered enlightening her about human grief. 'You've got a lot to learn about humans.'

'What's to learn? They're weak, fickle, easily manipulated, and disingenuous.' Alix smiled. 'Did I miss anything?'

'It's a little more complicated than that.'

'Do tell,' purred Alix suggestively, as though she'd somehow found a wicked double entendre in Ron's words.

'Plenty of time for that,' replied Ron before leaping away from her to land on Callum's suitcase. The impact forced the case free of Callum's grip and down to the floor. *Bang!*

'What?' Callum looked to the fallen case. 'Oh, it's you, Ron.'

'Oh, it's you, Ron? What kind of greeting is that?'

Callum grabbed the handle of his suitcase and lifted it off the floor, by which time the queue had progressed. He dutifully walked forward, stopping after a few paces. 'Have you put on weight?'

The woman in front of Callum in the line was standing at a right angle to him. At his words she turned her head and smiled at him. Ron remembered when Callum would not speak to him in public for fear of what others would think of him; these days, however, he was decidedly unabashed. The woman's smile was sympathetic, as though she suspected Callum was talking to himself rather than asking her a question. A logical response from a stranger, although it must have been hard for the woman to not take it personally given her obesity. Humans, females in particular, Ron had noticed were good at taking offense. They could be quite precious.

'I don't know, Callum,' said Ron. 'Do I look heavier?'

After a careful study, Callum concluded. 'Yes.'

'Okay,' said Ron. 'It was either those extra kilos, or my landing was an inexplicably clumsy one. I'm usually quite good at sticking my landings, even on small surfaces.'

The woman turned away, then moved out of the line, beckoned to a service desk by a hairy hand waving from behind it. Callum moved into the space she vacated, holding his tongue much to Ron's disappointment.

'Do you want to talk about your father?' said Ron.

'No.'

'Do you want to know why I have expanded my physical imprint on the earth?'

'No.'

A slender bejewelled hand gestured for Callum to come forward, which he did, handing over his passport as he arrived at the counter.

Ron thought about his size. He hadn't noticed it, but Callum was right, he must have grown. He would have to be mindful of that when operating in the corporeal realm. He wondered if Alix had noticed any difference in him between their first and second meetings. Although she hadn't said anything at St. Mary's, she was observant, and it was unlikely she would miss such an obvious change. He skipped back over to where she waited, to find her producing beetles to entertain herself and to horrify passengers entering the terminal.

'Having fun?'

'Not really,' she said, holding out her hand to receive a collection of her insect friends, assimilating them into her body as they crawled onto her hands and up her arms.

'That is such a cool trick. I'd love to know what it's all about.'

Alix smiled. 'Yes, I'm sure you would.'

Deciding not to press the point, Ron switched to the other topic of interest to him at the moment: his growth. 'Alix, do you think I'm bigger now than when we met at the hotel?'

Alix placed her palm on his chest, then scraped her nails down to his stomach. Ron gulped. She then took his chin between her thumb and forefinger, lifting his head. She brought her face close to his, so close he could feel her breath on his lips. It smelled awful which caused him to feel suddenly aroused. Paralysed, Ron waited to see what Alix would do next. Disappointingly, she withdrew, releasing his chin. 'A little bit,' she said finally, with a note of indifference.

Finished at check-in, Callum was making his way back towards Ron, but turned sharply to continue his march through the terminal towards the security checkpoint. Ron said to Alix, 'Let's go.'

Alix slinked along beside Ron as they followed Callum, accelerating to catch up to him. 'Are we really going to Australia?'

'What an adventure we'll have,' replied Ron. 'I can't wait. There's so much I want to show you and share with you.' Overcome with enthusiasm for the journey ahead, Ron pressed on, overlooking Alix's predictable reaction. 'Let's do it.'

Truth be told, there wasn't much to distinguish one place from another in Ron's mind. Differences in climate, variations in scenery, shades of the same colours. Nor was there anything remarkable about the people. Whilst they might not look the same, their behaviour was almost identical. Capricious and confused, the majority had unfocused minds, regarding vice as virtue and vice versa. Alix was right to dismiss human sociology as an unworthy pursuit for a demon, yet ever since Callum's awakening,

Ron's opinion had been shifting. Some might have accused him of selling out. Others diagnosed *Homo sapienitis*, the human sickness which diluted the darkness in the devil's underlings. It was said that only the weak were susceptible to this infection. Ron considered himself strong. Although he was beginning to see strength through a different lens, this was a choice rather than a symptom of a disease.

At immigration, their progress was halted as another queue knotted the human twine. Callum stood patiently while Alix fidgeted beside Ron to whom a thought occurred.

'Alix,' he said. 'Was it you, following me and Callum at Chiang Mai airport?'

'You really do have a high opinion of yourself, don't you?'

Very familiar now with Alix's provocations, Ron was about to redirect her, without bothering to defend himself when he spotted something troubling ahead of them. Just beyond the immigration checkpoint, Ron detected a shimmering fuzziness in the light. He avoided staring, managing to monitor the distortion from the disinterest of his periphery.

'Don't look now, but on the other side of the checkpoint, can you see the light bending?'

'Yes,' said Alix.

'Can you do that?'

'Do you mean can I do it personally, or is it possible to do that?'

'I mean,' said Ron. 'Is that something we should

worry about?'

Alix slapped Ron's arm then bounded in the direction of the light distortion. He called after her, but she was too fast, too impetuous, too adorably reckless. Quickly following, ignoring Callum's question about where he was rushing off to, Ron joined Alix inside the distortion where they found an expanded space concealed within plain sight. Inside this cavern was a pack of level two demons, all of whom were shocked by the arrival of Alix first, then soon after, Ron.

'Hello,' said Alix airily, as though she was welcoming guests to a dinner party. 'What have we here?'

Ron counted six of them. There was zero chance of them being here for any other purpose than to...to what. To stop him? To slow him down? To distract him? To kill him? With the element of surprise stripped from them, the evil cohort seemed paralysed. They shifted uneasily where they stood, casting subtle glances sideways at each other, seeming to seek for a command from someone to proceed. What to do when Plan A failed and there was no Plan B? More cautious than he used to be, Ron pondered the options for he and Alix. Alix, on the other hand, decided to play it differently.

Charging the demon closest to her, directly in front of her, she knocked it flat on its back before whipping around to clobber another from behind. As it fell forward, grunting, Ron's instinct kicked in causing him to leap into the fray. From high in the air, Ron came crashing down on the fallen demon, reached for the demon's neck, placed both hands around it and squeezed with all his might. The demon shuddered and squirmed, but Ron was too strong, suffocating it quickly. Just as he released the lifeless body from his talons, a blow from the side sent him reeling. Tumbling first, then scrambling to his feet, he twisted his body away from the next attack. Repeating the action several times until he was able to put a little distance between him and his foe, Ron gained his balance and received the next assault with a deft block and a counterstrike. The demon on the receiving end was unaffected by Ron's punch so he stepped closer and hit him again, twice in the face before stepping away to strike with his foot at the demon's knee. As it buckled, Alix appeared from behind, breaking its neck with a rapid twisting motion of her small but impressively strong hands.

There was no time to celebrate the death of two of their adversaries though. Demons three and four rushed at Alix from behind, rolling straight over her to crash into Ron. Sent sprawling, Ron managed to push off one of them as Alix tore the other away, flinging it backwards as though it were made only of paper. She smiled at Ron, who returned the gesture. In that frozen moment, Ron felt something strange, an alien emotion for which he could not find a name. It felt welcoming, warm, and terrifying at the same time. As he tried to identify the feeling and attach a label to it, Alix fell on him. Through her body, Ron felt the blow which hammered her back. She buried her head into his armpit before lifting it, turning it, and smiling again.

'Double kick now,' she said before rolling off him.

Ron obeyed, sending the demon who had struck Alix sailing through the air to land on the far side of the battleground. Alix sprung up, rushing across the space which separated her and the demon, appearing in its face as soon as he regained its senses. Ron was immediately beside her, lifting up the demon to make it easier for Alix to box its head until it collapsed in on itself, and the demon died.

The next assailant was joined by the other two remaining demons to launch a combined attack on Alix and Ron, but they lacked skill, coordination and they were also disheartened. It was with a duck and an open palmed uppercut that Ron dispatched the first. Alix side kicked the other in the stomach before dropping her elbow to the back of its head.

'Nice work,' said Ron.

'I'm guessing these recently deceased clowns were hiding here to ambush you, right?'

'Or you.'

Alix shook her head. 'I don't have enemies, but even if I did, I doubt they'd be setting elaborate traps and sending dispensable grunts. More likely they were sent by one of your friends in high places who, if we are to believe the stories told about you, have been put offside by your behaviour…and your mouth.'

'My mouth?' said Ron, feigning indignation.

'Listen,' said Alix. 'While you're trying to think of something clever to say, we should think about how to get out of here. I was thinking it ought to be as easy as it was to enter. If not, then it was probably designed to be a one-way experience.'

'You enter and then you die.'

'Exactly.'

Ron looked around the space, for the first time noticing how indistinct its boundaries were. There weren't walls as such, not a defined area, but neither was there any sense of transparency or porousness. They might have been standing in the hollow centre of a solid cloud. To test his theory, Ron walked into the wall and found it unyielding. Moving around the perimeter and repeating his probing demonstrated likewise. 'Either this space was generated by the dead soldiers, or externally by whoever sent them.'

'The grunts are dead so it can't be them,' said Alix.

'We'd better check that.'

'When I kill, it's permanent,' said Alix, sounding offended by the doubt placed over her lethality.

Ron laughed. 'Check them all anyway,' he said. When Alix refused to move, frowning at Ron instead, he added. 'Humour me, Alix. Just to be sure. If this space was created by them and they're all dead, then logically we should be out of it, or it should have simply disappeared. We need to rule that possibility out first. There's a chance we didn't finish them all off, so let's sort that out first. If we did, well let's just say the alternative is much more disturbing.'

He rolled one of the demons onto its back, cupped his hand over its mouth and nose for a few seconds. 'Definitely dead.'

Alix relented, joining Ron in the post-mortem,

albeit haphazardly. Kicking one, then another to satisfy herself, she announced two more confirmed deceased. Ron was unconvinced, but before he could suggest Alix take her examination more seriously, he found one of the demons unconscious; not dead, but knocked out cold from, if his memory served, one of Alix's headshots. 'Bingo!' said Ron. He placed his hands on its throat, commencing a death squeeze, which he happily admitted to himself, never failed to make him feel warm and fuzzy inside. It was better when there was resistance from the inevitable victim, but in this case, there was still sufficient pleasure. As it breathed its final breath, its eyes popped open, and the misty walls which surrounded them vanished. 'Bingo!'

'Stop saying bingo,' said Alix.

'I wondered where you'd got to, Ron,' said Callum. 'Been playing a bit of hide and seek, have we?'

It took Ron a few seconds to realize that Callum had just come through immigration and was walking towards the departure gate unaware, naturally, of what had happened. 'Something like that,' he replied.

Chapter Seventeen

'You what?'

Pitch shuffled his backside on the hard, metal chair and looked across the circular table at Ande's incredulous expression. He raised a red coffee mug to his lips, and broke the foamy surface to sip the hot coffee beneath. 'I know how it sounds, but I can only tell you what happened. What I saw.'

Ande leaned forward over her coffee. 'You'd been drinking, right?'

'Ande,' said Pitch. She could hear exasperation in his voice, but he was wise enough to not allow himself to become upset. 'When you try to offer rational explanations, or worse, dismiss first-hand personal experience, it's insulting. We don't know each other that well, but well enough, I think, for you to accept what I am saying.'

Visibly chastened, Ande looked down, sipped her coffee. 'You're right. What do you think it means then?'

'I've already been through the possibilities. An over-active subconscious, obsessing about beetles. A dehydration induced hallucination or poisoning by something which had the same hallucinogenic effect. I've never experienced anything like it before. Before I started tripping, I was definitely stung, or scratched by the beetle. I felt it, but I didn't see it happen. As there was nothing or no one else around me at the time, there's no other explanation.'

'Does this beetle normally do that?'

'No.'

Ande shook her head. 'So…'

'Have you noticed how unfazed Callum is by all the weird stuff going on here?'

'Like this, you mean?' Ande showed Pitch her mug.

'What?'

'See the scarab beetle in the foam?'

'I'm serious, Ande. You know what I'm talking about.'

A slice of pumpkin cheesecake sitting beside a massive dollop of cream on a white plate was placed on the table between Pitch and Ande. Ande thanked the waiter, pulled the plate closer to her and picked up a gleaming dessert fork. She was used to Callum's rantings and had become accustomed to the strange events that seemed to occur wherever he went. His recently discovered laconic attitude to supernatural occurrences had become almost endearing. Without taking him too seriously, she could humour him and enjoy the cute factor whilst simultaneously suppressing her own internal agitations. Focusing on *Callum* as the oddball enabled her to pretend not to notice what was really going on, at least for short stretches of time. She was unsettled by it all but determined not to let anyone know it.

Pitch was a scientist, by nature and profession, even more of a rationalist than Callum used to be. Now *he* was having bizarre personal experiences, and this one, getting stung by a harmless beetle then hallucinating about magical creatures with tusks, happened when he was alone. Nothing to do with Callum. Pitch was looking at her, waiting for her to answer him.

'This is the kind of story I expect from Callum, and I've seen some strange things myself. More, in fact, in the last few weeks with Callum than in my whole life prior to that. When I first met him, he was so straight. I couldn't talk to him about anything like this. Every time I went anywhere near religion or spirituality, he shut me down. Then we went to Thailand, and you know all about that. Now, here with all these beetles, after all the scorpions in Thailand, and I don't even like bugs.'

Ande paused to observe Pitch's face. She smiled.

'You haven't answered my question,' said Pitch.

'Yes, he's changed and yes, he seems to take it all in his stride.'

'As though it's normal.'

'Yes, although his instinct is still often to look for some rational explanation.' Ande thought for a moment. 'But he doesn't try very hard.'

'As though he's quite comfortable with it.'

'Yes.' Ande couldn't disagree with Pitch. 'Are you going to have something to eat? This cheesecake is amazing.'

Pitch shook his head. 'I want to get to the bottom

of this. As a scientist, I've seen incredible things. Had my mind blown by wonders beyond description, but there's always a reason. There's always more than what you see, but I'm happy to embrace the extraordinary in the context of the ridiculous variety and innovation of nature.'

'Nature?' Ande loaded another, larger slice of cheesecake into her mouth. She chewed slowly, savouring the taste, looking alternately between the remaining cake on her plate and Pitch.

'You know what's really surprising?' said Pitch. Without waiting for her to answer, then added, 'Is me meeting Callum and then you, and having these strange experiences. This latest one takes the cheesecake, though.'

'Good one, Pitch,' said Ande. She smiled. 'Don't you wonder that maybe fate has brought us together for a specific purpose?'

Pitch looked doubtful, almost dismissive. 'What purpose?'

'I don't know.' She ate some more cake, thinking about Callum. She felt a little lost without him. He'd only been gone a day, but she missed him terribly already. Missed his irritating flippancy. Missed his sporadic intensity. Missed his voice. Her assignment in Istanbul would be finished soon. She would have to move on to the next, in Greece. Callum might not return to Istanbul before she left. Then, who knew how long it would be until she saw him again. When she'd left Thailand, she hadn't wanted to see him again. Ever. She felt differently now.

As the last piece of cheesecake dissolved in her mouth and slid down her throat, she felt foolish at having reacted so strongly to hearing about him and the crazy woman in the taxi. They were friends, colleagues. She had no claim on him, yet jealousy had overwhelmed her and created a great wall of awkwardness between them.

'I've always wanted to be a detective,' said Pitch, breaking into Ande's thoughts. 'I could have done forensic medicine but decided to focus on entomology instead. I've never regretted that because I've been continually fascinated by bugs and studying them, which was a childhood hobby, has become my thing. My livelihood. I love it. Travelling, attending conferences, writing papers, contributing to books, consulting. It's a comfortable space, but not the kind of comfort that causes laziness or boredom. Do you know what I mean?'

Ande pushed the plate away from her, wiped her mouth with a napkin, laid it on the plate then placed the fork on top of it. 'I get it,' she said. 'Getting into hotel reviewing was accidental for me. I studied journalism, but couldn't really get into a job I wanted, which was probably because I didn't know what job I wanted. I wanted to write. I loved it, but I usually didn't know what to write about, and the few jobs I had with local newspapers and small magazines left me feeling hollow. I could write what my editors wanted me to write, and even with my occasional odd expressions, murdering English idioms— which I'm still learning—I produced professional work. But I never really felt passionate about anything.'

'Let's get out of here,' said Pitch. 'Do you want to finish your coffee?'

Ande threw the remnants in her mug in her mouth,

swallowing immediately. 'Done.'

'I'd like to visit Hagia Sophia?'

'Yeah, great,' said Ande. 'Callum and I went there. The largest cathedral in the Christian world for a thousand years and then it became a mosque, but it's still got all the Christian stuff in it. Fascinating. I think it's not far from here.'

'If you've already been,' said Pitch, 'We can go somewhere else.'

'No, no. It's amazing. I'd love to go again.'

'And on the way we can talk some more. I feel like we are supposed to be doing something now, while Callum is gone.' Pitch gestured for Ande to walk out of Coffeetopia before him. 'I'll pay and see you out front.'

On Arpacila Cd, Ande stood facing across the mall. A yellow taxi cruised slowly by, stopping the flow of the pedestrian stream temporarily. Pitch joined her, then they stepped away from the café, taking a place on the wide footpath. Ande turned back and looked up: *Fresh coffee is good,* it said beneath the name of the café. She looked at the customers seated in the al fresco area of Coffeetopia, smiling, chatting, relaxed. It was a charming place, not quiet but still peaceful. She googled Hagia Sophia, and discovered it to be just over a kilometre away.

'Which way?' said Pitch.

'It's a five-minute taxi ride, or we can walk if you like?'

'I like.'

Ande started walking and Pitch fell in step beside her. 'Thanks for the coffee and cheesecake,' she said.

'No worries, mate.'

'That's such a strange saying.'

Ande used Australian slang even if she didn't always understand it. In her early years of living in Australia and learning the language, she had decided to make every effort to speak like the natives. To copy their accent and use their funny phrases. If she got it wrong, someone would correct her, and she'd remember how to use it properly the next time round. If she heard one that she hadn't heard, she'd come right out and ask what it meant. She learned fast, impressing her parents and her teachers at the Intensive English Centre. She was told many times that making mistakes was the best way to learn, so she developed a thick skin, the ability to laugh at herself while she made the language of her new home, her language. Without dumping Swahili or losing her African accent, she quickly began to master Aussie English. Conquering the twin peaks of pronunciation and slang.

'How old were you when you moved to Australia?'

'Eight.'

'So that was…?'

'It's not polite to ask a lady's age, Pitch.'

Pitch smiled. 'Gotcha. Let's just say somewhere between ten and twenty years.'

'Let's just say it's not polite to—'

'Okay, okay,' said Pitch, raising his hands in mock surrender.

Although she'd become very proficient with the language, she was still uncomfortable talking about herself, so she changed the subject. 'What did you mean when you said you thought we should follow on while Callum's away?'

'The beetle infestation in particular areas and the behaviour of certain of them which we've seen is a supranatural phenomenon.'

'I thought you said you didn't believe in supernatural.'

'I said supra-natural, not super-natural.'

'What's the difference?'

They turned right to follow Arpicila Cd, crossing the road where it intersected Yali Kosku Cd and passing Ziraat Bank on their right. The people walking to and fro were dressed casually in modern styles. No one wore shorts or short skirts though, despite the heat.

'It's a subtle difference,' said Pitch. 'Basically, supernatural means above or beyond nature whereas supranatural means natural but rare. Very rare.'

Ande stopped walking. When Pitch realized, he also stopped, turning around to look back at her. 'You're still saying these are *natural* occurrences. Billions of beetles suddenly appearing in public places to bury people. You getting stung, by a normally harmless rhinoceros beetle and having hallucinations? What about Corpulent and Elephantine?'

'Huh?'

'Oh,' said Ande. 'I didn't tell you about them.' She laughed, started walking again. 'This will convince you once and for all.'

As they continued their journey to Hagia Sophia, Ande began to recount the events following Mass at St.

Mary's.

Pitch listened politely, but Ande felt the vibe of a parent listening to a child waffling on about some flight of imagination, until suddenly he interrupted her.

'Wait a minute!' said Pitch. 'What happened at St. Mary's?'

'Oh,' said Ande, 'I didn't tell you about that either?' She guessed he was humouring her but was ready at the end to remind him of how he'd been offended by her not believing his story about his trippy beetle experience.

'I think you'd better go all the way back to the start,' said Pitch.

'Okay. Callum and I went to St. Mary's.'

'Was that St. Mary of the Mongols?'

'No. St. Mary of Sakizagic.'

'Well, that explains everything,' said Pitch.

Ande stopped walking again, and glared at Pitch. 'Do you want to hear this story or not?'

'I certainly do.'

She frowned at him, before saying. 'I understand why you and Callum are friends. Peas in a puddle.'

Apart from when Ande was temporarily distracted by the incredible and enticing display of cakes and sweets in the front window of Hafiz Mustafa Café, she told Pitch everything, fluently and in great detail, from the first sign of beetles at the church, to the invasion which quickly led to mass panic. Pitch noted the pun, but Ande didn't understand. She described how determined Callum was to do something, as though he somehow felt responsible for what was happening. She told how he didn't initially appear to know what to do, until suddenly he did. She related how the stained-glass windows above the altar at the front of the church smashed, but only in a small specific pattern, like a basketball had been shot through it.

'Actually it wasn't round like a basketball. It was more irregularly shaped, like it had legs.'

Pitch shook his head. 'Go on.'

'We left the church, but not immediately. The police were there, and people hung around as though they weren't sure if they could leave or not. Maybe they were in shock. I know I was.'

'How was Callum?'

'Really calm as usual. I mean as usual for the new Callum. He was telling me about the beetle problem and how it was going to get worse in the same way he might have described a blocked toilet.'

Pitch laughed.

They continued to walk at an easy pace, now on Hamidiye Cd, until they reached Turk Telekom and one of its opponents across the road: Vodaphone, at the intersection with Zahire Borsasi Sk. Ande went on to tell Pitch about their first meeting with the odd couple, and how they'd decided to walk back to the hotel, but it had become a little weird because of how quiet it was. Then the strange couple appeared from nowhere, and it was during this part of the narrative that Pitch was visibly affected. He kept stopping and looking at Ande as though he thought he'd misheard her. Clearly, her personal experience of witnessing human beings, or at least what appeared to be human beings, turn into beetles connected with his vision of the sorcerer's tusk. Ande had finally presented the piece of evidence to push Pitch off the cliff. When she finished her story, Pitch fell silent.

They reached Captain Candy, a small, but eye-catching store with its front lined with wooden chests filled with a dazzling array of candy and chocolates. Ande couldn't resist. She walked inside, eyes wide, mouth open; the literal embodiment of the metaphoric a kid in a candy shop.

'Looks like you found heaven, Ande,' said Pitch.

'Wow!'

Inside the store was a kaleidoscope of coloured wrappers and lollies bursting from even more rustic barrels. She didn't know where to begin, but heard Pitch say, 'Knock yourself out.'

Finally recovering her shock at the serendipitous discovery of Captain Candy, Ande said to Pitch. 'I don't know what that means, but I'm going to carefully choose a very large collection of these exotic-looking sweets and I might even share them with you.'

'That's big of you,' said Pitch. 'I'm going to buy some water.'

'Sure. And while we're gorging on lollies and chockies, you and I are going to stop pretending we aren't caught up in something way beyond us and our understanding.'

'Okay,' said Pitch, but Ande heard the uncertainty in his voice.

'Fate is calling us to become paranormal investigators,' said Ande, beaming at Pitch. 'Paranormal investigators! How cool is that?'

Pitch swallowed and turned away, leaving Ande to her deliriously pleasurable mission to discover as many new, sweet treats as she could handle.

Chapter Eighteen

Callum was not unaware of the irony of how much time he was spending in churches now. True, on this occasion, his father's funeral, it was not by choice, but still, when he'd studiously avoided such Christian edifices for so long, it was hard not to draw the conclusion he was being pulled back, deeper into a world which was once so familiar.

He reached for his mother's hand as she sat beside him in the front pew of St. Luke's Anglican church. When he lightly squeezed her hand, she returned the gesture, turning to smile at him albeit with clear strain. Her face was over-made up in a concerted effort to cover the signs of grief. On the other side of her sat Callum's brother Darren, and next to him his wife. The distance Callum had created between them, as he forged his own way in life, finding himself outside the prism of expectation and disappointment, shrivelled to insignificance as they united in grief. He would come to see this, and numerous subsequent events in his life as signs of personal transformation.

Built in 1882, the church also known as the Osbourne Memorial Church of St. Luke, had once represented all that Callum didn't like about his parents' religion. Thoughtlessly indentured to tradition, addicted to clichés, and mired in impractical irrelevance, they'd religiously rejected the term religion, preferring to talk in terms of faith and relationship. It was easy now to see how he spurned what they offered out of nothing more than rebellion. The standard teenage package of striving to figure himself out by himself. Of happily taking the loving care and provision of his parents whilst biting the hands that fed him. Every now and then, making decisions to attempt to assert his authority, to maintain control or at least maintain the illusion of control. Callum understood the illusion now. The clever and subtle deception.

Feeling his hand becoming sweaty, Callum let go of his mother's. She quickly took it back. 'I love you, Mum,' he said quietly, watching a solitary tear roll down her cheek.

The small church was crowded, full of mourners and sacred furniture, together with the ghosts of parishioners past. Reverend Stephens approached them, radiating compassion, getting his smile just right. The smile which said' I'm sorry to see you under these circumstances. I know this is difficult for you. I understand.' The smile of polite, yet genuine comfort. He took Callum's mother's hand in his, placed his other hand around it, held it for just the right length of time, then let go.

'Hello Callum,' he said, extending his hand. 'It's good to see you again. Very sorry about your father. He was much loved by his family here, and his Father in

Heaven. He's at peace now.'

Unable to speak or even muster a smile, Callum nodded his head and looked away. He felt Reverend Stephens' eyes linger on him briefly, before shifting his attention to Darren to whom he said nothing. Callum felt singled out, chastised, then foolish for being so cynical. He swallowed and turned his gaze to the walnut coffin. He imagined the discussions over which wood the casket should be constructed from. Callum was glad he'd missed the planning. Had he been there, he would have had uncharitable thoughts about funeral homes profiting from grief. What difference did it make what a corpse was interred or cremated in? Instead of spending thousands of dollars on a single use, disposable item, inexpensive, eco-friendly caskets should have been rented out. Everything about funerals was for the benefit of those left behind, even if the whole service, the whole shebang, every last detail was organized prior to death by the deceased. It was all designed to ease the pain. Callum swallowed hard, suppressing tears and spiteful thoughts, beneath which lay his own overwhelming grief.

Callum noticed how the closed casket glistened under the church spotlights. A small wreath and a photograph of his father sat on top of it, in the centre. As Callum stared at it, Reverend Stephens moved to the lectern which was positioned to the right of the casket. He adjusted the height of the microphone, looked at Callum's mother, smiling that same warm sincere smile.

'We are gathered here today to celebrate the life of John Alfred Steele. As Christians we believe God created us, breathing life into our lungs and that all our days are numbered by him. We believe we have been created out of love and born for a purpose. The intentional and inspirational life of John Steele is what we are celebrating here. Whilst acknowledging the sadness of lost, especially for his wife Kathleen and sons Callum and Darren, we do so in hope of the resurrection to eternal life. Thank you for joining us today. Darren will now bring the reading.'

As Darren rose from his seat and slowly walked to the lectern, Callum continued to stare at the shiny box which contained his father's corpse. That was a body lying there inside a wooden tomb. Just a shell. If he looked, it would appear to be his father, but it wouldn't smell like him and it wouldn't be able to hear him or talk to him. Callum would never get to do that again. The knot in his throat expanded as he tried to focus on his brother's words.

'Usually,' began Darren, 'the readings at funerals are from Old Testament books like Ecclesiastes in which Solomon tells us that there is time for everything including a time to be born and a time to die. Classic New Testament verses include Romans chapter eight in which Paul explains that not even death can separate us from the love of God.'

Callum wished his brother would just read his assigned verse and sit down. As usual, just like their father, Darren was seizing the opportunity to deliver another sermon. God's gift to the broken-hearted. God's gift to the lost. God's gift to the lonely. God's gift to the sick. Callum glanced at Reverend Stephens, searched for signs he was feeling slighted at potentially being upstaged. To Callum's disappointment though, he looked perfectly serene. Angelic.

'In the Book of Revelation,' continued Darren, 'John speaks of a new heaven and a new earth which the children of God will inherit. These are all great verses. All very inspiring and relevant, but Dad wanted to share a different passage with you.'

Callum wished he was facing the guests in the church so he could see their faces. A wall of silence pressed against his back

'This is from Job, chapter 19:23-27:

Oh, that my words were written!
Oh, that they were inscribed in a book!
That they were engraved on a rock
With an iron pen and lead, forever!
For I know that my Redeemer lives,
And He shall stand at last on the earth;
And after my skin is destroyed, this I know,
That in my flesh I shall see God,
Whom I shall see for myself,
And my eyes shall behold, and not another.
How my heart yearns within me!'

'Dad was a man who lived as though he believed these words to be absolutely true.' After standing, still and dramatically quiet for a few moments, Darren returned to his seat.

Hearing a stifled sob from his mother, Callum again took her hand.

Reverend Stephens took Darren's place at the lectern. 'John's family has prepared a slide-show for us to watch while we listen to his favourite song. After the song we'll hear from John's eldest son, Callum.' Stephens nodded and stepped aside, as the screen on the back wall above the casket came to life with an announcement. Stark black type on a white background:

> *'Whatever may pass,*
> *And whatever lies before me,*
> *Let me be singing*
> *When the evening comes.*
> *Bless the Lord, oh my soul.'*

The music began and the slides rolled slowly through. Childhood photos; alone, and with family and friends. The stages of John Steele's life displayed for all to see the boy grow into a man. Mum appearing in shots from his late teens. The background changing from the wild greens of Scotland to the exotic temple-studded mountains of Mae Sai, to the open spaces of Australia. Callum's baby shots. Deliriously proud parents. Callum's brother. His wedding. Fewer photos of Callum. More of the rest of the family. Dad ageing wonderfully like fine wine. The beautiful song supporting the images, evoking gratitude.

> *'For all your goodness,*
> *I will keep on singing.*
> *Ten thousand reasons for my heart to find.*
> *Bless the Lord, oh my soul.'*

When the song finished, the church was blanketed by reverent silence as a final photo, the same which adorned his father's coffin, remained on the screen. John Steele, smiling peacefully. He was terribly sick at the time, and probably knew that only divine intervention would extend his life. Despite his faith, John was not given a miracle, but Callum knew that even death would not have shaken his father's trust in the benevolent sovereignty of his God. Assuming he passed from life into eternity, into the arms of his Father in heaven, John would simply have thanked Jesus for bringing him to his true home. Naturally, Callum had no way of knowing what happened to John after he breathed his last, but faced with the canyon created in his life by his father's death, Callum found himself unable to accept, as he had once easily done, that death was the end of life. Regardless of whether it was true or not, Callum wanted to believe in the immortal soul. He yearned to know John Steele had received his prize, that his faith had been rewarded.

Callum suddenly realized the collective spell cast by the song and photographs over the mourners had broken. Reverend Stephens was looking at him, nodding imperceptibly. Darren appeared before him, crouching, placed his hand on Callum's knee.

'Do you want me to come up with you?'

The correct answer, the truthful answer would have been yes. 'No,' said Callum. 'I'm okay. I'll be fine.' As he stood, his brother's hand moved from Callum's knee to his shoulder and then to his back as Callum walked away from him towards the lectern. He carried the sensation of his brother's comforting touch with him as he stood to face the assembled mourners. He hadn't prepared anything, confident in his ability to speak from the heart and say what he needed to say, what needed to be said. He swallowed, wiped his hands on the front of his trousers. Staring down to where he would have laid his notes if he'd had any, Callum couldn't think how to start.

He looked at his mother, then his brother, then around the church, taking in the faces, seeing the expressions of pity, empathy, encouragement.

'My father, John Steele...'

Callum had been quite sure his grieving was over. Remembering how much he'd cried and cursed the God he didn't believe in when John's terminal diagnosis had been delivered. Recalling how the anger had dissipated into a film of bitterness which lined his insides, colouring everything he did and thought. Eventually, he'd accepted the folly of allowing resentment to rule his life, but there had been many times when he'd felt more anguish at the prospect of his father's death. Moments when he'd almost called to apologize or make amends, or to at least say, that despite everything, Callum still loved him.

'I love you, Dad.' It was barely a whisper: a strangled breath wrestling with words. 'I'm sorry.'

Through blurry eyes, Callum looked to the ceiling of the church, then to the back where he saw a totally unexpected vision. The angel who visited him at his awakening. The same heavenly hero who rescued him and Ron from Harut's wrath in Mae Sai. There he was, standing silent and still. A towering sentinel of impossible beauty and peace. Callum felt a huge weight lifted from him, sensed powerful arms encircling him, embracing him.

'My father John Steele loved with such earnest power because he had a relationship with Love. Capital 'L' love. Love personified. He wasn't a perfect man. Given to extremes, he could be immovable at times, but this stubbornness should perhaps better be described as zeal.'

And so, Callum continued, eulogizing his father effortlessly, and remarkably for him, without sarcasm. He spoke of positive childhood memories, not needing to ignore the bad ones because they didn't come to mind. With the one exception being his recount of the time John schooled him on the value of having a relationship with God as primary guidance in decision making. He told gathered friends and family, he had always drawn strength from, almost delighted in, a twisted version of the story which had made him more confident in himself rather than in God or the Bible.

'I will always remember his words: *You will know.*'

The angel was still standing at the back of the church, watching him, and Callum knew that without the angel's presence he would not have been able to deliver the eulogy.

'I guess this confidence he instilled in me nearly undid me today. I didn't prepare a speech because I thought I would know exactly what to say. I rehearsed it all in my head, over and over until I was sure I had it right. Then I sat there.' He pointed at the pew space beside his mother. 'I sat there and looked at those photos of Dad and heard, as you all did, that remarkably beautiful song of thanksgiving which, because Dad chose it, very clearly represented him. His attitude to life. And I forgot everything I wanted to say. I know now that I didn't want to say what I planned to say. My plans were upset and I'm happy about that.' Callum shook his head, laughing in a mild self-deprecatory way.

'I'm rambling now. Let me finish by simply saying this.' He turned to face the walnut casket, noticing again how it shone, quickly glanced to the radiant angel at the back of the church. 'I love you, Dad. Thank you for being God in my life. I'm sorry I didn't get it while you were around, but if you're listening, I reckon I'm starting to cotton on now.'

Callum returned to his seat where his mother grabbed his hand, kissed his cheek, and laid her head against his shoulder.

'Very nice, Callum,' said a muffled masculine voice from under the pew. 'I told you the big guy would come back one day.'

'Where are you?'

'What, dear?' said his mother.

'Nothing, Mum.'

Reverend Stephens was back at the lectern. 'John's sister, Frances will now bring the second reading.'

'Where are you?' Callum said again, almost inaudibly.

'Under the pew,' said Ron.

'Why?'

'Are you serious?'

Aunty Frances took her place behind the microphone, fumbling first with it, then with the bible.

'Do you think I'm going to show my face when he's around?' said Ron.

The angel would have most certainly known that Ron was here. Him trying to hide was funny, but now was not the time for laughter.

Frances began. 'Romans 8. Verses 37 to 39 says this:

> *'None of this fazes us because Jesus loves us.*
> *For I am absolutely convinced that*
> *nothing-nothing living or dead, angelic or*
> *demonic, today or tomorrow, high or low,*
> *thinkable or unthinkable-absolutely nothing can*
> *get between us and God's love.'*

As Aunty Frances resumed her seat, Callum pondered the specific phrase; nothing living or dead, angelic or demonic. By the time Reverend Stephens had finished his sermon, Callum's awakening was almost complete.

Chapter Nineteen

Immediately catching Ande's attention, which was some feat given the ridiculous volume of sweets in a riot of colours, were frogs. As the store had been open for some time already, it was clear no one had yet touched this mountain of mock amphibians. Green bodies and perfectly proportioned yellow legs lay stacked on one another in the glass container perched on one of the barrels. The frogs were all facing outwards as though ready to leap off the pile to capture passing flies. Ande searched for a sign to say what kind of candy they were. She first discovered one depicting a hand with a red line through it, then noticed a conveniently positioned silver scoop. Again, an indication that no one yet had taken any. Did this suggest they weren't any good? Unpopular despite their cuteness?

The tangy jelly frogs had hard shells and soft sweet centres. Ande frowned, looking elsewhere for something more to her taste. Beside the frogs were blue sweet jelly sharks. There were red, blue, black, and white batons which apparently could be eaten or used to tie things up. Red marshmallows in the shape of strawberries with white crowns. Dark, milk and white chocolate balls containing hazelnuts, almonds, and coconut centres. *Now we're talking*. Ande pulled a paper bag from the dispenser, grabbed the scoop, and loaded it up before pouring her haul into the bag.

Ande moved on past a mound of miniature tennis balls which were labelled chewing gum, to another barrel which housed candy bugs. Deciding instantly to not even bother reading of what sweet tooth's seduction they were made of, she nonetheless found herself entranced by the colours. As one stares into flames, transfixed by their dance of blended light, so Ande inched nearer, leaning down, mesmerized. On closer inspection, she saw they were a mix of very lifelike beetles.

'You're not going to eat them, are you?' said Pitch. 'I'm sure you've had more than enough.'

'Enough what?'

'Bugs,' said Pitch, then without waiting for the conversation to continue along those lines added, 'Can we go soon? The unique Hagia Sophia awaits. Unlike lollies and chocolates which you can find everywhere.'

'Everywhere?' said Ande, without bothering to look at Pitch. 'Not like this.' She gestured at the insect shaped candies. 'Surely these are unique and exclusive to Captain Candy.'

'Yes, but Captain Candy is a Czech franchise. You can find these stores in other countries with exactly the same collection of sweets.'

'Is that right?' said Ande, who despite her intention not to, found herself feeling an urgent need to taste one of the sugar-laden confections at her fingertips. At least one. She thought maybe it was a nice way to reverse the demonization of beetles which had occurred in her mind as a result of several unpleasant run ins with massive numbers of them. On the way home from St. Mary's, she kicked a couple of human imposters, literally to pieces, so what now if she ate them? What if she could do that in front of some others? Like a warning to the diminutive devils that they should not take her on. Sure, these were lifeless lollies, but the symbolism of devouring them would certainly not be lost on the real ones. Maybe she could buy some and save them for future encounters with beetles. She could carry them in her bag, and when real bugs appeared to disturb her or bother anyone with whom she happened to be, she could whip out one of these replicas, maybe even a handful, and stuff them in her mouth. To show the invidious insects she was not afraid of them. Would that work?

'If you're going to buy some, can you get on with it?' said Pitch. 'I can give you a hand if you like.' He reached for the scoop, but she gently slapped his hand away.

'I don't like,' she said curtly, 'but thank you.' She held out her bag of chocolate balls to Pitch, 'Can you hang on to these, please? Have a look around. Maybe you'll find something you like.' She wanted to outline her clever plan to Pitch and suggest that he buy some candy bugs for himself, but she dared not. To Callum, she might have, but not to Pitch. He wasn't quite in the same headspace as her and Callum. Not yet anyway. As she helped herself to a scoop of bugs, she wondered if she and Callum were actually occupying a place distinctively theirs. An esoteric cocoon of shared experience.

'I'm not really a fan,' said Pitch, 'but I might give the candy bugs a whirl. Feels seductively ironic.'

Ande replaced the scoop, and closed the top of her bag of beetles. 'What does that mean?'

'Never mind,' said Pitch. 'Are you done? Can we get going?'

'Patience. Patience.' She smiled, turned away.

'Wait!' said Pitch. 'Look at this.'

Ande followed his gaze and his finger to the hole in the insect mountain which she'd created. Inside the crater she made with the scoop, the bugs were moving. 'That's just gravity Pitch.'

Pitch shook his head. 'Look again.'

Pushing out of the crater, unmistakably living bugs were thrusting and squirming their way out, displacing their candy counterfeits. Ande scrambled to open the bag and pulled out as many insect sweets as she could fit between her thumb, fore and middle fingers, pushing them quickly into her mouth.

'What are you doing, Ande?'

'How do you like that, suckers?' Ande chewed furiously while glaring at the expanding mass of insects. Pressed against the edges of the container, the candy bugs were forced up and over the side, falling to the floor, soon cascading like a thick technicolour waterfall. Ande stepped forward, crushing them underfoot. She pulled more candy bugs from the bag and stuffed them in her mouth. 'I'm not scared of you little dogs.' She ground her shoe into the lollies under her feet.

'Ande? Ande!'

Soon more bugs pushed out from the centre of the sugary hill, to the extent that candy beetles were falling to the floor from all sides of the container. Bursting from the centre. Live beetles, bristling and clicking, forced the fakers out and away, flowing like lava down the slopes of an erupting volcano.

'I think we'd better go,' said Pitch, grabbing Ande's arm, attempting to pull her away.

They headed for the door, Ande reluctantly allowing Pitch to lead her although she was fuming. Mortified that even as she'd discovered a sweet heaven, the damn bugs had found a way to turn it into a sour hell. Part of her wanted to stay and fight because she was tired of running. Leaping in fright. They were tiny and weak after all. Nothing to be scared of. How could they hurt her? Wanting to kill them all, she kept stomping on them as Pitch dragged her out of the store.

'Hey. You haven't paid for those sweets!' called the sales assistant.

'You need to get out of here now,' said Pitch to her. When she scowled at him, he added, 'We'll pay you later but seriously, you need to get out. Right now.'

She looked ready to protest before an explosion from one of the containers drowned her words in a scream. A colourful burst from one of the containers was followed by a confetti like shower and a buzzing sound. The air filled with flying insects, the beetles stretching their wings, flitting, and zooming in random patterns around the enclosed space of Captain Candy. The shop assistant fled along with the last handful of customers, all of whom were swatting bugs from their faces. More eruptions followed as one by one each of the containers spewed their lollies everywhere, releasing a deafening chaos of swarming bugs. The shop assistant left the door open, allowing some of the insects to escape. Pitch quickly shut it without checking if anyone else was still inside. By now it was almost impossible to see anyway. The insects were so thick, banging into each other and into the glass, then bouncing off to resume their mad rush to nowhere.

A horrified face appeared, pressed against the inside of the glass.

Ande screamed.

The woman's cheek was flattened by the pressure of God knew how much insect mass. She tried to move, down, up, or back, anywhere to escape, but the bugs wouldn't allow it. Whether by design or accident, she was trapped, and they were clearly going to take advantage of her plight. A beetle entered her ear. Her eyes widened. Another crawled up her nose. She opened her mouth to cry, but no sooner had she done so than bugs filled this cavity. Her cheeks bulged as insects continued to cram into the space. Her skin changed colour.

Ande looked away. 'Oh my God, Pitch.' She trembled within his arms, burying her face into his chest. Eventually she managed a sob. 'Is it over?'

'Hell no. I can't see her anymore, but those little suckers are still going off. I can't see anything in there except the bugs. Where the devil did they all come from?'

'That's exactly right, Pitch,' said Ande. 'From the

devil. What are we going to do?' It was a stupid question.

'There's nothing we can do.'

'Are you sure you can't see the woman anymore?'

'Yes.'

Ande broke the embrace and looked in through the window of Captain Candy, marvelling, astounded by the ferocity of the insect storm she was witnessing. She thought she saw a crack forming in the glass. 'Get down everyone,' she shouted, diving to the footpath, pulling Pitch down with her.

Suddenly, with an impossibly bright flash of light, the glass shattered with a thunderous spray of deadly shards and slivers, firing like missiles across the street. Cries of agony, groans and frightened exclamations filled the air as the swarm blasted into the free airspace, immediately dispersing, forcing those bystanders who hadn't been taken down by glass darts to flee or duck for cover. Many beetles dropped to the ground after brief flights, their tiny wings perhaps exhausted by an extraordinary amount of flying. Ande viewed the horrific scene, horizontally from ground level. After several frantic, insane minutes it was over. Many of the bugs had disappeared, many more were creeping over the road, the footpath and the people who lay prone: victims of their short reign of terror.

One of those was Ande, who felt bugs on her arms, legs and back. She stood quickly, brushing them off. Pitch did likewise, and soon after, everyone who could, also stood to join the macabre amusing insect removal dance. Ande stomped her way through the routine, making sure she crushed as many as she could. She turned to look inside Captain Candy, which was empty now, aside from thousands or maybe hundreds of thousands of dead bugs, saw the woman's corpse lying in twisted repose between barrels. She too was covered with insects, and Ande noted candies as well, all mingled in with the remaining beetles.

'What a mess!' said the shop assistant. She said something in Turkish, then looked at Pitch. 'Should I call the police?'

'There's nothing they can do now, but yes, you should report it. We'll need some ambulances as well.'

The woman didn't respond, so Pitch repeated himself. She looked at him blankly. Ande saw the shock on her face. She and Pitch had developed some resilience, having already been exposed to supernatural phenomenon, but this poor lady couldn't deal with what had happened. Ande put her arm around the woman's shoulders, causing her to crumble into Ande's full embrace.

While comforting the traumatized shop assistant, Ande spoke to Pitch. 'We've got to do something about this, Pitch. We've got to stop it!'

'What exactly do you think we can do?' said Pitch. 'This happened,' he waved his hand at Captain Candy, 'without warning and ended without our intervention. We're all victims here.'

Ande nodded into the shop assistant's head. 'I guess the question is victims of what or who?'

'Are you suggesting someone was behind this?'

'Yep.'

'No. Not possible. This was just a—'

'Come on, Pitch,' said Ande, as she released the shop assistant who nodded, smiled, then wandered slowly around inside the store, looking at the catastrophe which was once not only her livelihood, but perhaps her pride and joy. 'Don't tell me you think this was one of those supranatural events? What we just saw never happens. Should never happen.'

'It could.'

'Pitch!' Ande stamped her feet, placed her hands on her hips, glared at him. 'Get out of the river! Smell the coffee.'

'Huh?'

'It's time we stopped pretending that any of what we've been dealing with is normal. It's not normal and it's not good, and we need to do something about it.'

'Why do we need to do something about it?' said Pitch. 'Why us?'

Ande had a memory of Callum impersonating someone from a movie called *Taxi Driver*. She tried to remember the exact quote but couldn't. 'There's no one else.'

Sirens wailed into the scene as at least a dozen emergency vehicles arrived at Hamidiye Cd: police and ambulances in universal blue, white and red. Ande and Pitch watched them come to screeching halts, parking wherever they could, spilling loads of uniformed occupants who fired into action with urgent and intentional movements.

'There's a number we should remember for next time,' said Pitch. 'And there will be a next time. One, one, two to get the Turkish boys and girls in blue.'

'Thankfully, someone called them,' said Ande. 'Let's have a quick look inside before they close it all off and tell us to get lost. Maybe we can find some clues.'

'They'll want to talk to us first,' said Pitch. 'I'm sure. But as for clues, I have no clue.'

Ande shook her head, proceeded inside Captain Candy without any further conversation. She reckoned if she could grab a few handfuls of bugs, dead ones in a bag, and take them away to have a look at, maybe Pitch could do some scientific stuff on them. A post-mortem. Maybe he could figure out if they were normal insects or if there were other factors at play. Maybe he could see if they were on drugs. They acted like it. Like people who go on violent uncontrollable sprees of mayhem because of crystal meth. There might be an insect version of that. She scratched around for a paper bag then loaded it with bugs as fast as she could. She took a second bag and repeated the process.

'Outside please, miss,' said an authoritative voice. 'And leave everything exactly how it is.'

Quickly stuffing the paper bag in her coat pocket, she stood and walked out, passing a tall police officer with a serious moustache. He put his hand on her shoulder, just before she was out of reach. 'This bag for me?'

'Which bag?'

The moustache didn't move an inch. 'Give me this bag now, miss.'

Ande looked into his eyes, decided against giving him any further trouble. 'This bag?' she said, retrieving only one of the bags from her pocket and handing it to him.

She held her breath as he took the bag, hoping he hadn't seen the second one. He studied her for a long, uncomfortable moment.

'Thank you miss,' he said. 'You wait outside please. We are talk.'

The officer nodded his head very slightly to indicate he was finished speaking with Ande. Having dismissed her, he drew a small silver case from his pocket, opened it, then selected a cigarette from it. He placed it in his mouth and lit it with a lighter which appeared from nowhere.

Outside the store, Ande found Pitch chatting with another officer with an even more intense moustache. He stood toe to toe with Pitch, never once looking at him as he recorded whatever information he deemed useful, in his notebook.

'Thank you, sir,' he said, closing his book and walking away.

'These cops are pretty scary, aren't they?' said Pitch.

'What about those moustaches?' Ande agreed, shaking her head. 'Wow!'

'I'm very envious,' said Pitch. 'Did you find any clues?

'No,' said Ande quickly, 'but I collected some samples for you to examine.'

'To examine for what?'

Ande was getting closer to slapping some sense into Pitch. She didn't know him well enough to do that though, or to figure out whether he was being deliberately dull-witted or not. 'You said you wanted to be a cop when you were young,' she said. 'Here's your chance. Think like a scientist and a cop and get some answers for us. When Callum gets back, we're going to come up with a plan. We're going to get serious.'

'Serious like the cops' moustaches?'

Ande granted Pitch a smile. 'Way more serious than that, my friend. Way more.'

Chapter Twenty

There was a huge difference between arriving somewhere for the first time and returning to that place. The initial thrill of curiosity and nervous tension evaporated, heated by familiarity. Callum reflected on this as he watched the lights of Istanbul unfurl beneath the plane as it descended through the clouds on approach to the airport. He'd only been gone for a week, so Istanbul would not have changed at all. Neither would Ande or Pitch have changed. One could reasonably assume that a week was insufficient time for anyone or anything to change. However, Callum had changed. When faced with a series of inexplicable events, encounters with supernatural beings, and confronting mortality with the death of his father, Callum had fallen into a raging river. Echoes of rebellion were ineffective against his weakening will to resist. With so much out of his control, it had become increasingly futile to try to hold on to his personal sovereignty.

'Back to business, right?' said Ron.

'How do you keep from being detected now that you've grown so…'

'Robust?' suggested Ron. 'Powerful? Imposing?'

'I was going to say big,' said Callum. 'You've grown so big, and you never did get around to explaining to me why that happened.'

'You've been a little preoccupied, you know, so I was simply being respectful. My post-pubescent growth spurt is not really very important compared with your loss. Compared with anything, actually.'

'How remarkably respectful of you, Ron.'

'You say that as though I've never been or am not usually respectful.'

'We'll be on the ground in twenty minutes. So why don't you tell me all about it now. And speaking of being respectful, when are you going to introduce me to your girlfriend?'

'She's not my girlfriend,' protested Ron.

'Okay,' said Callum. 'Your lady friend.'

'I asked her to be discreet,' said Ron. 'To keep her distance.'

'It's tricky finding the right way and the right time to introduce your girl—sorry your lady friend to your parents.'

'Huh?' Ron dug his talons into Callum's arm. 'What are you talking about?'

'Just being facetious. Having a little fun.'

'I wasn't sure if you could see her actually,' said Ron. 'Or hear her?'

'Why wouldn't I be able to? If I can see you, why wouldn't I be able to see and hear her?'

'Ah, my young padawan. You have much to learn.'

'Hello Callum, my name is Alix. With an 'i'.'

Callum turned his head, glancing at Ron and Alix who were sitting on the two passengers beside him. Ron on the middle seat. Alix in the window seat. Callum still hadn't figured out how they could be in the same space as humans without the humans being aware, without them feeling anything. He knew demons could be both ethereal and corporeal, but to see them sitting, kind of overlaying the humans in those seats was hard to process. Naturally he couldn't look at them either. The woman in the window seat happened to turn her head at the same time, necessitating an awkward exchange of smiles between her and Callum. At a different time, Callum might have tried, most likely unsuccessfully, to read something into the smile. For now, he quickly turned away.

'Nice to meet you, Alix with an 'i'.'

'We've met before,' said Alix. 'Once before.' When Callum raised his eyebrows rather than reply, she added. 'At the hotel. The day you got the news about your father.'

Callum nodded. 'Ron says you're not his girlfriend. Can you confirm his denial?'

Alix giggled, surprising Callum. He didn't know demons giggled. 'I haven't decided yet,' she said.

'Tell me about your growth spurt, Ron,' said Callum.

'Humans have them during childhood and adolescence as you know. Once puberty has had its wicked way, they get their adult bodies, albeit trapped inside embarrassingly puerile brains ill equipped to handle the demands of adulthood.'

'Thanks for that information,' said Callum, deadpanning in a tone to make sure Ron knew he wasn't grateful at all. 'I'm pretty well versed in human biology.'

'It's much the same with demons except it happens more frequently and is also much less longer lasting.'

'Shorter,' added Alix.

'Much less longer lasting,' continued Ron. 'In fact, it can occur in as little as a few hours, and again, unlike what happens with humans, our spurts can also happen while we are active. Sometimes at the most inopportune times.'

'I was once in a fight with a smaller opponent when my legs suddenly grew longer, causing me to lose balance and suffer a humiliating defeat.'

'What sort of growth are we talking about?' said Callum.

'Maybe five centimetres.'

'Five centimetres! That's impossible!'

'Old habits die hard, don't they, Callum?' Ron waggled his index talon in front of Callum's face.

'Okay,' conceded Callum, unable to refute the truth of Ron's words. So much of which he would have considered impossible before his awakening was now not only possible, but in many cases, completely normal. 'Please continue.'

'He's so polite,' said Alix. 'It turns my stomach.'

'The spurts continue at irregular intervals throughout our lives until we reach physical maturity.'

'And when is that?'

'It depends, but it's usually around a hundred.'

'A hundred?'

'Yes,' said Ron.

'Forgive me for never asking,' said Callum. 'But how old are you?'

'Ninety-nine.'

Callum laughed as politely as he could.

'I know,' said Ron. 'It's an awkward age, but what can you do?'

'Not quite a centenarian,' said Alix. 'Not according to the numbers anyway.'

Callum thought he heard flirtation in those comments, but what did he know? Conversations with Ron were always entertaining, albeit occasionally mind-boggling, and always helped to pass the time. Now with Alix along for the ride, things were bound to become even more amusing. 'We should have a big bash for your one hundredth birthday then. When is it?'

'I don't know what a bash is, but I presume,' said Ron, 'that you are suggesting we hold a celebration of some sort, a party?'

'Yes, of course, it's a huge milestone to achieve.'

'Maybe for humans,' said Ron dismissively. 'Alix, tell Callum how old you are.'

'Two hundred and three.'

As the plane wobbled its way onto the tarmac, Callum realized his otherworldly companions had disappeared, without so much as a whisper of a farewell, leaving him to his own thoughts again. He longed most of all to see Ande, and wondered how she was, what she'd been up to in his absence. Wondered too whether she'd missed him and hoped they…he wasn't sure what he wanted. Not exactly, but he knew he missed her, and that spoke volumes about where his heart was.

Had there been any more beetle events? Or were they only for his benefit? Ande would probably have called him out on the self-centeredness of that question. She could be annoying, but like the irritant which invaded some species of oysters causing the secretion of a fluid to alleviate the discomfort and protect itself, the result was a beautiful pearl. Ande was a pearl, no doubt. Or maybe her effect on him was less subtle—more like the ocean throwing rocks together in an excessively rough-and-tumble massage which produced smooth stones. Whichever analogy worked best, Callum knew that his relationship with Ande would ultimately make him a better man. This was possible now, he realized because he had changed, not because she had. Callum was content to allow the transformation instigated by his circumstances and to reap the benefits in whatever shape they presented themselves.

The showdown at the Scorpion Temple in Mae Sai had been a dramatic example, but there were other, more subtle agents of alteration. He thought suddenly of the scorpion's breath, the otherworldly mist which he and Ande had seen together the first time they climbed those stairs of death. While immersing themselves in the ambient sunset, the temperature dropped, and the mist appeared. The mist was comprised of tiny bubbles with scorpions inside which both he and Ande had inadvertently swallowed. Callum had spent so long denying that, pretending that even if it had actually happened—that they *had* ingested miniature arachnids—it surely would have no impact on his life. Ever. Not physical repercussions, nor spiritual. At the time, he could barely even say the word 'spiritual' without gagging on it. Callum made a mental note to ask Ande if she thought the scorpions had affected them in any way. Very likely, he thought.

Callum disembarked the plane and strolled through the airport to the immigration counters where he stood in line, waiting patiently.

'I've been thinking,' said Ron, appearing in front of Callum. Alix was absent. 'About your idea for a birthday party for me.'

'Now where did you get to?' said Callum. 'And where's your girlfriend?'

Ron clenched his fists, stiffened then exhaled heavily. 'She's not my girlfriend.'

'Right,' said Callum. 'Because she hasn't made up her mind about you yet?'

'That's not what she said.' Ron sighed, then shook his head. 'Anyway, about my birthday party.'

'What about it?'

'I don't know exactly what day I was born, but let's just say it's today.'

Callum laughed. The line moved forward as he and Ron discussed how to celebrate his birthday—not today, but perhaps tomorrow, because, as Callum explained to Ron, good parties take time to plan. They discussed cultural differences and whether there would be any conflict. It wouldn't do to offend anyone. Callum was fascinated to learn that demons didn't celebrate birthdays with their friends, mainly because they didn't have any, but chose either solitude or very large groups of strangers. Callum did his best to convince Ron to have a more human celebration which surprisingly Ron did not reject out of hand, but listened to, debating the pros and cons.

Without coming up with anything other than a vague plan, Callum exited the gate to find Ande waiting for him and instantly forgot all about Ron and his party plans. She smiled. He smiled back. He felt his heart jumping, butterflies going ballistic in his belly. He waved. She waved back. Then they were face to face, and before he could speak another word, Ande had planted a kiss on his lips and wrapped her arms around him. He hugged her back, smelled her skin and her hair, loving it.

'Hi,' she said.

'G'day.'

'How are you?'

Callum had kept in touch via Messenger while he had been away. They hadn't spoken, but that had been okay with both of them. He gave her what he could, and she didn't ask for more. He hadn't talked about how he felt, not in any great detail. His reporting to her was brief, light on detail, devoid of emotional content. More like a logbook than a journal. She hadn't pressed him, respecting his space, and he appreciated that.

'Thanks for giving me some room while I was gone,' he said. 'I'm sorry I didn't have much to say.'

Ande placed her hand inside his arm as they

walked, keeping close to him. They fell into an easy, harmonious step. 'You don't need to apologize, Callum. Just tell me you're okay, and if you're not, tell me why. I'm here for you whatever you need, whenever you need it.'

Callum stopped. 'Are you okay, Ande? You seem...different.'

She smiled. 'I've been thinking.'

'About?'

'About life,' she said, pulling on Callum's arm, restarting their exit from the airport. 'Are you cool to meet Pitch for dinner tonight?'

'Sure. In the meantime, you can tell me all about your thoughts on life. It sounds big.'

'We had another beetle incident.'

'I was wondering about that.'

'Pitch and I were on our way to visit the Hagia Sophia, but we only made it as far as Captain Candy when I got distracted.'

'I'm guessing the source of your distraction was the candy. Captain Candy's a lolly shop, right?'

'Oh Callum, not just any lolly shop. Actually, it's closed now because of the incident and to be honest, I'm not sure if I'll ever be able to go to a candy store again.'

With Callum's encouragement, Ande began to share all the gory details. They climbed into a taxi and made their way slowly to the hotel, Callum listening in amazement. It further surprised him that his reaction was excitement, not concern or horror. Tinged with a modicum of disappointment because he had missed it, but excitement, nonetheless. The beetle activity was ramping up and they were perfectly positioned in the thick of it. God only knew for what purpose, though.

The taxi pulled up out the front of the hotel. Ande paid the driver, thanked him, then climbed out. Callum retrieved his small travel case from the boot of the taxi. 'Have you ever had the feeling that you're a part of something much bigger than yourself?' said Callum.

'That destiny has seated you in just the right place at just the right time?'

'Yes,' said Callum, 'although I'm not sure destiny has anything to do with it.'

'Whatever forces are at work, I would love to know what it's all about.'

'Let's find out,' said Callum. 'What time are we meeting Pitch?'

'At seven.'

'Can we make room for more?'

'Sure. Why?'

'I've got a couple of friends I'd like you to meet. I reckon they'll be very helpful in our quest.'

Ande cooed. 'We're on a quest now?'

'Yes, we are.'

Chapter Twenty-One

Professor Berat Sakarya hurried out through the Baby Door of the South Campus of Bogazici heading for the car park where his fifteen-year-old BMW waited. He tried to remember if he'd hung up the receiver and locked his office door on the way out. He also wondered if he'd closed the lid on the specimen jar on his desk. If not, he'd have to return and take care of that. Finally, after replaying the scene in his mind a few times, he was satisfied his prize catch was secure. His hasty departure was forced by an unbelievable coincidence, one which involved an unexpected telephone conversation and an invitation to dinner. Despite the very short notice—usually sufficient reason for the professor to decline such invitations, he accepted because he felt compelled to.

Reaching his car without interruption, Berat opened the door, threw his case on the passenger seat and climbed in behind the wheel. He picked up his phone, entered the address he'd been given for Divella Bistro, then waited for the directions from Google maps. He noted this highly rated restaurant, which he'd never heard of, was near the Hagia Sophia. That was helpful. Less helpful was the mad rush to get there. He should have said no.

Should have picked a time more suitable for him. He'd become carried away with the excitement of being contacted and asked for help. His long, long night in the forest of obscurity might soon be over. He would finally receive the recognition he deserved. The honour for which he'd worked so hard. Thoughts of future glory made him giddy, wearing away his hard, circumspect edge. By the time he arrived and found parking near Divella Bistro, Professor Sarkarya had shaken off the vulnerable foolishness and fully switched on his defences.

Berat left his BMW and walked a block back to the restaurant. When he was standing across the road, he paused, gathering his thoughts, steeling himself once more. His delivery would have to be flawless. It was unclear whether he was dealing with professionals or hacks. Real investigative journalists or curious wannabes. He would act as though these people knew what they were doing. He didn't have much information to do otherwise, not even close enough. A hotel reviewer named Callum Steele and a couple of his friends who were interested in talking about beetles, specifically in relation to the August beetles and other unusual insect events. It was the latter reference which piqued his interest most. He'd asked how Callum got his number and received a reasonable answer about a mutual associate. He'd asked for more details about these unusual events, but had not received a satisfactory response. It was a tease. Irrespective of this Callum's intentions, Berat was being seduced. Sucked in, to put it more crudely. Such appeals to his ego were irresistible. There was more risk attached than the professor would normally accept, but he had good reasons to at least play along, or so he convinced himself as he stood across the road from Divella Bistro.

Professor Berat Sarkarya would spin a riveting, poignant and ancient tale sure to both captivate and ensnare his listeners.

He crossed the road casually, not wanting to draw attention to himself. Once inside, he searched the restaurant, over the shoulder of the maître d' who was duly informed that Professor Sarkarya was meeting a man called Callum Steele and two others for dinner. The head waiter quickly checked a list on the table before him before informing Berat that Mr. Steele had not yet arrived.

'Let me show you to your table, Professor.'

'Thank you,' said Berat, following the man to a table towards the end of the bistro, adjacent to the window. He took his seat and ordered his favourite drink: Scotch whiskey.

He had barely enough time to settle himself before an odd-looking trio arrived at the table, courtesy of the maître d' who invited them to sit and asked if they would like to order a drink.

'Three Heinekens, thanks,' said Callum. He faced Berat, holding out his hand. 'Professor Sarkarya, I'm Callum Steele. Thank you for joining us. These are my friends, Ande and Pitch.'

Everyone stood and shook hands with Berat, in turn, before seating themselves. Obligatory small talk followed until a waiter appeared with their drinks, advising them he would return in ten minutes to take their orders.

'We were at the conference together, Professor,' said Pitch.

'Yes. Please call me Berat.'

'It still blows me away how incredible new species are still being discovered.'

'Quite,' said Berat, sipping his whiskey, keeping his eyes mostly on the table.

'You mentioned when we spoke on the phone,' said Callum, 'that you had a story which might shed some light on the supernatural events that have been going on here in Istanbul. We're interested in putting an end to these beetle invasions.'

'Supernatural or possibly supranatural,' said Berat, overlooking the explicit arrogance in Callum's words. 'The Sorcerer's Tusk is an ancient story. It's mythological. Myths are useful for helping us understand ourselves. Humans have always told stories to each other as a way of sharing history and building cultural identity. Whether these myths are true or not is immaterial. From a sociological point of view, their value lies in what they say about human nature, and how they consciously or subconsciously inform behaviour, within the context of cultural and moral norms. By the way, did you know the word mythology literally translates from the Greek as *the spoken story of a people?'*

He continued, not waiting for an answer. He noticed them nodding with what appeared to be genuine interest. 'These stories were traditionally used to explain phenomena and origins, of humans, animals, and places.

They deal with various elements of human nature by explaining and describing historical events.'

'I once heard a man say that if you didn't know the story, you didn't know the man,' said Ande.

'Precisely,' said Berat. 'The Sorcerer's Tusk is just such an important foundational story for Turks.'

The waiter returned as promised but no one had yet looked at the menu. The professor ordered in Turkish, then smiled at Pitch, Ande and Callum as they hurriedly grabbed their menus, searching for something recognizable and safe. 'Perhaps a few more minutes,' said Berat to the waiter who bowed slightly.

'Sorry, Professor,' said Callum. 'Give us a moment. You ordered without looking at the menu. Have you been here before?'

'No.' Berat looked away to avoid the next question, hoping to defuse it, to redirect them back to the menu.

Callum closed his menu, as did Ande, while Pitch continued to flick through the pages. 'I have no idea,' he said. 'Unique and forgotten tastes which were presented in the Ottoman empire between the fourteenth and eighteenth centuries. What the heck is that?' He looked up, face screwed in puzzlement.

'You're supposed to be picking something to eat,' said Ande. 'Not sharing the history of the restaurant, which is all very interesting, I'm sure.'

In a moment of magnanimity, Berat decided to help Pitch. 'You can't go wrong with stuffed vine leaves. They do them with cherry and levzine.'

'I love levzine,' said Callum.

'Of course you do,' said Pitch. 'What are they exactly?'

'No idea,' admitted Callum with a wry grin.

'An Ottoman dessert made from almonds, butter and sugar.,' said Berat.

'So, that would be dessert,' said Pitch.

'As you wish,' said Berat. 'Lamb shanks are also a safe option.'

'That's where I was going,' said Callum.

Pitch looked at Berat, then at Callum, 'Bring on the shanks.' He raised his hand to catch the waiter's attention.

Berat nodded and smiled at Pitch, sipped his whiskey. Once the waiter had taken their orders and left the table he began. 'Let me tell you the story of the Sorcerer's Tusk.

'Many hundreds of years ago, there was a small village in what is now Hakari, the eastern region of Turkey. It was mid-autumn and the village chief had arranged a wedding for the following spring. His daughter was to marry the son of a king from a much larger neighbouring village. It was seen by all to be a wise plan by the Chief because it would safeguard his village from attack and ensure a share in the prosperity of their neighbours. However, with the winter fast approaching, sickness came to the village, and one of its early victims was the Chief's daughter who lay prone on her bed in deadly peril from the mysterious contagion.

'As more and more of his people were struck down by the sickness, including the infants and the elderly who seemed particularly susceptible, the Chief held counsel with the village elders and the shaman. At the meeting, the shaman declared that after much prayer and consideration, he believed the sickness was a curse brought about by the pending union of the Chief's daughter and the king's son. Tengri, said the shaman, was displeased.'

'Tengri?' said Ande.

'Tengri was the pre-eminent deity worshipped by the people at that time,' replied Berat. 'The Chief was horrified but held his temper in check. How could Tengri be unhappy about a wedding pact which would undoubtedly bring prosperity to his village? Ignoring the terrible pride underpinning such thoughts, and the folly of challenging destiny, of resisting a god, the Chief determined to find a way to outwit Tengri.

'*What is the solution?*' the Chief asked the shaman.

'The shaman was reluctant to answer, fearful of the wrath of his chief, but equally certain he must speak the truth as revealed by the holy ones. *First, you must send one of your sons to inform the king the wedding has been cancelled. When asked why, the messenger, your son, will simply say 'Tengri does not approve of this union.'*

'*It will be done*, said the Chief who sent one of his servants to bring his eldest son to see him immediately. He then said to the shaman, *And what of the sickness? Will it end once this message has been delivered to the King?*'

'*Yes,* answered the shaman. *However, all of those who fall ill until then, and all those currently afflicted will die.* The shaman paused, allowing the full weight of his words to fill the shocked silence in the meeting room.

'*Including your daughter.*'

'The Chief choked on his reply, angry almost beyond his strength to contain it. Knowing the power of the gods and of the shaman, however, the Chief bit his tongue to avoid further punishment. Just then the eldest son arrived, at which point the chief dismissed everyone but his son from the room.

'*The shaman has angered me with his words of doom and damnation*, said the Chief. *He has condemned your sister and our village to death and poverty. He has instructed me to send you to the King to inform him the wedding has been cancelled because it displeases Tengri.* The Chief waited for his son to recover his surprise. "*I told the shaman I would obey his instructions my son. But I will not.* He gripped the young man's shoulders firmly and gazed into the eyes of his first born. *I will challenge the shaman.*'

'Wow!' said Ande. 'That's ballsy.'

Immersed in artful storytelling, Berat had quite forgotten he had an audience. Although he looked at them while he spoke, he was not mindful of them, concentrating on the power of the narrative and his skilful delivery of it. It helped that interruptions had been sparse. Steele and his friends drank and listened, and when the food arrived, they ate. Ande's outburst had broken the spell. 'Quite so,' said Berat, curtly. 'May I continue?'

'Please do,' said Callum.

'The Chief's son did not argue the merits of resisting the will of Heaven, but merely asked how his father proposed to do so.

'I will summon a genien and enlist its help in the name of justice and mercy.' The Chief went on to explain to his son how the genien were neither good nor bad, but simply operated at the whim of their emotion. If they were moved to a cause, they would fight for it, irrespective of any rights or wrongs attached to such action by others. He then heard his son's concerns about the trustworthiness of such creatures, and questions about their power, before laying out his plan in full.

'Go, my son, said the Chief, *in the direction of our neighbours as though you are going to carry out the shaman's directions but go instead to the Stone Pillow which is two hundred metres northwest of the Tree of Life. Wait for me there. I will come soon.*

'The Chief met his son at the appointed place where he used an incantation to summon a genien. He welcomed it and thanked it for coming, bestowing lavish complements on it for he knew these creatures were easily flattered into cooperation. When the genien suggested a contest, the chief was puzzled.

'I will make the arrangements on your behalf, said the genien. *The curse will be lifted, or it will remain depending on the outcome of the battle.* When the Chief enquired who the combatants would be, and why they would fight over a small, insignificant village such as his, the genien was matter of fact.

'It is Erlik's pleasure to fight so he requires no cause other than an invitation. Tengri is a defender of good, the creator of life and the Lord of Heaven. It is his pleasure and duty to defend the Kingdom against any

attack. Your insignificant village will be a pretext for another in an eternal series of battles between good and evil.

'The Chief was unconvinced. Why would Tengri and Erlik want to go to so much trouble for him and his people? However, the genien persuaded him that if the Chief willed it, the contest would certainly take place. All the Chief had to do was agree, and the genien would take care of the rest. The Chief gave his consent and was advised to wait for word from the genien.

'*When will this happen?* asked the Chief.

'The genien replied, enigmatically with the trace of a smile on its lips. *It will not be long.*

'Three days later, the Chief was roused from his sleep by the genien, inviting him to come to the village square where the combatants would soon meet to fight for the future of his village. On his way to the square, the Chief was intercepted by the shaman who wore a look of intense and fearful displeasure.

'*This will not end well, he said.*

'*You know of it?"*

'*The Holy Ones have revealed it to me. Your deception and your hubris will bring about the destruction of you and our village.* They walked on, side by side. *However, it is too late to warn you, for you must have suspected it to be so. Let us see what comes of this dangerous nonsense.*

'Had the Chief been fully awake, he might have trembled or wavered in his determination to save his daughter and his village by any means. As it was, he simply gaped at the sight before him in the village square. The moon was unwilling to witness the event, so it was a dark night, requiring torches to light the square in which the fight was to take place. On opposite sides of the square stood two giant beetles.'

'Get out of town!'

'Ande,' said Callum. 'Can you try and curb your enthusiasm please.'

Berat prepared a mouthful of food, ate it, sipped his whiskey, waited. He remained calm though he was impatient and hungry.

'On the Chief's left,' continued the professor, 'was a giant stag beetle, while on the right a giant rhinoceros beetle. Both were the size of houses, their metallic-hued carapaces reflecting and refracting flickers of torch light into the darkness. The shaman explained to the Chief, *Erlik has assigned an abasi to take the form of the stag beetle, the thunder bringer. Kayra represents Tengri and Heaven in the form of the rhinoceros beetle, the Hercules of the insect world. The fight is until death or submission. There will be no external interference and the combatants are forbidden from using any supernatural powers. It is to be a contest of strength, guile, and determination.*

'And so, the battle commenced and raged for hours with neither beetle gaining any advantage. When once the abasi was tossed on its back, Kayra moved quickly to seize the opportunity to attempt a fatal blow. The shaman, impatient and seeing the threat, sprung to the defence of the stag beetle, grabbing one of its legs, attempting to help flip it over. Unaware of the shaman's presence, the mighty stag lashed out, slicing the man's forehead vertically with one of the razor-sharp hairs on its leg. With blood instantly spurting from the gaping wound, the shaman fell to the ground. The abasi, although not remotely sorry about the injury it inflicted, was impressed by the shaman's show of loyalty and courage. It secreted a liquid on the wound and sealed it, saving the shaman who nonetheless remained unconscious.

'The battle resumed, lasting another half hour before Kayra finally found an opportunity to thrust its horn through the underbelly of the stag beetle, between two hard exoskeleton plates, into its heart, piercing the outer muscle wall and puncturing the organ. With the gushing release of blood and water from the beetle, it died, releasing the abasi who immediately disappeared.

'Kayra transformed from enormous insect to humanoid and addressed the Chief. *The curse is lifted. Your daughter will recover fully and marry the King's son in the springtime.* The abasi gestured towards the shaman. *Nurse him to full health, then inform him he is to instruct your son in the ways of the Holy Ones. The training shall last until the beginning of the next winter, at which time you will banish the shaman from your village. Before I leave, I will heal his wound. However, he will sleep for three days, and wake drained of energy. He will also wear a curse on his body which will reveal itself once the wound has fully healed. It will remind him forever of his foolishness. He is not to be punished beyond what I have said.*

'The Chief prostrated himself before Kayra. *I too*

have been foolish. What is to be my punishment?

'The angel laid its hand on the chief's head. *Your days on this earth will be cut short.* Without another word, it disappeared, and so the village was saved, the wedding took place, and the shaman taught the Chief's son the ways of the Holy Ones before being sent into exile where he bore the mark of his ignominy: a ten-centimetre, curved tusk-like structure which protruded from his forehead.'

'That is the coolest story I've ever heard,' said Ande.

The professor proceeded to eat his dinner, which unfortunately for him had grown cold as he talked.

'Not exactly sure how it connects with what's going on now,' said Callum. 'There was a beetle battle…'

Ande giggled. 'Sounds like a line from *Fox in Sox.*'

'Could you try to focus, Ande?' said Callum. He turned to the professor. 'Sorry, Berat. It's a cool story, but how does it help us?'

'The exiled shaman wore the Sorcerer's Tusk until he died,' answered Berat, 'but legend has it that the abasi which had fatally wounded him resurrected him, granting him immortality and thus the opportunity to seek revenge on the followers of Tengri.'

Callum leaned forward in his seat. 'Are you saying the shaman is responsible for what's happening now? In Istanbul?'

Berat nodded. 'Most likely.'

'This fits with that story I told you before Callum,' said Ande, sitting forward in excitement. She turned to Berat. 'How do we stop him?'   The professor looked at

Ande

The professor looked at Ande, Callum, then Pitch. 'First you must find him. He will be present in the swarm, not physically perhaps—that would be too obvious—but probably inhabiting a stag beetle. There might be many stags in the swarm, but the one you are looking for is the Alpha. It will be larger and will behave differently.

'Suppose we find this Alpha beetle,' said Callum. 'What then?'

'Capture or kill it.'

Berat returned to his meal, satisfied his work was done.

Chapter Twenty-Two

Berat's story resonated strongly with Callum, long after the sage professor had left their company. There was an undeniable authenticity in his words and there was no doubting his credentials. Hearing the ancient tale of the Sorcerer's Tusk was another watershed moment for Callum, enabling him to not only see a way forward through the current beetle apocalypse, but also instilling in him a sense of moral compulsion. A feeling that he, after many years of dabbling in this and that, had finally found his thing. If he could bring Ande and Pitch on board, they would be a formidable team. Despite the necessity of the *ad hoc* reactive approach they had been using, it had reached its use-by date. It was time to get serious.

'What are we going to do with this information?' he asked his friends.

Pitch sipped his beer, then looked away. Ande held Callum's gaze momentarily, before lowering her eyes.

'Not quite the response I was looking for,' said Callum.

'Obviously, we should keep our eyes open for the alpha beetle, and if we see it, kill it,' said Ande.

'Obviously,' replied Callum. 'Pitch?'

'Obviously.'

Surprised by Pitch's reluctance to speak, Callum allowed him some time, without pushing.

'The trick is,' said Ande, brightening up, her tone suddenly enthusiastic as if she'd only just caught the vision and been inspired by it, 'identifying the alpha beetle. The professor was a little vague. I didn't really get a clear idea. It's bigger and acts differently. What does *acts differently* mean? We've already seen so much abnormal behaviour. How can we know which specific weirdness will tell us we've found the alpha beetle?'

'Remember we're looking for a stag beetle. They are distinctive, so we need to study up on them. That's where we'll be depending on Pitch's expertise, right?'

'Obviously,' said Pitch.

'What's wrong, mate?' said Callum. 'This is right in the pocket for you. You're usually much more excited by this stuff. You set us up with this guy, but you acted like you wanted to be somewhere else. Not only not your usually chatty self, but barely polite to a man who I thought you respected. Something's bothering you.'

'No,' said Pitch. 'I'm a little tired, that's all.'

Callum studied his friend for a few moments to satisfy himself that Pitch was telling him the truth. Pitch had suggested they talk to the professor, but while they had talked to him and listened to the story, Pitch had seemed disinterested at best, dismissive at worst. It didn't make sense. 'What did you think of the Sorcerer's Tusk?'

'A remarkable coincidence given what I saw in my vision,' said Pitch still without enthusiasm.

'Your vision? What vision?' said Callum.

After Pitch filled him in on the details of the story that he'd already shared with Ande, he resumed his meal without any further comment.

'Wow,' said Callum. 'The pieces of this puzzle are falling into place very nicely.'

'Remarkable and exciting,' said Ande. 'Makes me feel like we are the right people gathered together at the right time in the right place.'

Pitch groaned

'There's just one thing,' said Callum. 'Your vision involved a rhino, not a stag.'

'And I'm sure that's very significant,' said Pitch.

'Mate,' said Callum, disappointed by the sarcasm in Pitch's voice. 'I respect that you don't want to tell me what's wrong, but this doesn't sound like you. Do you want to try again? Maybe dial up the enthusiasm a bit. We're talking about kicking this dream team of paranormal investigators into gear. We can't simply walk away from all this.'

'I'm sorry,' said Pitch. Downing the last of his beer, he looked in turn at Ande and Callum, shaking his head slowly. 'I can't commit to this. What you're suggesting is not something I'm…it just isn't me.'

'What do you mean, it isn't you?' said Ande. 'It's exactly you. You're an entomologist and we've got some supernatural beetle business going on and we're right in the middle of it. I'm with Callum. This is totally us.'

Pitch finished his drink and stood up. 'I'm heading home tomorrow evening. Let's meet for lunch tomorrow.

I'll give you all I've got on stag beetles, then I'll wish you well and leave. Okay?'

It wasn't okay, but Callum knew there was no point pushing the issue now. Maybe, after a good night's sleep, Pitch would come around. There was definitely something on his mind, but for whatever reason, he was keeping it to himself. That in itself was disappointing, as Callum felt they were better friends than that. Callum had often confided in Pitch and come to see him as something of a father figure. With his own father distant, geographically and emotionally, and now dead, Callum wanted to maintain his friendship with Pitch more than ever. They'd hit it off at their very first meeting on the plane to Thailand. They'd already been through so much together in such a short period of time. Callum might have been reading too much into it, but Pitch seemed to be withdrawing not only from the project, but also from their relationship. Callum felt they were an awesome trio, a perfect combination of skills and personalities. The idea of becoming paranormal investigators was thrilling. Why couldn't Pitch see that? Why was he resistant and negative? It wasn't like him at all.

'No worries, Pitch,' said Callum. 'See you in the morning.'

'Good night, Pitch,' said Ande.

Pitch mock saluted them, then left after saying a brief farewell.

Ande placed her hand on Callum's arm. He turned to face her. 'Something's not right there,' she said.

'I wish I could say that I reckon he'll come good in

the morning, but that was so dramatically out of character,' said Callum. 'We can go on without him, but his knowledge will be hard to replace. We'll be forced back to Google. Roaming the internet, staring at our screens, sifting through information, unable to sort the wheat from the chaff.'

'I don't know what chaff is, but I get your point. What did you think of our professor?'

Callum realized Ande's hand was still on his arm and was aware of their proximity. Anyone looking on would have seen lovers engaged in verbal foreplay. He moved away. She didn't react.

'They're a weird mob, those academics, but he sounded believable.'

Ande smiled. 'I thought he was full of himself and his storytelling was an attempt to convince himself as well as us.'

'Wow,' said Callum. 'You thought he was pretentious and putting on a show?'

'Full of himself,' said Ande. 'Like he thought he was better than us. Did you see his face when you ordered beer for us?'

'No.'

'He was drinking whiskey.'

'Yeah, so?'

'And he ordered his food in Turkish without looking at the menu.'

'Yeah, so? He's Turkish.'

Ande playfully slapped Callum's hand, then left her hand on his. 'Didn't you say you wanted us to be investigators? You aren't very observant. You have to notice details like that. The things a person does, or doesn't do, can say more about the person than their words.'

Callum smiled, pulled his hand from beneath hers, and grabbed his glass of Heineken, raising it to toast. 'Here's to us. The dream team. Paranormal investigators par excellence.'

Before Ande could raise her glass, Callum's glass was removed from his hand and placed back on the table, forcefully. 'What?'

'Are you going to keep us waiting all night?' said Ron.

'Sorry,' said Callum.

'What's going on, Callum? What just happened?'

'Oh, the glass thing?'

She punched his arm this time, which made him laugh. 'Callum, your glass was taken out of your hand and slammed on the table. Can you explain that?'

The plan was for Callum to introduce both Ron and Alix after the others had left. Callum felt that only Ande was ready for such a meeting. She seemed way more open to supernatural stuff than Pitch. In fact, way more open than Callum himself had been. He remembered fondly her zeal at the Triple Four café in Mae Sai. She'd been jumping out of her seat to get to the mysterious heart of all those coincidences. He was dismissive then, unable to process what was happening, unable to accept it, but she was right all along. Ron was next level though. How would Ande react? It was now or never.

'Yes, I can,' said Callum, looking at the seats

vacated by Pitch and Berat where he saw Alix and Ron fidgeting. They were invisible to Ande at the moment, but they would appear when he formally introduced them. 'Give me a minute or two to prepare her, okay?' Ron and Alix both gave him the thumbs up.

'Who are you talking to?'

It seemed sensible to provide some background before springing the existence of demons on Ande, so he went all the way back to the falling coffee cup in their office before the Thailand trip. From there he went through all the interesting and bizarre events. They'd talked about all this before, but Ande seemed pleased with the recount, nodding, and smiling, touching him briefly here and there. Perhaps it was the way he told it without ridiculing every second thing as childish superstition.

'Is all this really necessary?' said Alix. 'It's sickening.'

Ron said, 'It's a human thing. Be patient.'

Callum ignored their exchange, continued the build-up, including the first encounter with the angel in his hotel room, but omitting any mention of Ron. 'The angel appeared again at Dad's funeral.'

'Wow! Really?'

'I was standing up front about to deliver the eulogy and I couldn't think what to say. I couldn't get started, but then I saw the angel at the back of the church, and I felt instantly encouraged and peaceful. The thing is, Ande, I've accepted the reality of this angel, and because it's real, there must be the possibility of there being other angels and…demons also. More than possible, actually.'

'I'm glad you haven't met any of them.'

'Other angels?'

'No. Demons.'

'You're assuming they're all bad.'

'Aren't they?'

The moment had arrived. Ande naturally had pre-conceived ideas about demons. Generally, although most people had not had genuine encounters with the Devil or his servants, they had been exposed through popular culture to various characterizations and caricatures of them. Irrespective of the medium, the thrust of the polemic was essentially that demons were bad. One way of dealing with the terror and potential harm which might be instigated by little Lucifers was to lampoon them. It would be fair to say that the majority opinion was that there were no such creatures as demons.

'Callum?'

He'd drifted away, wondering about Ron, marvelling about the fact the first demon he met was Ron, who was by all accounts a very unconventional member of his species. One who might or might not have initially intended to harm Callum in some way, but was now…what? A friend?

'I'd like you to meet a friend of mine,' said Callum, gesturing across the table. Ron materialized on cue. Ande gasped and fainted. Callum grabbed her as best he could to prevent her from falling off her chair and hurting herself. He looked at Ron, smiled sheepishly.

'That went well,' said Ron.

'Imagine if we'd both appeared at once,' said Alix.

'Ande,' said Callum gently into her ear. 'Ande, it's okay.'

Slowly, with evident reluctance, Ande raised her head off the table, staring at Ron. He approximated a smile. 'Hi.' Ande's eyes shifted to take in Alix. She fainted again, this time before Callum could save her from hitting her head on the table, right beside her drink which was knocked over by the impact, spilling on the tablecloth.

'That went well,' said Alix.

'Imagine if we'd both appeared at once,' said Ron. He and Alix looked each other, giggling in two-pitched stereo.

A waiter appeared to clean up the mess as Ande was making her second recovery. Holding Callum's hand tightly, she lifted her head and focused on the demons sitting opposite her. 'Hi,' she said.

Callum beamed with pride.

'What are you grinning about?' asked Ron.

'The lady said "hi" to her first pair of demons,' said Callum. 'I feel proud of her.'

'She fainted twice,' said Alix.

'She's still here,' said Callum.

'Are you going to hurt us?' said Ande. It was a genuine question, but Ron and Alix simply laughed at her.

'Ande,' began Ron once he'd composed himself. 'Do you think Callum would have introduced you to us if he thought we were going to hurt you? Either of you?'

'You might have tricked him,' said Ande.

Callum beamed again. 'That's my girl.'

Ron smiled, standing on his seat. 'That's true. I

mean that's what we do, right?' He looked to Alix for support.

'We are deceivers and liars,' she said. 'Certainly not to be trusted.'

'And yet,' continued Ron, smoothly slotting in with Alix's line of reasoning. 'Callum does trust us.' He looked at Callum. 'At least he trusts me.' He looked at Alix. 'Sorry. I guess you have to earn your stripes.'

Alix stood on the chair beside Ron, who also stood up, causing Ande to lean back, creating more distance between herself and the two demons which were now towering over her and Callum. Alix looked annoyed. 'I have earned my stripes,' she said, displaying the scars on her shoulder.

'Sit down,' said Ron, laughing. 'You know you lost your one and only scar, remember, and anyway, our rank scars don't mean anything in the human world.'

'The human world doesn't mean anything in my world.' Alix disappeared.

'She's a bit of a firecracker,' said Ande.

Callum beamed.

'Callum, please stop making that ridiculous face every time Ande speaks,' said Ron. To Ande he said, 'Alix is still learning how to deal respectfully with humans.'

Ande turned to Callum. 'Is he for real?'

'Yes,' said Ron. 'I am for real, and I'd appreciate a little more respect. Thank you.' Ron disappeared.

Callum sighed. 'That went well.'

Chapter Twenty-Three

'Now that you've met Ron and Alix,' said Callum, 'and in light of the terrific and illuminating Sorcerer's Tusk tale, do you agree that what we've witnessed *is* demonic activity?' He looked at Ande. 'It's got nothing to do with August beetles. Even though it is August and there is a lot of natural seasonal activity by these Antalya beetles, there's something way bigger than that going on.'

Seated at a small table in the al fresco dining area of the Miran Nargile Café, Callum and Ande were waiting for Pitch. He was late, and Callum would not have been surprised if he called to excuse himself, or simply bailed altogether. Based on his behaviour at dinner the previous night, anything was possible. Callum hadn't seen Pitch act so out of character since…come to think of it, he'd never seen that side of Pitch. In fact, he didn't know he had such a side.

'I read quite a bit about the August beetles before I came,' said Ande.

'Flying cockroaches,' said Pitch, arriving to join the conversation without apologizing for his tardiness.

'Cockroaches are the worst,' said Ande. She shivered involuntarily. 'The most disgusting creatures on

God's earth. I would rather swim in a sea of beetles than have to deal with a single cockroach.' She finished her rant, sitting in her familiar arms akimbo pose, a look of extreme indignation on her face.

'How very Anatolian of you, Ande,' said Callum.

'What's that supposed to mean Mr. I-know-a-lot-of-fancy-words Steele?'

'Anatoly is the westernmost protrusion of the Asian continent. A region which makes up most of modern-day Turkey. The arms on hips, legs slightly apart stance is a common motif in Anatolian artwork. In your case, it's just a bust.'

'Lovely. Thanks for sharing,' said Ande, still smoky of tone. She thought for a moment. 'That kind of rings a bell actually. Anyway, I have some interesting information. The rhinoceros beetle is endangered in Turkey, and thanks largely to Turkish media adding further fuel to the fire of rumours concerning the beetle's status, its value to collectors is said to be the equivalent of one hundred thousand dollars.'

'Damn,' said Callum.

'In other news,' said Pitch. 'There's a scorpion plague in Northern Thailand. Just read about it in my news feed.'

'Stag beetles,' said Callum. Scorpions were the last thing he wanted to talk about, or even think about. 'Let's focus on stag beetles. According to the professor, our alpha beetle will be a specimen of unusual size and behaviour, so what can you tell us about stag beetles Pitch?'

Pitch's coffee arrived on cue. 'I just want to point out that my hallucination featured a rhinoceros beetle, not a stag beetle.'

'And according to the professor's story,' added Ande, allowing no time for Pitch to answer Callum's question, 'the rhinoceros beetle was the representative of Heaven. I interpret that to mean that you are one of the good guys, Pitch.'

After taking the skimpiest of sips, almost a pretence, Pitch said. 'It was just an hallucination.'

'A fascinating and remarkably timed one though,' said Callum. 'I agree with Ande that it was a portent.'

'I thought a poor tent was what a poor camper put up in the bush,' said Pitch.

Callum and Ande sighed in response to the terrible joke.

Pitch cleared his throat. 'Anyway, my fellow good guys' he said. 'There are around fourteen-hundred species of stag beetles in the *Lucanidae* family which have been scientifically described and named around the world. They can be found on every continent except Antarctica. There are forty-one species in Europe, and the most well-known of these is *Lucanus cervus*. They aren't terribly common in Turkey though, so the swarms, theoretically, and in a natural sense, shouldn't have many stags in them.'

'Making them relatively easy to spot,' said Callum.

'Theoretically,' added Ande.

'Also making them easier to spot and more to the point,' said Pitch, 'more helpfully, I mean, is obviously their disproportionately large jaws which resemble the antlers of a stag. Hence the name. Only males develop these oversize mandibles which are primarily used for courtship displays and fighting other males. These saproxylic beetles are heavily dependent on the presence of rotting wood in their habitat because the larvae feed on it, below ground, for the first three to five years of life. In fact, the beetles only emerge for a few weeks in the summer to find a mate and reproduce. As a result of their specific ecosystem needs, they are listed as endangered.

'*Lucanus cervus* features prominently in European mythology, particularly in the stories and superstitions of Germany in the Middle Ages. They were routinely denigrated as things of the devil, emanating from Hell and always accompanied by fire. It was even said they could summon fire from the sky—lightning, in other words.'

'Bingo!' said Ande.

'We've seen a single lightning strike occur at the end of every beetle swarm, right?' said Callum.

'You know it.'

'Stag beetles look spectacular, but they are quite harmless,' said Pitch. 'And of course, there's no truth to any of the superstitious nonsense believed about them.'

'They're harmless, yet responsible for an unknown number of deaths,' said Callum, still studying Pitch for signs of a personality resurrection. Pitch had a faraway look in his eyes though. He seemed to be performing out of obligation. Reciting scientific facts as though he was reading a shopping list, in a horrified stupor at the prospect of actually having to go and buy the thing on the list.

Callum waited for Pitch to respond but was

D. A. Cairns

disappointed when he finally did. With the remnants of his coffee in his stomach, Pitch stood, extended his hand first to Callum, then to Ande.

'I'll see you two later. Time for me to head to the airport. Enjoy the rest of your time in Istanbul.'

It was so unlike Pitch, neither Callum nor Ande could do anything other than shake his hand and say good-bye. 'What's wrong with him?' said Ande, after Pitch walked briskly away.

'I don't know,' said Callum. 'But I wish he was hanging around to help us.'

'On the other hand, not having him here means we can roll out the demon sidekicks.'

'Hey!' said Ron.

Callum laughed.

'I can see why you like her, Callum,' said Ron. 'She's just as cheeky as you are.'

'Maybe more so,' said Callum. 'Wait! Who said I liked her?' He looked at Ande who smiled affectionately at him. 'I do like you, but...but.' Overwhelmed by the awkwardness and suddenly tongue-tied, Callum couldn't finish his sentence.

'Okay, Callum,' said Ron, patting his back not very gently. 'It's okay. Take a breath.'

'Where's Alix?' asked Ande.

Ron shrugged his shoulders, fluffed his wings a little, before settling in his chair. 'Said she had an errand to run.'

'It's so funny how you talk,' said Ande. 'Like you're normal. Like you're human.'

'Callum,' said Ron. 'Can I hit her please? I really want to hit her. Please.'

'What did I say?'

'First you suggest I'm not normal, which I most definitely am…most of the time, and second you say I'm acting human: a disgusting insult. Appalling. Extremely offensive.'

'Calm down, Ron,' said Callum. 'It's not that bad. Keep your shirt on.'

'Yeah,' added Ande, 'Don't get your shirt in a knot.'

'Idiom killer,' said Ron. 'Language butcherer.'

Ande stood and glared down at Ron. 'English isn't even my first language. How many languages do you speak?'

Ron glanced upwards. 'Let me think.'

'You're real funny, Ron.'

Ron finished his beatific sky gazing. 'Forty-seven, I think.'

'A real comedian.'

'*Ninakupa tu jibu la uaminifu. Sio kujaribu kuchekesha,*' said Ron.

'Now you're just showing off.'

'What did he say?' said Callum. 'Was that Swahili?'

'He said he's not a comedian, he's a truth teller.'

Callum laughed and looked at Ron. 'That is the most ironic sentence I've ever heard from your mouth, my friend.'

Ron bowed. Ande scowled. Callum said, 'Let's get

back to business. Ron, what did you make of the Sorcerer's Tusk. Have you heard that story before?'

'Of course. It's a well-known legend.'

'Meaning it's just a story?'

'Meaning,' said Ron, 'that's it's a well-known legend and probably every word of it is true.' He paused. 'If you're asking if there could be a connection between the beetle swarms in Istanbul and the cursed shaman, then I would say it's likely. I talked to Alix about it last night, but she was oddly dismissive, which is really strange given her presence at two of the swarms. Not to mention the fact she claimed to be controlling the bugs at the hotel, and at St. Mary's. I must admit I found her coyness arousing.'

'Be that as it may,' said Callum, 'she wasn't at the cafe swarm or the one at Captain Candy.'

'Just because we didn't see her, doesn't mean she wasn't there,' said Ande.

'You're right, Ande,' said Callum. 'In every other way, the four swarms have been identical. Roughly the same duration and scale—'

'St. Mary's was way bigger,' said Ande.

'Okay,' said Callum. 'Same duration. Same diversity of beetle. And of course, there's the lightning strike.'

'Which we now think is caused by the alpha stag beetle,' said Ande.

'Ooh,' said Ron. 'The alpha stag beetle.' He smiled a twisted little grin. 'Remember that scorpion in Mae Sai Callum? I'd love to see that death match.'

'Unfortunately for your macabre fantasies, that

sucker bought the farm.'

'Thanks to that giant, shiny creature,' said Ron. 'That mysterious friend of yours.'

The hairs on the back of Callum's neck stood up, his skin prickling at the mention of the angel: his saviour. Three times he had appeared to Callum. Three unforgettable, life-changing moments. He'd never summoned him, never cried for help. There was no stereotypical desperate scream from a pathetic lost soul destined for damnation, pleading for salvation. He hadn't said a word. Not even thought about seeking help from a celestial being. Of course, back then he hadn't even believed in such creatures, so naturally he wouldn't have, but the second time? It was most likely a case of denial the second time, and the third time? It was possible now, quite possible, that he was reaching out with some hidden part of himself without even knowing it. The instinct to pray, which was what his parents had always done, was developing some muscles. Good news or bad, the Steele family had included God in their conversations for as long as he could remember. Maybe Callum had simply fallen out of the habit. Perhaps it was a decision he made somewhere along the line to ignore such religious thinking.

'Callum?' Ron's voice broke into his thoughts. 'Are you still with us?'

'Yes.' Another thought occurred to him. 'Why are you still hanging out with me, Ron?'

'I could be offended by that.'

'If you didn't have such thick skin.'

'If I didn't have such thick, tough and awesome skin,' said Ron emphasising the *tough* while fading a little on the *awesome*. It didn't sound right coming from him, but in any case, he had successfully deflected Callum's question between the slips, as Pitch would say, by way of being complimentary.

'I'm going to get a refill,' said Ande. Callum had forgotten her temporarily. 'We're going to be here for a while, right?'

'Didn't you want to do some more sightseeing?'

'Yeah, but there's no hurry. We've got all day. I'll just have another coffee, then we can head off, have a look around, then grab some lunch afterwards.'

Callum smiled.

'You asked why I've been hanging around,' said Ron. Callum nodded for him to explain. 'Until your awakening, everything made sense to me. I'd been given an assignment, which was to stop your awakening.'

'Good job on that one.'

Ron bared his teeth, shaking his head as though he was mauling Callum. 'I'll admit to being ill-prepared for the encounter with the angel, then subsequently allowing circumstances to overtake me. Some personal business kept me off track as well. By the time we got to the Scorpion Temple, I was already getting the idea that there was much more to the story than I'd been told. I didn't realize, for example, that so many heavy hitters knew about you and were interested in you. I completely underestimated your importance in the overall scheme of things. The big picture was fuzzy. Still is. I…' Ron rolled his head around on his shoulders, arched his back, stretching his arms out in front of him. 'It's complicated.'

'You got that right,' said Callum. 'Let me summarise for you.'

'Go ahead.'

'You and me have unfinished business.'

'Exactly.'

'Just call me the nutshell master.'

Cocking his head, grinning at some hidden amusement, Ron said, 'Okay, nutshell master.'

'Callum!' Ande called from the door of the cafe. 'Come and check this out. There's just been another swarm.'

Callum joined Ande quickly, as she led him to the TV mounted high on the wall inside the cafe. 'At the airport,' she said answering Callum's question before he had time to ask it. 'What time was Pitch's flight?'

'I don't know,' said Callum, taking his phone from his back pocket, finding and dialling Pitch's number. He kept his eyes on the television screen while he waited for Pitch to answer, but he didn't.

'Voicemail,' he said to Ande, before ending the call without leaving a message.

The sound was turned down on the television, and the captions were in Turkish. Someone had taken some footage during the swarm, on their phone, and shared it with the television station. It showed a swirling mass of insects, concentrated in a corner of the terminal. Although Callum couldn't see clearly, they were certainly beetles. The vision lasted ten seconds before a jagged rod of lightning pierced the ceiling above the beetles, cutting into the heart of the swarm. The person filming screamed then dropped their phone, and the pictures stopped; replaced by the face of the news anchor.

Callum and Ande looked at each other. 'All the swarms we know of happened with at least one of us present,' said Callum. 'So I'm going to assume Pitch was there.'

'Call him again.'

Pitch answered after several rings. 'Yep.'

'Are you all right, mate?'

'Yep.'

Infuriated by Pitch's reticence to talk, Callum raised his voice. 'Where are you? Did you see what happened? There was a swarm. There at the airport'

'Yep,' said Pitch. 'Listen, I have to go. I'm boarding soon. I saw the swarm, but didn't see any stag beetles. It was all over pretty quick. I'm fine. Good luck with your investigations. See you later.'

'Pitch?' Pitch had hung up. 'Ron, do you have any idea where Alix might be? Do you think she might have gone to the airport?'

Ron did an annoying impression of Atlas. 'It's an extremely suspicious coincidence otherwise. You two kids go sightseeing. I'll find Alix.'

Callum wanted to protest, but Ron had already vanished.

Chapter Twenty-Four

'They say that Istanbul is where the East meets the West,' said Callum, as he and Ande stood side by side admiring the impressive gardens of the Hagia Sophia. Complete with majestic water fountains, the extensive lawn forecourt of one of the great religious architectural wonders of the world beckoned them to worship.

'Do they?' said Ande.

'They do,' said Callum, stepping forward. 'Napoleon himself is quoted as saying that if the whole world was a state, Istanbul would be its capital. Shall we go inside?'

'I think that's why we came here.'

'Again,' said Callum.

'I know we should have done the tour the first time, but it's worth a second look isn't it,' replied Ande. 'Amazing.'

They walked slowly along the wide path which led to the main entrance, enjoying the heat, the hum of humanity and the pleasant feeling of togetherness. It seemed they had built a bridge over the Mae Sai incident, and they were now happily strolling along the other side of the river. Elephants in rooms didn't usually disappear, but Callum was thankful for the miracle. Unless it was a bucketload of denial facilitating their blossoming relationship.

'You booked us on a tour, right?'

'Yes, Callum.'

'What about the Blue Mosque?'

'What about the Blue Mosque? They're the same thing, aren't they?'

'Same place, but not the same thing. Didn't you ask any questions when you made the booking? You know, it's kind of what we do. Ask questions. Do research.'

Ande hadn't stopped when Callum did, so she was soon lost in the crowd. She seemed distracted. Callum guessed she should have been more than distracted in the circumstances. Ande had only just met her first demon. Her reaction had been surprising considering her background and the fact her sister was a witch doctor of sorts. How do you get your head around that sort of thing? When you have neither choice nor time, you just do.

'I've had a few things on my mind lately, Callum,' said Ande. She cocked her head and stared at him as though he was an insensitive tool.

'It's easy to be consumed by stuff, Ande. You just need to break out of that, shake it off.'

With a wry smile, Ande said, 'Okay Taylor, help me shake it off.'

'Taylor?' Callum laughed, then took her hand; impulsive and verging on romantic, the action took Ande by surprise. The sound she made was like a squeal, but there was probably a better word for it. In any case, she offered no resistance, allowing herself to be pulled along as they headed for the entrance of the Hagia Sophia. They went to the information counter, gave their names, and said they had booked a tour.

By the time, the customer service officer had found their names, Callum noticed Ande's hand was still inside his. Suddenly self-conscious, he released it. Ande didn't comment. Soon, they were greeted by a stooped, scaly-faced man who looked a hundred years old, but spoke with the timbre and enthusiasm of a fifteen-year-old. He was to be their guide. The subsequent two hours passed in a leisurely blur of visual wonders, fascinating history, and funny anecdotes. Callum and Ande talked little but touched and smiled often as they followed the old tour guide around the Hagia Sophia for two hours, listening to his professionally energetic commentary. It was breathtaking.

'What about all the gold?' said Ande.

'Thirty million tiles,' said Callum. 'Did I hear that right?'

Ande answered yes but had clearly lost interest in Hagia Sophia factoids. 'Look', she said, then added quickly. 'Not now. Don't look.' Callum had already turned his head but snapped it back on command.

'What am I not looking at?'

Staring, fixing her eyes on something or someone in the distance, Ande whispered absurdly, 'Slow and casual'

'Huh?'

'Turn your head slowly and casually and look over by the far wall near that thing, that statue. There's a group of people, but some of them aren't people. Maybe.' Ande lowered her voice further. Impossibly. 'Tell me if you recognize the skinny couple.'

Callum obeyed Ande's instructions, eventually searching for what Ande said she could see. It couldn't be. He'd seen Ande kick those two wraiths into a pile of beetles which had scattered to the four corners of the city, being absorbed by the darkness, leaving no trace of the counterfeit flesh they'd hidden themselves within.

'Don't stare!' said Ande.

'You're staring,' snapped Callum, not annoyed with Ande, but unnerved by the return of Corpulent and Elephantine: the weird non-couple from St. Mary's. 'You've been staring for a good two minutes.'

'How can they be here?' said Ande. 'You saw what I did to them?'

'Do you think they want to talk again?'

'I think,' said Ande, taking hold of Callum's hand, pulling him towards the exit. 'They are more likely after a bit of revenge. I would be too. They offered us a friendly warning and we attacked them.'

'You're rewriting history, Ande. And I think the word you're looking for is killed, not attacked.'

'Let's go,' she said.

With a feeling not too different from trying to leap across a flood-swollen creek, Callum consented to being dragged away. He knew if Corpulent and Elephantine had spotted them, there would be no running away. They would dispense with relatively moderate threats and warnings and do precisely as Ande thought they would. Exact some retribution. Could they though? If they were only made of beetle-stuffed skin, approximating human form with near perfect accuracy, how much damage could they do? They looked like stick men, so maybe they possessed the strength of dry twigs which was why Ande was so adroitly able to dispatch them. She was still wearing a bright pink badge of pride to celebrate that mighty deed, but Callum suspected the spectacular end of Corpulent and Elephantine had more to do with their weakness than Ande's power. When they appeared in front of Callum and Ande, ending their escape, Callum was not at all surprised.

'G'day, skinny fake people,' said Callum. He'd learned a few things from Ron's ability to deliver casual quips in the face of danger.

The beetle ghosts looked at each other. Corpulent turned his head slowly and spoke. 'We don't know what that means.'

Ande lashed out with her right foot, but Corpulent dematerialized, meaning Ande's foot hit nothing and achieved nothing other than to drag her whole body forward and throw it on the ground. She grunted in an appreciably feminine way. Callum moved to help her to her feet, offering his hand which she took, smiling up at him.

Elephantine spoke next, after Corpulent had re appeared beside her. 'You were warned to leave.'

Ande feinted with her right foot, then pivoted,

swivelling on her heel, before dropping the right foot quickly to the ground as an anchor for her left foot which she thrust quickly towards Elephantine. Sadly, it too missed the mark. Ande sprawled ungracefully once more.

She laughed. 'That was my best move.'

Corpulent shifted beside Callum as he stooped down to help Ande up. When Callum pulled, Ande remained exactly where she was. Callum tried again to no avail. Corpulent said, 'You were warned.' He lifted his hand in the air above Ande forcing her flat on the ground, her head twisted to the right side. The cheek depressed, a fearful look transforming her smile into a horrible grimace.

When Callum attempted to stop what Corpulent was doing by pushing his arm aside, he himself fell victim to an invisible restraint. Ande's mocha skin whitened under the pressure as though she was a cup of coffee to which Corpulent was adding milk. 'Ande,' said Callum, 'stupid question I know, but are you okay?'

Unable to move due to the imposed tautness of her muscles, Ande blinked twice, which Callum assumed meant yes although it could have meant no just as easily. Callum wrestled the invisible chains restricting him, but it was futile. Soon, he felt his knees begin to buckle, then, unable to push back, he collapsed. It wasn't pain he was experiencing, just unbearable pressure. He took comfort from that as he inevitably found himself on the ground beside Ande. If he wasn't hurting, then she probably wasn't either. He closed his eyes and did something he never imagined he would do. Something which he hadn't tried yet. Something simultaneously daring and embarrassing. He prayed.

'God, help me please.'

'Common first prayer, but well done,' said a strange, but somehow familiar voice. Callum realized in that moment he was free. Ande too, beside him was liberated, and Corpulent and Elephantine were nowhere to be seen. Callum checked thoroughly.

'They're gone, but they might return. I suspect they lack the intelligence to accept the futility of their actions. Threatening God's children?' The angel looked more human than ever before as he spoke. 'Come on.'

Surprised by the appearance of the angel, the answered prayer, the angel apparently referring to him as one of God's children, and speaking like a regular person, Callum was dumbfounded. It was a lot to take in. This was not the first time the angel had appeared to save him, or in the case of Callum's father's funeral, to comfort him, but this was the first time he had spoken directly to Callum. The first time he had arrived as an answer to a prayer. Prayer worked. Okay, it was a very moderate sample on which to base an opinion, but it was a pretty striking example. Hard to refute the power of personal experience.

'Have you finished your analysis?'

'Not by half.'

The angel smiled. 'Until next time.' He nodded his head slightly, a stiff and awkwardly formal gesture, then disappeared.

Having forgotten Ande, Callum now looked at her. Gently, he placed his finger under her chin and closed her mouth. 'Are you okay?'

Ande frowned, apparently searching for the right words. 'You know what I really don't understand?'

'What's that?'

'How I, how we, take all of this on our stride.' She waved her hands around. 'All of this weird stuff that's going on. Shouldn't we be in a permanent state of shock? How are we coping with all this so easily? I mean it's just like your brushing teeth, right?'

Callum laughed. 'Okay, I wouldn't go that far, but I get what you're saying. It's *in* our stride by the way.'

'Huh?'

'We take things *in* our stride, not *on* our stride.'

'Whatever, Mr. English professor.'

Suddenly Ron joined them with an announcement. 'An insect swarm has been reported at Dolmabahce Palace.'

'Where've you been?' said Callum.

'Looking for Alix.'

'Why? Was she missing?'

'I had a suspicion about what she might be up to, so I thought I'd check it out.'

'And?' said Callum.

Ron seemed quite chirpy. Callum wondered how long he'd been around. Had he seen the angel and kept his distance until it departed or was it a case of lucky timing on his part. His tone suggested Ron had either good news on Alix, or no news. He would have certainly been snarkier had whatever suspicions he'd held been confirmed.

'And…it's a good news, bad news scenario.'

'Go on,' said Callum.

'The good news is that Alix was not involved in the airport swarm. She's been at two of the previous swarms—'

'That we know of,' said Ande.

Following a funny little bow, Ron agreed. 'That we know of. Also, the fact she belatedly absented herself from breakfast made me suspicious.'

'But she wasn't there at the airport.'

'Correct.'

'Are you sure?' said Ande.

'Yes, but…'

Ande rolled her eyes. 'Here we go,' she said. 'This will be a big but, I'm sure.'

'There was someone there, in the thick of it so to speak. Directing insectoid traffic. Orchestrating the beetacular procession.'

'Knock it off, Ron,' said Callum. 'Who was it?'

'Someone who looked a lot like Alix actually. Someone—'

'Ron!'

'Keep your shirt on,' said Ron. 'I don't know who it was, but she looked exactly like Alix. Like a doppelganger. Maybe a twin.'

'You've got to be kidding me,' said Callum. His mind scrambled through the ramifications of this new information. Ron was telling the truth about what he saw and about it not being Alix. Callum was certain of that. An evil double. Wait. Self-correction. Was it possible for a demon to have an evil twin? The supposition depended on the assumption that a demon could be good. That wouldn't do. A demon who had a twin was surely the equivalent in satanic terms, equally evil. Or were there shades of evil? Were good and evil relative terms or absolutes? Now those were a couple of juicy questions for the philosophers. Unfortunately, there weren't any philosophers present.

'I guess Alix has never mentioned having a twin?'

'No,' said Ron, 'but we don't know each other that well. I don't think we've had a conversation about siblings. It's not one of my favourite topics, and probably not Alix's either, especially if the demon I saw at the airport is her evil twin.'

'You'll probably need to have that conversation now,' said Callum.

A hole opened in the discussion, allowing Callum some more thinking time. He remembered Ron's mention of the latest swarm. 'We'll worry about the Alix and her evil twin situation later.'

'Or we won't,' said Ron.

'When you arrived, you mentioned at swarm at a palace? By the way, it would've been helpful had you arrived much earlier.'

'Why, didn't your angel mate do a good job of whatever it was he was doing?'

So, Ron had seen the angel and delayed his arrival to avoid the shiny white one. Fair enough. 'It would've been good for you to meet Corpulent and Elephantine.'

'Oh yes, they sound like real charmers. I'm so looking forward to meeting them. When will they be back?

Soon, I hope.'

'Oh my God, Ron,' said Ande. 'You're like a seventh dan blackbelt in sarcasm.'

'Thanks.'

'I thought Callum was good, but you're next level.'

Their chat was running off the rails and Callum wanted to get them back on topic. 'You were saying?' he said. 'About the palace swarm?'

'Yes, one of three others today.'

'Three?' said Callum. 'Besides the airport.'

'Dolmabahce Palace. Eminonu Pier and the Miniature Model Park.'

'Things are heating up now,' said Callum. 'I suggest we visit those places and have a chat with any witnesses.'

'For what purpose?' said Ande.

'For starters, we need to confirm that each involved a lightning strike and see if there are any other similarities.'

'But what's that going to achieve?' said Ande. 'We missed the events, and how come, when the swarms are all happening where there are lots of tourists, how come there was no action here? Why'd we miss out? Are we going to try to do something to stop the swarms? To take out whoever's responsible? If there is anyone behind it, that is.'

'Oh, there's definitely someone behind the swarms. We just don't know how to find him,' said Callum.

'Who's that?'

'The Sorcerer with the tusk.'

Ande laughed unconvincingly. 'We're going with that theory, are we?'

Callum was dead serious as he looked into Ande's eyes. 'We just need to be there when a swarm happens and find the alpha stag beetle. Then I'm sure we'll get to meet this Sorcerer.'

'You make it sound so simple,' said Ande. 'What do you think, Ron?'

Ron was gone.

'Food first, then we'll go to the nearest of those attractions where swarms occurred today and check them out. Agreed?'

'Food, I agree with,' said Ande. 'The rest of your plan sounds like a wild duck chase.'

Callum smiled to himself, resisting the urge to correct her. 'Okay, my friend, let's go duck hunting.'

Chapter Twenty-Five

'I see you two have already met,' said Ron, attempting to hide the alarm he felt on seeing confirmation of his theory in the flesh. This explained so much while simultaneously opening up a detestably large can of worms.

It wasn't until Alix spoke that Ron knew who was who. That was what happened with identical twins. 'Ron, this is my sister Twistix.' Nodding at her, she added, 'Twistix, this is my boyfriend Ron.'

Alix's eyes twinkled as they often did when she stabbed Ron with the primal intensity of her gaze. Ron searched for a safe place to fall over, maybe scurry away into a dark crevice. Since being assigned to Callum Steele, Ron's life had escalated in complexity and intensity. He was used to tension, found it pleasing it fact, but mainly when he was causing it as opposed to having it pulled down over his head like an undersized woollen beanie. His head was preparing for self-destruction. He was Alix's boyfriend, and it was time to meet some of her family.

'Hello, Twistix,' he said, then to Alix: 'My love, oh my love.'

Twistix frowned beyond acceptably safe levels of

displeasure and confusion while Alix rolled her eyes, skin flickering dark purple spots in embarrassment.

In an effort to breach the discomfort, Alix spoke next. 'We were just discussing how pleasant it is to sit at a table chatting and not be bothered by anyone.'

'It's a cool little trick,' said Twistix. 'Cursing the space surrounding us with a repulsive fragrance of palpable fear so that whichever dumb human tries to invade our space is instantly driven away.'

'Cooler still,' added Alix enthusiastically, 'is they have no idea what's going on. The look on their faces is priceless. Here comes one now.'

A tall man with a dark grey business suit stretched over his enhanced muscular structure hit the no-fly zone as though walking into a closed door. Fear filled his eyes, his human handsome faced blanched, his knees buckled. Ron watched his right hand reach desperately for his heart, before he spun around and returned from whence he came. Ron had to admit it was quite entertaining.

'You see?' said Twistix.

'I do,' said Ron, drawing out the words, procrastinating as he tried to figure out what to do now. It was so typical of the latest version of himself to be terribly disorganized. Once upon a time, he would never have stalled, for he always strived to project a casual air irrespective of the circumstances into a situation for which he lacked a solid plan and a hefty back up plan. His reprieve came courtesy of an invitation from Alix to join them. Upon his acceptance, they lost interest in him, resuming their previous conversation which, as Ron had suspected, was all about the Sorcerer.

When Ron had seen a demon who looked exactly like Alix at the airport, he had known it wasn't her. She'd told him where she'd be, and as far as his kind could trust each other, he trusted her. Damn, they were a thing, an item. Ron had never imagined having such an intimate and exclusive relationship, had never known that type of thing was possible for demons. Naturally, he was unprepared for it, and no doubt theirs was a rough start with the fight at St. Mary's, but somehow the two of them had found their way along an unmarked track. It wasn't simply that she'd told him where she was at that time, but he'd sensed it wasn't Alix as well. He'd seen Pitch there too, but as great an entomologist as he was, and undoubtedly a good friend to Callum, the man was one of the human somnambulists—those who wandered around through life with their spiritual eyes closed. In any case, he was clearly leaving and was in no way threatening, even if he was staying.

Alix's twin, for again Ron intuited this truth, was another matter. He was too shocked to take her on at the airport, but as she had been in the thick of yet another swarm, she was high on his agenda for his next private discussion with Alix. Ron's main question was whether Alix was still creating mayhem. If they were operating together in coordinated mischief-making, then Ron had a significantly bigger problem than he had first thought. Identical twins were notorious pranksters, always looking to take advantage of the confusion caused by their looks. If they, being evil, had put their heads together, then Ron was to face an impossible choice. He was about to be impaled on the horns of a dilemma. To stand with his mate Callum, or allow the continuance of disturbances, or take Twistix out of the picture and probably Alix as well. Their deaths would be the end of his first relationship. It was a distressing thought. Perhaps there was another way. Deciding it was time to get off the bench and into the game, he turned back into the conversation, seeking a gap to insert himself.

'So,' he said loudly enough to cause both the sister's heads to spin in his direction. 'What's the go with all these beetle swarms?' Looking at them in turn, he added, 'Is it just the two of you amusing yourselves? Or is there something bigger going on?'

Sometimes silence was a sweet, peaceful thing, a thing to be enjoyed and savoured. Other times it was an angst-filled agony of suspense, a thing which made stomach muscles tighten and heart rates rise. In the absence of words, without an amiable atmosphere, silence threatened to spew forth carnage. Ron physically felt the danger in the quiet which followed his questions. It was as though he had walked in on a top-secret conversation behind closed doors, asking, with no authority, to be included. Two pairs of scornful eyes admonished him, rebuking his insolence, warning him to stay out of other people's business. Refusing to be intimidated, Ron decided to get on the front foot.

'Fair question, is it not?' said Ron taking time to glare at each of the sisters, willing invisible fire to erupt from his eyes to scorch theirs and incinerate the delusion they held that Ron was easily pushed away. 'One way or another,' he continued, 'I am going to have to do something about this situation.'

Twistix laughed out loud, mocking him. 'Is that so, Ronny?'

'Ronny?' He turned to Alix, searching for some sign that she would take his side, even against her own sister. She stared at him briefly, before turning away.

'Why don't you stick to your patch, Ronny? Leave this to the experts. We all know what we're doing, and whether you know about it or not is neither here nor there. You certainly won't be able to do anything to stop us.'

The poisoned air comprising the cocoon in which they sat seemed to be leaking into Ron's skin, creeping into his bones. He fought to ignore it, focusing instead on keeping Twistix talking. He'd allow her arrogant ranting to inadvertently reveal some of the information he was seeking. 'There are,' said he, 'perhaps bigger forces at play here than you can handle or even understand.'

'You mean Callum's angel?' Twistix laughed again, derision exploding into the space between them. 'You have a lot to learn.' Suddenly she leaned closer to Ron. 'I would have thought your experiences in Thailand would have eroded your embarrassing naivety. You were in over your head there as well. You and your boyfriend, Callum Steele.'

Ron wondered who told Twistix about the events in Thailand. Alix was an obvious choice, but surely, she wouldn't have betrayed him by sharing his war stories with her sister. They'd had confidential conversations,

Alix and he, many of them, but he never suspected she was merely gathering intelligence rather than building their relationship. The idea was as shocking as it was now evident. Smacking him in the face was the undeniable truth that Alix had played him. Ron smiled and nodded, directing his attention to Alix. 'I see.'

'I know,' continued Twistix, leaning back in her chair, speaking in a ridiculous seductive tone, 'about the angel's offer for you to switch sides and how, even now you are considering it. How you've been contaminated by human frailty, the confusion of passion, the muddy waters of morality?' She paused, smiled broadly. 'You've allowed yourself to be trapped in a no man's land, fooling yourself all the while that you are in control.'

Slapping Twistix's face felt great. It also achieved the pleasure of silencing this witch. Her skin changed colour, rolling through several dark shades as she scrambled to deal with Ron's unexpected assault. He watched to see if she would retaliate. Or indeed if Alix would leap to her sister's defence. 'You talk too much,' he said, raising his hand again, looking for signs of fear. 'You're going to tell me everything I want to know, or I will beat it out of you.'

'Like hell I will.'

The second blow was harder, knocking her off her chair, yet still she restrained herself from fighting back. As she rose from the ground to resume her seat, Ron punched her in the throat. Twistix grasped her neck, gasping for air, while Ron positioned himself to inflict some more damage.

'That's enough, Ron,' said Alix. 'Stop it.'

Ron turned on her. 'I should pound you as well, you slimy Judas.'

'What do you mean?'

'I'm seriously upset now,' said Ron. 'I don't know where the two of you get off being so disrespectful to me. Acting like a couple of repulsive brats, trying to bully me into backing off. I could snap both of your necks in a flash and send you to permanent oblivion. I wouldn't even lose my breath to do it. You were mining me the whole time, while you and your twisted bitch of a sister played lackey for the Sorcerer.'

He glanced at Twistix, her heaving chest, her sullen rage, and felt nothing but contempt. Until the mention of the Sorcerer, Ron's words had seemingly not gained any traction with Alix. Now he saw a flicker of something. Surprise, perhaps. Why should she have been surprised that he had made the connection between the beetle swarms and the Sorcerer? She'd been there when Professor Berat had told the ancient story. Ron had not immediately connected Alix with any of this because he didn't want to. He preferred, because of his ill-founded affection for Alix, to believe that her being present at the swarms was coincidental. She certainly had some power, but her antics were circus tricks, the kind of nonsensical gallivanting bored and unattached demons were famous for. This was what he had believed right up to this moment, when the overconfidence of the demon sisters pierced his pride and reignited some devilish fire within him. His anger made him feel strong, like his old self. He would have liked to kill them both for the sheer pleasure of it, for the satisfaction gained from destruction. The old Ron was back.

Ron flexed his wings to their full glory, took a deep breath, then stomped on Twistix's head. Her groan was rewarding.

'Ron, please,' said Alix.

'Beg, my foe,' he said. 'Beg for your life, Sorcerer's slut. Beg me to back off.'

It was so easy, the power and the control burning, boiling his blood. This was good. He could afford to relax now he'd shown them both what he was capable of. Alix had previously fought him tooth and nail at St. Mary's, but he had eventually subdued her there. She had plainly chosen a different tactic following that defeat. She couldn't best him physically, so she tried to cosy up beside him and snake her way into his heart. It had been effective, very effective. He had swallowed the bait she laid out, allowing himself to relax into a fantasy.

'The only words I now want to hear from you, Alix, are words of explanation. Tell me what you know of the Sorcerer's plans. What's his game? What does he want? Is it simple revenge? Or is he another megalomaniac like Lutevo? You will fill in all the gaps in my knowledge and I will arm myself to prevent whatever he has in mind. After you've told me everything you know, I'm going to kill your sister, and probably you as well.'

He glared at Alix, leaned in close, breathed his fetid breath heavily into her face. 'Go ahead, I'm listening.'

Chapter Twenty-Six

'I guess I owe you an explanation.'

Callum leaned back in his chair, stared out the hotel window. Although he hadn't expected it, he was pleased to hear Pitch's voice. It had baffled Callum at the time, but with all that had been going on, he hadn't really thought about Pitch: neither his sudden departure nor his off demeanour. The almost instant affinity between them since they first met on the doomed QANTAS flight 444 to Thailand, and the comradery and intimacy they'd built since through their shared experiences had elevated Pitch in Callum's mind. Lifted their relationship beyond association, above professional interaction, deeper than friendship. Callum missed Pitch: his humour, his steady, even-tempered unflappability, his pragmatism, his knowledge. Ande liked him too, and together they had become a team in the truest sense of the word. More like family.

'I was wondering,' said Callum. 'Are you okay? You sound better. When are you coming back to help us knock over this Sorcerer and his beetle gangbangers?'

The silence was enough of an answer, though not the one Callum wanted.

'Do you have time to talk?'

'There are currently no swarms. Ande is busy working on her article for the magazine, and I've seen enough of Istanbul for now, so…plenty of time for you, old mate. What's been going on?'

Another pause from Pitch, heavy with something, maybe sadness, maybe guilt, maybe both. Callum knew that place of fear and uncertainty, when there was much to tell but little understanding of how to tell it. You want to come clean. You feel you should, that confession will be good for you, but you worry if it will be good for the other person. You're concerned with how what you say will colour the other person's view of you. Irrespective of how close you are, there's always a streak of worry, a voice which warns you that your words will bring judgment and rejection. It only has to happen once for a person to be perpetually impacted, even if peripherally. There's always a place of doubt. There's always a voice suggesting you stay in the darkness, cut and run, burn your bridges, and flee to the imagined safety of hidden places and superficial relationships. Callum knew it. He sensed it in Pitch, somehow.

'What's happened?' Callum said.

'I've been married for thirty-one years.'

And that was all Pitch needed to say for Callum knew where he was heading. The tone of voice did not suggest a celebration of a milestone, but rather dripped with regret as though it was the end. Pitch hadn't previously talked much about his wife, so Callum had assumed, perhaps erroneously, that it was a solid partnership. He assumed this but, as he waited for Pitch to say what he needed to say, Callum realized he could have assumed something else just as easily. When a man does not speak about his wife, does not bring her in, or attempt to bring her into to every conversation, regardless of the topic, surely this speaks volumes about a disconnect. People in love, in happy and secure relationships litter the landscape with their partner's name, opinions and anecdotes because the one they love is never far from their thoughts. While it's effortless to speak of them, it's equally natural to keep quiet when the cover does not match the contents. Callum cut to the chase in an attempt to make it easier for his friend to spill his guts.

'What's her name?'

'My wife?'

'Cut it out, Pitch. Send it down straight.'

'Her name is Annie.'

'Go on.'

'I rushed back to Australia to deal with the fallout when my wife found out about Annie.'

'It's been going on for a while?' said Callum. 'The affair?'

'Nearly a year. I met her at conference in New Zealand. I didn't intend for anything to happen, but me and Margie had hit a rough spot, and I was feeling bummed. Annie and I got to talking, and I invited her to have dinner with me. It was so easy to talk to her, I just opened up, which was dumb given we'd only just met, but I needed to talk, and she had a way of making me relax. And we were drinking.'

'And one thing led to another,' said Callum, not

unsympathetically. He recalled how the wrong combination of feminine seduction, personal weakness and booze had caused more than a little drama for him in Mae Sai.

'We didn't go there,' said Pitch. 'I didn't want that. I wasn't thinking about sex. I just wanted someone to talk to. Someone to listen to. Margie had switched off and I reacted by withdrawing. We both stopped trying. I don't know why that happened, but I felt lonely as a result. Lonely in my marriage. Sex was one thing, a big thing of course, but she was emotionally frigid too. She'd turned into a different person, but I hadn't noticed. I must have changed too. Maybe it was my fault.'

'It's not usually the fault of just one person when relationships breakdown.'

'I wasn't only feeling the alcohol that first night with Annie. I was drunk on her, the attention she gave me, the smell of her perfume, her breath across the table. I could tell that I was the only person in the room for her. I could have been the only person in the world. You talk about intoxication? Nothing smashes a man like a woman who wants him.'

Callum thought of Ande, shifted in his seat, stood up and walked to the window. He knew exactly what Pitch was talking about. He'd be hard pressed to find a man anywhere on earth who didn't want to be the centre of a woman's attention, the object of her desire. Fragile male egos pursuing strength through sweet words of flattery. 'I get it,' said Callum. 'I understand.'

'After the conference, we stayed in touch, but I

kept it secret from Margie. She didn't ask about the conference when I got home, but that wasn't unusual. There was a time when she'd lap up my post-travel reports. I'd regale her with exaggerated stories of larger-than-life characters, slotting them all into neatly labelled boxes. The men. The women. The bugs. She used to love that stuff, but as I said, for whatever reason she lost interest. Before I even touched the ground back in Oz, I'd decided I was going to stay in touch with Annie. I told myself it was friendship, but I was kidding myself. I'd controlled myself that night after dinner, but back in my room, I got a hard-on and took care of business, if you know what I mean. I was thinking about her the whole time. I was too often thinking that way whenever I felt upset or tired or frustrated. Annie became my medicine and all the while we maintained contact on Messenger. She would flirt with me, but I couldn't quite go there, so I brushed it off when I was with her, but when I wasn't, I lapped it up.

'Is she a Kiwi?'

'Yes, from Tauranga on the North Island. The conference was down in Christchurch.'

'So, you were chatting for a bit, and you were pretending you weren't having an affair.'

'It wasn't an affair,' protested Pitch. 'We hadn't done anything. Just talking.'

'Rubbish,' said Callum. 'Just because you hadn't had sex, doesn't mean you weren't having an affair. You'd grown emotionally dependent on her, which paradoxically made it easier for you to stay in an unhappy marriage. You probably even had a conversation with yourself about how having another woman on the side would help you survive your unhappy marriage.'

'Bloody hell, Callum,' said Pitch. 'Where'd all this come from?'

Callum had to think about that. He wasn't married. Had never been married. Wasn't in a relationship, although some could argue the point about him and Ande. He wasn't speaking from experience except in relation to the feelings aroused in him by a woman which often left him feeling dazed. Self-reflection was bringing some clarity, but he was really stumbling in the dark like most men. Slaves either to their penises or their emotions whilst projecting self-controlled, logical strength. No doubt Ande was sharpening his edges. Even though they weren't together as such, there was no question of him having ever felt closer to a woman than he did to her. She pushed him, pulled him, stirred him up and challenged him. Callum decided to avoid answering Pitch's question.

'It makes sense, doesn't it?' he said. 'You understand what I'm saying, right?'

'Finally, I couldn't handle the fantasy anymore. I wanted to make it real. The next conference was scheduled for Jiangxi, in China. Local entomologists were looking to garner some international support for research into the *Cassinadae* beetle, which they said was being underreported in Longnan compared to neighbouring provinces. It was all political bulldust of course. In inviting international scientists, the event organizers hoped to push their government into action by embarrassing them. The underreporting they referred to in the promotional material was for foreign eyes only and was clearly code for lack of money. I never really found the *Cassinidae* beetles especially interesting, although particular members of this species were wreaking havoc on vegetation and based on the stats, whether they were reliable or not, they were rightly being described as pests. A control and /or eradication program was being spouted, but—'

'Hey Pitch!' said Callum. 'I thought we were talking about you and Annie.'

Pitch laughed self-consciously and mumbled an apology. 'Annie and I arranged to stay together.'

'That was risky.'

'Yep.'

'I guess risk goes with the territory when you're in that place.'

'Yep,' said Pitch. 'Anyway, to cut a long story short, Anne and I carried on for a while, initially meeting at scheduled conferences, then making up events to attend as cover for us to be together. I learned she was also married, but equally unhappy and looking for…'

'Something better.'

'We talked about how we might work things out. I was happy to continue in secret, but she became increasingly pushy about me leaving Margie and making a proper go of things with her. I didn't want to do that because, for one, I didn't want to hurt Margie, but I didn't want the hassle either. I've heard enough horror divorce stories to want to stay clear of it, so I kept putting her off. Some of our time together, limited as it was, was being consumed with discussing this issue, and those discussions started to turn into arguments. She'd accuse me of using her and I couldn't really refute that, but I reckoned she was using me too.''

'You didn't say that though?'

'Of course not, but I started to try to think of a way to escape.'

'Let me guess,' said Callum. 'Annie wasn't going to let go easily.'

Pitch sighed. 'She started to make threats about exposing our relationship. Telling me I didn't love her.'

'Did you love her?'

'I don't know. Remember what Tina Turner said? Anyway, the party was over, and I needed to find a way out of it. I was pretty convinced by her threats so I reasoned I should be the one to tell Margie. But how do you have *that* conversation?'

Callum knew his friend had buried himself in a box. These things rarely end well. Such passionate affairs of mutual need make for great drama in the movies, and in real life. The difference was that real life had real consequences. Pitch ignored sound judgment, making a series of choices which led him in to a vast and dangerous wilderness. He'd fooled himself into thinking he could control the situation and keep a leash on Annie.

'I knew I didn't want to stay with Annie, especially when, in her desperation, she'd shown me a previously well-hidden side of herself. Spiteful and nasty, she demonstrated a willingness to do anything to get what she wanted and to hell with the consequences. In the end, I didn't really have a choice. I decided to confess to Margie and ask her forgiveness. I knew that would mean falling under the wrath of both women, but that would have happened anyway. I just needed to stay in control, try to navigate through the storm. It wasn't going to be pleasant.'

'Wow,' said Callum. 'There's an understatement if I've ever heard one. Where are you at now?'

'Unfortunately, Annie beat me to the punch. She found some contact details for Margie and sent her a message revealing our affair, stating among other things, that Margie wasn't good enough for me, and I was happier with her and that I was planning to dump Margie. Margie sent me an email letting me know that she received a message from my girlfriend, and that as far as she was concerned, I could stay in Turkey permanently. She said our marriage was over and when she calmed down, if she calmed down—she underlined *if*—we could talk about the divorce.'

'How'd you feel?'

Pitch whistled but said nothing.

'That's why you were acting weird, and why you left in a hurry,' said Callum. 'How'd you keep a lid on all that? Why didn't you pull me aside for a chat?'

'I don't know what to tell you, mate. I've barely slept since then. I can't eat properly. I've spent quite a few nights on the tiles. Fat lot of good that does though. Margie's not talking to me, and neither is Annie. Her last words were quite damning and final. She really gave it to me in a long expletive-riddled message. I blocked her, then tried to figure out how to save my marriage. That's what I'm doing now, but like I said, Margie's not talking to me and won't let me near the house. All our mutual friends have either taken sides or ditched us. Her friends are demonizing me, sending me messages to leave her alone, blasting me for being a selfish arsehole. My friends are commiserating as best they can, even though most of them agree that I'm a tool and I'm getting exactly what I deserve. I just don't know how to get back from this. I'm genuinely sorry. I'm drowning in regret, but my apologies are meaningless to everyone except me.'

'Damn,' said Callum. He thought for a moment about what he should say. Whatever words he chose, however he delivered them, Pitch was going to be in a world of pain for the foreseeable future. 'Pitch,' he said. 'Do me a favour? Don't give up. And keep talking to me, or if it needs to be someone else. Whatever. Just keep talking. Don't spend too much time inside your own head. Will you do that for me? Let's keep talking.'

'I've still got my work to occupy me so I'm not totally adrift, but everything feels pointless now. Life seems pointless.'

'It isn't, mate. I miss you. We miss you. You're important to us.'

Silence.

'Let's change the subject back to a safe happy place. Let me update you on the situation in Istanbul. There's been a bit of action since you left and we're expecting things to hot up even further.'

'Tell me about it,' said Pitch, but his voice was as flat as a pancake.

Chapter Twenty-Seven

All that remained of Twistix was a memory contained in the suppressed rage written large on Alix's face. Ron's decision to let Twistix go was his last attempt to win Alix back. Futile and inexplicably charitable as it was, the result was hardly surprising.

'Mercy, Ron,' said Alix, spitting the word through gritted fangs. 'Is that what you've become? So far from the calling, so lost in a muddle of misguided and ill-informed destiny.'

Ron slapped her, taking care to leave a mark with an extended talon. 'I'll get what I want with or without you,' he said. 'I had hoped we could walk this path together.'

Alix laughed. 'And you thought beating up and humiliating me and my sister would bring me on board with your sick, sycophantic mission.'

'Sycophantic?'

Ron was already frustrated and disappointed by Alix's duplicity, hurt even, but now with this display of bloody-mindedness, his desire to see it through was collapsing. His hopes being pounded into splinters against the jagged rocks of Alix's vehemence. He felt the attraction, the passion draining away with every acridly tense moment. It seemed increasingly pointless to interrogate Alix now that he had ceded the advantage of dominance of Twistix and his threat to kill her. He should've just done that, and if Alix continued her bitter resistance, he would finish her quickly to save time.

'Sucking the ass of humanity,' she said.

'Crude,' remarked Ron, releasing his grip on Alix's arm. 'Has it ever occurred to you that our whole existence is based on slavery? Bending our will. Surrendering ourselves. Obeying orders, irrespective of what we think of them. Sweet-talking stronger demons of higher rank, but lesser character. Have you ever thought about that? We spend nearly every second kowtowing. How is that any different from what you're accusing me of? You should know me well enough by now, Alix. The reason I'm so unpopular is because I don't suck up to demons I don't respect. Even when I'm in danger of excruciating physical suffering or worse, I say what I want, and I do what I want. I do whatever suits my purposes and I take whatever advantage I can, from whoever, whenever. I belong to me. I call the shots.'

'You're pathetic!'

With such a disappointing response to his passionate and well-argued speech, Ron decided to quit this nonsense. He announced his intention with a clubbing blow to the top of Alix's head which caused her to fall from her chair. The wound gushed putrid liquid onto the ground, pooling around her. Squatting down beside her, bringing his face close to hers, he said, 'Last chance ex-lover of mine. Tell me everything you know about the Sorcerer and his plans, and I'll see if I can organize some treatment for your headache.'

Her eyes shifted slowly, moving from his, around the space, searching for something, perhaps considering whether to live or die. Ron allowed this contemplation, hoping against hope that Alix would finally come around. When her eyes rolled to the back of her head revealing vacant red orbs, Ron feared he had blown away his last shot by hitting her too hard. She closed her eyes, swallowed, coughed herself back to consciousness.

'Twistix came to see me one night while I was on a job in Thailand,' said Alix, her voice soft, raspy, blood gurgling in the back of her throat, oozing from the side of her mouth. 'At that time, I was still working for Slerfgerg. She told me she had received a job offer which promised a promotion if completed successfully. An extra scar. She was excited, fired up, more intense than I'd ever seen her. I threatened a minion with new, unimaginable forms of pain if he didn't cover me for a while so I could talk to Twistix. That squad was a rabble. Full of hyperactive minions with carrots in their ears. You know what that's like, Ron, right? That's why you got out of that, making yourself positively odious to Slerfgerg in the process. For whatever reason, instead of dealing with you like every other upstart in the ranks, he tried to find a way to take you out of the picture while at the same time utilizing your evident skills.'

As Alix talked freely, Ron relaxed, savouring the recounting of his breakaway move: the one which solidified his status while simultaneously inviting a constant stream of challengers and assassins, all looking to boost their own credentials by fixing the Ron problem for patrons who had their own agendas. The life of the demon was all about advancement. Naked and ruthless ambition was always commended by those inhabiting higher circles, even if often proved to be personally problematic for them.

'I realized what Slerfgerg was up to,' said Ron. 'Wanting to get rid of me, but I'll admit to not thinking that he was sending me on a mission impossible, aiming to have me killed in the line of duty. How convenient. I guess he felt threatened.'

'The rumour circulating at the time,' continued Alix. 'Was that you had a friend in high places. I mean inner-circle-type higher places which was why Slerfgerg had to be sneaky about how he removed you from the picture.'

Ron smiled, feeling the tension in his body ease as the adrenaline kick died. 'I never considered that.'

'What Slerfgerg didn't know was that you actually did have a patron, a fan if you like, who gave the assignment to Slerfgerg with the not-unreasonable expectation, based on your rocky relationship with him, that he would choose you, and of course that you would fail.'

Alix shifted from her prone position, grunting as she struggled upright. She seemed to have forgotten her injury as she continued talking. This was troubling for Ron for two reasons; firstly, it indicated his power was diminished or diluted by mercy which weakened his authority over Alix, and secondly, if his strength was not the issue, her steady recovery suggested she had access to some healing magic. He didn't want to have to hit her again, but if she was merely spinning a yarn to stall for time until she was strong enough to fight or flee, he would need to channel some heartless cruelty to wound her again or destroy her once and for all.

'Do you know,' she said, 'how few demons get assigned to human awakenings?'

Ron had to admit he didn't have any idea, but suspected it wasn't many. Otherwise, the question was redundant.

'The reason you have multiple targets on you is simply jealousy,' said Alix. 'Awakenings are only given to senior demons, not lower than three scars. And do you know why that is?'

Ron was uncomfortably aware of Alix turning the tables on this interrogation. She was asking a lot of questions to which he did not have answers and she clearly knew much more about him than she'd previously intimated. Unfortunately, Alix's resilience was exposing his flaws.

'Awakenings occur in the presence of angels. Most demons can't handle angels. Forget all the chest beating, the empty bragging and the hollow curses, when it comes to the pinch, angels are quite superior as we all know. God is superior to our Master, Lucifer.'

This was a shocking confession. 'I should knock your fangs out for heresy.'

Alix shook her head slowly, managing to wrestle a

pusillanimous laugh from her mouth. It was throaty and condescending. 'Everyone knows it, Ron. It's the truth and despite our pathetic efforts, truth always wins. Most humans and most demons tell themselves it isn't true. The more pitiable humans even deny the existence of God, while others keep him at arm's length, recasting him as an occasionally useful servant rather than Lord of Creation.'

More than anything else that had happened between Ron and Alix, greater than any conversation they'd had, her blasphemous confessions underpinned what he had been unable to define, the connection he felt with her. She was a kindred soul. Soulless they might have been, but they shared an affinity based on a deep sense of rightness, not wrongness, even though they were on the wrong side. Ron didn't know what to say. Manacles of guilt clipped around his wrists and ankles. If this was truly how Alix felt, why had he not known it? Why had she not shared it? And why had she resisted him to the point of suffering a near-fatal wound? She looked at him now, red eyes boring into his, communicating her heart, her unfiltered self for the first time in their tempestuous relationship.

'I don't know what to say,' said Ron.

Alix smiled.

'Let me sort out that headache for you.'

'No need, my love,' said Alix. 'I'll be fine.' She smiled again.

'Healing magic,' said Ron. 'Where'd you score that from?'

The wound, he noticed, had nearly healed and a

healthy grey tint returned to her skin. Ron knew the magic was not an immortality spell, but unless sufficient and persistent force was used against one protected by it, they would recover. He had unwittingly given Alix enough time for the magic to work. That was probably a good thing, now he thought about it. He hadn't wanted to kill her. Overcome with frustration, he'd allowed his feelings full vent. He shouldn't have cared, but he did and therein lay the true problem. After he had spent so much time hanging around Callum and Ande, their humanity had infected him. He was tainted, smeared with the weakness of pity. Now what?

'You shouldn't care, Ron,' said Alix, standing, staring at him. 'You shouldn't give a damn about me or anyone, especially human vermin. What happened to you?'

What happened to him? He knew full well, but despite Alix's unbridled scorn, Ron couldn't bring himself to feel anything other than pride. Although not in the same league as the master's audacious attempt to overthrow the King of Heaven, Ron had nevertheless carved a path of rebillion. He was forging ahead along a path of dedicatedly selfish resistance.

'You're not going to tell me anything about the Sorcerer, are you?'

'I'll tell you one thing for old times' sake,' replied Alix. 'The Sorcerer is about to up the ante. The swarms orchestrated so far have only been a prelude to the main show, albeit an impressive one. Twistix and I will be a part of something terrifyingly wicked and we'll be rewarded for it. Well rewarded. You and your friends can stumble around for as long as you like because in the end your efforts to stop the Sorcerer will be like a fly trying to bring down a tiger.'

'I'm sorry it had to end like this, Alix.'

'There you go again,' said Alix. 'Apologizing. You make me sick.'

Ron reached for Alix, a rapid, unexpected movement coinciding her with her departure. He concentrated his strength in his grip, latching on to her, twisting and pulling with all his might. A snapping sound preceded Alix's disappearance, leaving Ron with one of her arms in his hand, and the stench of defeat in his nostrils. Staring at the arm brought a wave of nauseating nostalgia, so he dropped it on the ground and headed off to find Callum to give him the bad news.

Chapter Twenty-Eight

A blazing fireball of light, accompanied by the hiss of electrical sparks filled the room, woke Callum from a dream in which he and Ande were becoming intimate on a private beach at sunset. Wrenched from this pleasure, he was understandably displeased.

'Couldn't you have waited a few minutes?' he said to the angel. 'A few minutes would have been enough.'

'Enough for what?' rumbled the angel.

The first time the angel had spoken to him out loud, Callum had been thrown off because previously, he'd heard, or at least thought he'd heard, his protector's voice inside his head. He'd been unsure whether the voice was his or someone else's, but as it made him more comfortable to believe the former, he generally went that way. After the angel rescued him and Ande from Corpulent and Elephantine, it was no longer possible to deny the truth. Nonplussed now, he held his tongue. Could he share his intimate dream with an angel? Maybe, he knew it already.

'You were dreaming?' said the angel.

'Yes,' said Callum.

'About what?'

'Can't you see my dreams?'

The angel cocked his head, squinted at Callum. 'I'm not God, Callum.'

When he appeared in the church at Callum's father's funeral, the angel had seemed less tangible than now. Callum wondered if he had some kind of internal, celestial dimmer switch. Studying the mighty one's frame filled Callum with awe. He seemed quite solid, perfectly proportioned and chiselled as though cut from stone by a master sculptor. Callum wanted to touch him.

'Go ahead,' said the angel, holding out his hand to Callum. 'It's okay.'

'I thought you said you weren't God. How did you know I wanted to—'

'I said I wasn't God, but I'm not stupid. I've had some experience reading people. You wanting to touch me is natural enough. You're impressed by what you see, and you want to see if I'm real. This is the first time it's been just the two of us. Where is Ron, by the way?'

It was too normal to be taken seriously. A casual conversation with an angel. Yet, what could he do but roll with it, as he had been doing for so long now it was very nearly normal. The idea that such a life could be normal for Callum would never have been acceptable in his old life. A peace came over him when he placed his hand on the angel's chest. The tension drained away as he attempted to squeeze his thigh sized bicep. The weight of anxiety fell from his shoulders through the mystical calm which passed from the angel through Callum's fingers into his soul. He was safe.

'Ron went to find Alix,' said Callum. 'He's been a little cagey lately in relation to that girlfriend of his.'

'You sound like his father.'

Of course, Callum cared about Ron. They had been through so much together, but perhaps brotherly concern was closer to the mark than parental angst. Was it that obvious he cared? Despite his protests, the angel seemed to possess a skill set which could only be described as divine. That should have bothered Callum as well. After all, he'd never really been able to build and sustain relationships within which the intimacy facilitated such perception. The old Callum had always kept his cards close to chest. He would have considered such cutting and personal statements to be intrusive. He smiled and looked at the angel who had turned his celestial lights down.

'Ron and I have been through a lot together.'

'He's quite special, that little demon.'

'He's not so little anymore,' said Callum. 'Have you seen him lately?'

The angel shook his head.

'I asked him about his growth spurt, and he explained it was a normal thing for his kind.'

The angel looked like he was going to move, maybe take a seat, but he remained steadfastly upright as though any shift in his posture would reflect poorly on his character. Maybe, he couldn't sit down. Maybe, he was unable to relax.

'He's yet to realize his full potential,' said the angel. 'He seems to be a having a bit of a rough time actually. Have you noticed how conflicted he appears?'

'I assumed he was just being shifty because demons are like that. Do you think it's a good idea? Him and Alix?'

'It will not end well.'

When the angel failed to elaborate, Callum decided to change the subject. He didn't want to think about a demonic break-up. Human ones could be nasty enough, but with these offspring of the devil who knew what devastating consequences might result. They weren't governed by any laws prohibiting violence, deception, or callous and disproportionate retribution. Death seemed inevitable for at least one of them. He wasn't sure what Alix was capable of, but Ron had demonstrated his ruthlessness on many occasions. Was Ron conflicted as the angel had suggested?

'Do you have a name?'

'Barachiel.'

'Does that mean anything?'

'It corresponds to Thursday.'

Callum harrumphed. 'That's a little underwhelming.'

'Would you be more impressed if I said I was one of the Seven?'

'The seven days of the week?' Callum chuckled. 'No.'

Barachiel's expression didn't change. His countenance was like the still blue water of an endless lake, simultaneously tranquil and mysteriously intimidating. 'One of the seven archangels.'

Callum instantly recognized his small-minded

error. He knew the Biblical significance of the number seven, made the connection between the seven days and the seven archangels. He'd heard the term before and despite only a vague understanding of it, he felt its weight. 'The inner circle?'

'That's one way of putting it. We are angels of the highest rank. God's oldest, longest serving, most trusted messengers.'

A dramatic slap of humility forced Callum to silence, almost to shame for having spoken so disrespectfully. He felt frightened, suddenly fearful of Barachiel's wrath. He'd always spoken to Ron as to an equal which had worked for them, but Barachiel was different in more ways than Callum could say. Callum studied the floor, keeping his mouth closed.

'Relax,' said Barachiel. 'We are not like our evil counterparts who take pleasure in throwing their weight around, humiliating people and other demons. For them it's all about power. Megalomania is a pandemic among their ranks. We are servants who do the will of our benevolent King. We always put ourselves last.'

Callum was reminded of his parent's faith, their efforts to guide him along the same path, their prayers and their good example. He would have to tell his mum all about his adventures one day. He could imagine her being amazed, but more than that, grateful. She'd believe every word of his fantastic tale, and she'd push him for details in which she would delight. How often had he heard his parents speak of surrendering to the will of God? Irrespective of what the situation looked like or how they felt about it, they accepted that God was good and therefore only wanted what was good for them. Callum hadn't understood it at the time, but truth be told he hadn't tried to. Latching on to anything remotely suggesting his freedom should be curtailed, he had rebelled against his parent's faith in dramatic leaps. He saw now how his life had consequently faded slowly, imperceptibly, to a shadow of what it could have been. He stumbled around in the dark for years, stubbornly clinging to the illusion of freedom and control. These simple words from the mouth of his guardian angel—*we always put ourselves last*—made Callum want to cry with appreciation and admiration. He found himself sliding off the edge of the bed, onto his knees before Barachiel.

'Stand up, Callum,' he said, gently lifting him to his feet. 'Do not worship me.'

'I'm sorry,' whispered Callum as he collapsed into Barachiel's powerful embrace. 'I'm sorry.'

'God has had his hand on you since your inception, Callum. He knew you before. He's always known you. He knows your heart. He forgives you and welcomes you to the Kingdom.'

There was so much to say, so much intense and conflicting emotion within him that Callum was unable to speak. He cried. Sobbed. Bawled his eyes out with heaving spasms, sniffing and gulping to breathe inside the cyclone. In solemn silence, Barachiel held him tight, holding him up, absorbing Callum's pain. As quickly as it passed from him to the angel, fresh waves flowed from deep inside. The pent-up confusion, fear and shame which he'd buried and ignored for so long was now a torrent.

After some time, Callum found himself lying on the bed. Opening his eyes, he searched desperately for Barachiel, to assure himself he hadn't been dreaming. The angel had gone, but Callum was certain the encounter had been real. He lay still, taking an inventory of his body and his mind. He recited a few facts to test his mental faculties, stretched his legs and arms, rubbed his temples. The room was dimly lit, but empty of anything save furniture and shadows. Although he couldn't put his finger on it, something had changed. Something felt different. He felt different. Fearful of disturbing the serenity, Callum lay still, feeling his heart beat slowly and steadily, listening to his breathing, tasting the air, reaching for more bliss within his cocoon. He closed his eyes, smiled.

'We need to talk about tomorrow,' said Barachiel quietly.

Callum experienced the archangel's words rather than heard them. Without opening his eyes, he spoke with humble confidence to the angel who he knew was very present. 'Will tomorrow be as good as this? It couldn't be. I've never felt so…' Despite his best efforts, he couldn't find the right word.

'Imagine always feeling this way,' said Barachiel. 'Imagine never worrying. Imagine being so content there was literally nothing you could wish for, nothing to desire but the continuation of this euphoria.'

'It's not euphoria,' said Callum. 'I don't feel elated.'

'Nirvana?'

Callum's eyes popped open, involuntarily. 'I wasn't expecting that word. Nirvana's not a Christian thing, is it?'

Moving gently into Callum's field of vision; materializing into time from eternity, the angel glowed, emanating soft, warm light. 'Have you heard of the writer C. S. Lewis?'

Callum shook his head even though there was some vague, cobweb-covered connection in his mind.

'He wrote the Chronicles of Narnia. *The Lion, The Witch and the Wardrobe* was the first in the series. One of his closest friends was J. R. R. Tolkien who wrote the *Lord of the Rings*. They were both gifted Christian writers.'

'Damn,' said Callum. 'Sorry. Tolkien was a Christian too?'

Barachiel nodded. 'Lewis' awakening, what is commonly referred to as his conversion to Christianity, happened after a chat with Tolkien and another friend named Hugo Dyson. Anyway, he went on to write some phenomenal books, albeit with more than a little help from above. He wrote what many consider to be one of the finest books on Christian apologetics. *Mere Christianity*. I suggest you read it.'

'I'm not much of a reader.'

Something approximating a frown, almost a look of condescension or exasperation, manifested on Barachiel's face. He might have been talking to a recalcitrant child, but Callum was not offended. Instead, he felt reassured for some reason.

'Okay, I'll give it a go.'

The paternal scowl dissolved into a smile. 'In the book, Lewis wrote that all religions contain elements of truth, but Christianity is the fulfillment of truth. He wrote at length on the topic of myth and had a very unique, you might say otherworldly view of myth. It's fascinating stuff.'

Every now and then Barachiel made a jarring drop out of formality into the vernacular. 'Fascinating stuff, indeed,' said Callum.

'Call it Nirvana, Utopia or Heaven, it's the same thing.'

For obvious reasons, Callum was reluctant to argue the point, but he was pretty sure, based on his rudimentary knowledge of spiritual matters, that Nirvana was an entirely different beast. *Poor choice of words*, thought Callum. Luckily, he hadn't voiced them. The angel appeared to be rambling a little now which ignited an old spark of impatience in Callum. He hoped it wasn't a sin to be disrespectful to angels, especially archangels. This doubt creased his face.

'It's passing already, isn't it?' said Barachiel. 'The feeling is slipping away. It can be so elusive, but remember, you wouldn't even know what it is if you experienced it all the time. Isn't it true that people mainly appreciate sunshine for the fact it isn't rain? People only comment about the light in relation to the darkness. Happiness can only be enjoyed because of its transience.'

'I understand,' said Callum, accepting the logic of the angel's argument, and discerning the message behind it. 'So, tell me about tomorrow. What's the big deal?'

Barachiel's sigh was a tranquil shaking of the air, like a warm summer breeze. 'I questioned the wisdom of giving you this information. After all, it isn't how we normally do it. Prophecy is a gift which should always be used with wisdom, which is why God doesn't like fortune tellers. It was funny'—Barachiel chuckled—'sad too, but mostly funny, how angry the deceased prophet Samuel got with Saul when he used a necromancer to speak with him from the other side. That's a terrible idea, you know. People have no idea how much deception occurs with that stuff. It's so dangerous.'

'You're losing me, Barachiel,' said Callum.

'The point is, it's better for humans not to know about their futures.'

'Why?'

'Mainly because it panders to inherent delusions, but it also has unpredictable effects on behaviour. Unpredictable for people, I mean, not for God. You know he's never surprised, never shocked. He never slaps his thigh and whispers about how he didn't see that one coming.'

Of course, God couldn't be caught off guard, and if Callum knew something bad was going to happen, he most certainly would move heaven and earth to avoid it.

'That's exactly why I didn't want to tell you.'

Callum frowned. 'Can you stop doing that?'

'What?'

'Reading my mind.'

'It's not mind-reading, Callum,' said Barachiel, again adopting a tone of parental remonstration. 'It's perception and anticipation.'

'You're just playing semantics.'

Barachiel's light brightened, his face paradoxically darkened. 'I don't play anything.'

Scratching his head, Callum decided to let the issue slide. 'Okay,' he said. 'Tell me what's going to happen tomorrow. How bad will it be?'

'Tomorrow's events will take you past the point of no return. You are defined by your choices. Everyone is. There comes a time when your response to a given situation, a challenge—regardless of whether you expected it or not, will mark a significant turning point. All actions have consequences, so the key to a successful life, to fulfilling your God-given destiny, is to consistently make good choices. Choices which take you in the direction you want to go. It's also about recovering from the fallout of bad choices. As you rightly said, if people know something bad is about to happen to them, they will do whatever they can to avoid it, or at least to plan how to deal with it. A job loss. A cancer diagnosis. A relationship breakdown. An unavoidable confrontation. There is sometimes an option to escape, to run away. People do that all the time because they lack courage, and they lack faith. If warned they would be walking into a situation which would certainly end life, most people will decide not to go there.

'But consider Jesus, whose death was inevitable and necessary for God's rescue plan to work. He knew he was going to be arrested when he returned to Jerusalem. He knew he would suffer and die a horrific death on the cross, yet he accepted this was God's will, that there was no other way. This is the power of the gospel message. Being fully God, he could have saved himself. In fact, he was often taunted with those very words, but he submitted to his Father's will and many men and women throughout human history have likewise bravely faced torture and death for the sake of their faith. The ultimate sacrifice for the glory of God.

'Tomorrow you will face off against the Sorcerer, and you will have to make this very same choice. You will need vision, to see things the way God sees them. You will need to see with God's eyes. To have an eternal perspective.'

When Barachiel finished his frightening prophecy and pep talk, Callum stared first at him, then at the floor.

'You can't be serious,' he said finally. 'There must be someone better qualified for the job. Who am I to take on the Sorcerer?'

'Who am I is a great question, Callum.'

'What's the answer? I need to know. I need to know everything before I can make a call on this one. I'm not ready.'

Barachiel placed his hand on Callum's shoulder, flooding Callum's body with warmth. 'You know all you need to know for now. You have all you need. You are ready, and tomorrow you will have an answer to your question.'

'This is…' Callum felt dizzy from the infusion of life-giving spirit. 'It's too much.' Darkness invaded his periphery, heat burned through his blood. As he fell, he felt Barachiel's hands take hold of him and lower him to the bed.

'Tomorrow you will learn who you are,' said Barachiel. 'Rest now, son of God.'

Chapter Twenty-Nine

Although not sensibly comparable to Barachiel, and albeit permeated with human affection, Ande also appeared to Callum as an angel. He smiled at her as she approached, standing to greet her, slightly unsure about what form of greeting was appropriate. Their relationship was still undefined, blurry around the edges, meaning at times they were comfortably unselfconscious while at other times it was quite the opposite.

'You look fresh, Callum,' she said. 'Better than I've seen you for a while now.'

'Thanks,' said Callum. 'You look…'

'Radiant?'

Callum wondered how long this tongue-tied, hyper-self-conscious state would persist. It had once been so easy to talk to Ande, but that was before he had fallen in love with her. Callum quickly checked himself. Is that what it was? Could he admit it now? He loved her. Best keep that under his hat for the time being. Things were awkward enough, for him anyway. Ande appeared as effervescent and warm as ever, apart from the incident at the hotel in Mae Sai when he showed up with a psychotic nymphomaniac, then vomited when Ande tried to help him. That was bad enough, but then he was too forthright, hammering her with truth in an astounding display of insensitivity. He shook his head.

'Are you okay?'

'Huh?'

'You just shook your head suddenly, like a fly landed on your nose and you couldn't swat it off.'

'You do look radiant,' said Callum, changing the subject. 'Quite beautiful.'

'Quite beautiful?'

'Have you had breakfast?'

'That would be a strange thing to do, considering you invited me to have breakfast with you.'

Averting his eyes momentarily, before being drawn inexorably back to Ande, Callum, mumbled, 'Yes, it would.'

Ande smiled. 'If you haven't picked a spot already, I'd like to go to Ciragan Palace. It's right on the sea, and although I saw a couple of reviews saying they didn't have much to choose from on the *a la carte* menu, I reckon a seat beside the Bosphoros is good enough. What do you think?'

'It's a probably a breathtaking vista.'

'Probably,' said Ande. 'Let's go!' She grabbed Callum's hand and pulled him towards the door and into the back seat of a waiting taxi. She told the driver where they were going, then said to Callum. 'Let me guess, the secret to your good night's sleep was whiskey.'

Fair call, thought Callum. 'Actually, I didn't drink last night.'

'Really.' Ande raised her eyebrows, twitched her chin a little. 'Good for you.'

After a promising quick exit from the hotel driveway, the taxi quickly became entangled in Istanbul's suffocating and perpetual traffic jam. As required by local custom, despite its futility, the driver began cursing and honking his horn. When the chorus reached a crescendo, gridlock occurred, leaving the driver slamming his palms on the steering wheel.

'Imagine being angry all the time?' said Ande.

'I doubt he's angry all the time,' said Callum quickly. 'Just when he's driving.'

'He's probably driving all the time. Builds up a massive head of water, then goes home to his family, and lets his frustration fire on them, after kicking the dog.'

Callum laughed. 'I'll give you half marks for that one.'

'What?'

'It's not a head of water, it's a head of steam.'

'But you kick the dog, right?' she asked with undaunted enthusiasm. 'I nearly said kick the cat.'

'Yep, kick the dog.'

The taxi lurched forward before stopping, then repeated the kangaroo-hopping for a couple of hundred metres. Callum leaned to the left to see beyond the back of the driver's large head and broad shoulders. Coincidentally, Ande leaned right at the same time, causing a spark of static to erupt from the contact point.

'Whoa!' said Ande.

Callum moved away from her, further than he had

been sitting previously. 'How far away is this place? Maybe we should walk.'

'It's nearly two kilometres.'

'I'm up for it if you are.'

'Great!'

Like the road, the sidewalk was packed, bursting, and brimming with city life, people in the throes of everyday madness. Callum and Ande walked in silence, past various shops, pharmacies, schools, mosques, and markets. A greater awareness tuned Callum into the minutiae as he looked and saw, listened and heard. He felt a different, clearer connection as though he'd been fitted with a first-class upgrade to his internal aerial. There were persons in the people. Voices in the babble of conversation. Lives in the living.

'Callum?' said Ande. 'Are you okay? You're very quiet.'

Callum wanted to tell Ande everything, right there and then, but he held back, still fearful, still uncertain. Barachiel. Could Callum speak his name? Could he share those wonderful moments, that odd conversation with Ande? Would she understand? She'd try to, but would she get it?

'I feel different today,' he said, dipping his toe in the water.

'You do look different,' said Ande. 'But what do you mean you feel different?'

Urged by some unknown prompting, Callum was about to put both of his feet in the water.

'Look at that rug!' cried Ande, stopping dead at a

storefront. 'It's so beautiful. Look at those patterns.'

Shrugging off the tinge of disappointment at the stolen focus, Callum embraced Ande's distractibility. She'd been there for him, encouraging him to open up, but her attention was then quickly captured by a rug. He looked at it, hanging in the storefront window, found it unremarkable apart from its size. Of course, in typical, almost cliched Anatolian style there were beetles and geometric patterns all over it. He looked up to read the name of the store above the window, reading it out loud.

Mehmet Tekstils

'What's that? Like John's Fabrics,' said Callum.' Not a very cool name.'

'The rug, Callum,' said Ande. 'Look at the rug. It's a genuine work of art.'

'How do you know that, Miss Rug Aficionado?'

'How do I know it's genuine?'

Callum nodded.

'No hawkers,' said Ande. 'That's a sure sign this store deals in the real.'

'Deals in the real,' said Callum. 'That's cute. Did you make that up?'

'You know at the Grand Bazaar, for example, where all the tourists go. There are hawkers everywhere. You can hardly take a step without some loudmouth sweet talker in a fez getting in your face to tell you he's got the best rugs in Turkey.'

'Voice of experience?'

'Yep.'

Callum studied the rug with a fresh perspective. One of the beetle motifs came to life, scurrying across the rug from right to left, then disappeared, melting back into the hand-woven fabric.

'Did you see that, Ande?'

'See what?'

Another two beetles made similarly rapid journeys across the rug.

'Do you think its ano—'

'Do I think what?' said Ande.

'That,' said Callum, pointing as a riot of insects erupted before their eyes. 'That! That!'

'Here we go again,' said Ande grabbing Callum's arm and pressing her face into his shoulder. As the window filled with an unimaginable melee, Callum concentrated on staying calm, remembering the need to identify the alpha beetle before the inevitable lightning strike signalled the end of the event, and yet another lost opportunity.

People fled the store, stumbling and sprawling on the sidewalk and into the street, cars screeching to sudden stops to avoid hitting them. Store customers mixed with pedestrians and nearby store holders and their customers in a horrible mash. Drivers yelled from behind steering wheels or leapt from vehicles to wave their fists and shout their disapproval. It was chaos, but Callum stayed still, centred.

'Ande, look!' he cried. 'There it is.'

In the middle of the maelstrom, near the bottom of the window, a large stag beetle sat sedately as beetles whizzed around the surrounding airspace. Callum stared at it, not wanting to lose it, not knowing what to do either. He had to capture it, but that was impossible. Impossible or not, he had to try.

'Ande,' he said. 'Can you see it?' He crouched down, pulling Ande with him, pointed at the alpha beetle, tapped on the glass. 'Can you see it there?'

'Uh-huh.'

'Keep your eye on it. Don't look away. Don't lose it.' He started to move but felt Ande rising with him. 'Stay there, keep watching it.

'Where are you going?'

'Inside.'

'Inside? What?' She attempted to stand to her feet, but Callum quickly pushed her back, as gently as he could, given the urgency of the situation. 'No. Callum. Don't.'

'Stay there,' he ordered, dropping any veneer of civility. 'Stay there and watch it.'

In a flash, Callum was inside, looking through the swarm at a pixilated version of Ande outside the glass. She wasn't looking at him, though. *Good girl*, he thought, as he stepped up and into the window display, to the right of where he had seen the Alpha beetle. Ignoring the beetles, he crouched once more, twisting his body to the left searching for the alpha beetle. He saw it, then caught Ande's fear-filled eyes. His smile was interrupted by a bug hitting his mouth, then another. He reminded himself to keep his mouth closed, to breathe only through his nose. Beetles began landing on him but were few in number at first, so he ignored them too. Soon there were more.

Evidently emboldened by Callum's passivity, they started landing *en masse* and were soon crawling through his hair, into his ears and his eyes. When one went up his nose, it broke his concentration and he finally flicked his head, swatting and scraping beetles off his face and out of his hair. Frantically resisting them now, he forgot the alpha beetle.

With a blinding flash of light, a sizzle of electricity sliced through the air, shattering the window. The beetles were gone. The rug burst into flames, sending Callum flying backwards into the shop. Thick smoke filled the air. He coughed as he reeled out through the door onto the sidewalk. In a demented symphony of sirens and voices, concerned and curious faces looked down at him. Ande?

'Ande?' said Callum scrabbling to his feet with the help of two of the onlookers. 'Ande?' He pushed through the morbid circle surrounding him but stumbled immediately into another. 'Ande?'

'Callum?'

Without care, Callum removed human obstacles from his path, pushing and pulling until he reached Ande and found her lying on the footpath, covered in blood.

'Oh my God. Ande,' said Callum. 'Are you—'

'I'm sure it looks way worse than what it is,' she said.

'Stay there,' said Callum regretting his choice of words instantly. That's what he'd said to her before entering the rug store, and now look at her. This was the result of her loyalty. Her faith in him. Callum felt sick with guilt. 'I'm sorry, Ande,' he said, kneeling beside and taking one of her bloody hands in his. 'I'm so sorry. This is my fault. It's all my fault.'

'You move now,' said a stern voice, accompanied by a strong grip, yanking Callum away. 'We look her.'

Forced to his feet, Callum shuffled back a few steps. He stood observing a hi-vis wall surrounding Ande. A head adorned with close-cropped silver hair turned to him. 'Not deep much. Okay.'

'But what about all the blood?' said Callum.

'Yes,' said the man, standing now to face Callum. 'Have many cut but not deep much. I think is okay.'

The man was a good thirty centimetres taller than Callum, who noticed the red crescent on the other's chest, as he listened.

'Take she hospital. Clean up. It's okay, I think.'

Callum nodded dumbly, shocked by the volume of blood on his beloved. His beloved? Yes, he admitted to himself, he loved her.

The hi-vis wall suddenly gained height as the crew of paramedics stood in unison, wheeling Ande on a collapsible stretcher, along a corridor they made through the crowd as they marched toward the ambulance.

'Which hospital?' asked Callum, as he trailed them, the corridor of people collapsing behind him.

The tall man opened the barn doors at the back of the ambulance allowing the others to slide the stretcher in. Callum looked at Ande as she lay there being brave, covered in blood. She raised her hand. He waved back, blew her a kiss.

'Which hospital, mate?' Callum asked again, with

more urgency and greater volume. 'Where are you taking her?'

'Uskudar.'

Callum repeated the name several times as he watched the barn doors close, and the ambulance slowly move away. He looked around, noticing fragments, shards, and larger pieces of glass all over the sidewalk. Police were on the scene now, attempting to move people away, but it was like herding cats. Their grisly curiosity was a force too strong to overcome. He looked at the blood too; mostly Ande's, he surmised. As he surveyed the scene more carefully, he saw more injured people with many suffering cuts from the torrent of shattered glass. None seemed as serious as Ande though, but she'd been right there, with her face in the window, watching that damned alpha beetle, just like Callum told her to.

He mumbled the name of the hospital to himself continuously as he re-entered Mehmet's Tekstils. A man sat in the corner of the store wearing a mask of disbelief. Callum hadn't noticed him before, but it had to be Mehmet himself. Going up to him, dispensing with formalities, Callum asked for a pen and paper. When the man seemed to not understand, Callum resorted to gesturing, miming the act of writing. The man muttered something unintelligible to himself, while waving his hand towards the counter on his left.

At the counter, Callum wrote down the name of the hospital, guessing at the correct spelling. He called to Mehmet. 'Where is the Uskudar Hospital? How do I get there?

Mehmet sat, silently staring at what used to be his storefront and perhaps one of his best rugs. It was only then that Callum realized the fire which engulfed the rug had not spread. Despite the suffocating smoke and the intensity of the fire, nothing else in the store had felt the lick of fiery flames. He walked to the window, looked down. Ash from the rug, broken glass and countless scorched insect carcasses were all that remained. It wasn't so bad. Mehmet's insurance would cover it. Callum walked back to the shaken store owner.

'I'm sorry about what happened,' said Callum, feeling as though he should offer the man some comfort instead of just focusing on his own needs.

Mehmet threw his hands in the air. 'What is this happen?'

Callum shook his head. 'It's long story, mate,' he said.

Mehmet looked at Callum dumbly.

'My friend,' said Callum, deciding now was not the time for fantastic explanations of supernatural events. 'My friend she's been taken…she go…hospital.' Callum showed him the piece of paper on which he'd written the name of the hospital. 'Where is this? How do I get there?'

'What is this happen?' said Mehmet, hands in the air with more head shaking.

Back on the street, the police had succeeded in dispersing the crowd, and although the lane closest to the curb was roped off for fifty metres in either direction, traffic was moving again. Very slowly, but moving, nevertheless. As Callum hurried to hail a taxi, he saw a policeman in his periphery. He was coming towards Callum, calling to him. There was no time for questions. A taxi stopped, Callum got in and it moved off. Callum looked over his shoulder to see if the police were coming after him, but he could no longer see the officer who'd shown interest in him. Everyone had more urgent matters to deal with, especially Callum.

'Uskudar Hospital.'

The driver grunted.

Callum could only pray that the tall paramedic was right about the extent of Ande's injuries. He hoped he'd find her all cleaned up, covered in Band-Aids, and smarting from all those cuts but otherwise okay. He could only hope and pray. He did that now. He prayed, but not mechanically or faithlessly—he believed his prayers were heard and would be answered.

Chapter Thirty

The Bosphorus was majestic, framed with a dazzling blend of ancient mosques with their spires reaching to heaven, and modern skyscrapers, some bristling with twenty-first century confidence, others draped in cranes and scaffolding. Callum lamented not being able to sit peacefully on her banks, dining with Ande. It would have been an idyllic way to spend the morning.

'Are you okay, Callum?' said Barachiel.

Callum hadn't seen him materialize but there he was sitting in the backseat, filling it. The driver would have gone off his brain had he been able to see the giant angel blocking his rear view. Callum didn't turn around, just glimpsed Barachiel in the vanity mirror on the back of the sun visor.

'I'm not the one who was ripped to shreds and nearly bled to death.'

There was a hint of bitterness in his answer, but he reckoned it was justified. Where had his pop in/pop out celestial guardian been when he was needed?

'Where were you? You're like some FIFO protector.'

'FIFO?'

'Fly in. Fly out, said Callum. 'Like remote mine workers who fly in for two weeks of nose-to-the-grindstone labour, then fly out for a week of rest, not giving a rat's about the job. Just thinking about the coin.'

It was difficult to figure out these supernatural beings. These angels, the one he knew at least, had incredible power but apparently only used it selectively. Callum thought the whole idea of the guardian angel was to provide twenty-four-seven protection. They had to be on standby to swoop in and save the day, at any time of day. That had not been his experience. It was the same deal with Ron. Sometimes he was around, but others time not. Like now. Callum had not heard from him or seen him since when?

Barachiel sat silently while Callum pontificated, wallowing a little. 'Well,' he said finally. 'Where were you? You know what happened to Ande, right?'

'Ande will be fine,' said Barachiel, absorbing Callum's anger as easily as a thirsty man drinks water. 'It's you I'm more concerned about.'

'I'm fine.'

'Good. Stay strong, son of God.'

'Don't call me that,' said Callum turning his head, ignoring the driver's questioning mumble. Barachiel had gone. 'It feels wrong,' said Callum.

'Who you talk to crazy man?' said the driver.

'My guardian angel, Barachiel.'

The driver mocked Callum with a laugh, then muttered to himself.

'Ron!' called Callum. 'Are you here?'

'Hey crazy guy!' said the driver. 'Who you talk to?'

Callum snapped back. 'Mind your business, mate!'

'What my business, mate?' The driver was about to injure his neck by switching so quickly back and forth between Callum and the road.

'Watch the road,' said Callum, pointing ahead. 'And be quiet.' He used his thumb and forefinger to close an imaginary zipper on his lips. 'Mind your business.'

'Ron?'

'I remember when you would never talk to me in public because you were worried people would think you were crazy.'

'Different times,' said Callum.

'How'd you know I was here?'

'I sort of know when you're around. I can feel it.'

'That's a bit creepy.'

'Where have you been?'

Callum's question wasn't specific enough to avoid Ron's gift for dissembling. He was asking whether Ron found Alix and if so, what was the outcome of the meeting. His gut told him Alix and her twisted sister were up to their eyeballs in the Sorcerer's grand plan. He didn't know how they fit in, other than acting as ringmasters, for many, if not all, of the swarms, but he was hopeful Ron was bringing him some much-needed intel.

'Did you know there are three bridges crossing the Bosphorus Strait?'

'No,' said Callum. 'But—'

'And this particular one, a fine example of a suspension bridge, is colloquially known as First Bridge. I bet you can't guess why?'

'Knock it off, Ron.'

'Did you find Alix or not?'

'Yes.'

'And was her sister with her?'

'Yes.'

If not for the fact they were separated by a generous bucket seat with an oversized headrest, Callum would have slapped Ron around a little. He wanted to give him a few of what Ron derisively called 'mosquito bites.' Even though his demon buddy was a big boy now, he still freely exhibited his teenage insensibility and insensitivity. Something about that kind of disrespectful, envelope-pushing behaviour made Callum furious. How on earth would he manage with children of his own? Did he even want children? Maybe not. What about Ande? As Callum's thoughts crashed into her, he accepted the collision, asking the question; did Ande want children? Was that part of her thinking when she considered her future? Surely, she was doing a lot of that right now as she lay in that hospital bed.

'Earth to Callum,' called Ron.

'I was just thinking about how to give you a beating, and how much you deserve one.'

'Okay,' said the driver suddenly, jumping on the brakes. 'Okay. Okay. You go.'

'What?' said Callum. They were stopped in the middle of the bridge. The incessant honking of horns reached new levels of sonic wrath.

'You go. Get out.'

'Drive the car, mate,' said Callum, feeling the irritation rising, coming to the boil inside his words. 'Take me to the hospital.'

The driver reefed the handbrake and toggled the gearstick into neutral. 'Okay,' he said, getting out of his cab. 'I go.'

'What're you doing?'

'What's he doing?' added Ron.

'Get back in here and drive me to the hospital!'

'I dance for you,' said the driver. 'Look. Good belly dance.'

Callum watched, dumbfounded as his driver shook his considerable girth while twisting his hips and flapping his arms up and down like he was trying to fly.

'You must see the number one.'

Ron started laughing, then reigned his mirth in. 'Ah Callum, I think I know what's going on.'

'Do you, Ron?' snapped Callum, before climbing out of the taxi.

The driver was stopping traffic with his performance, but the honking of horns was not in appreciation of it. He ignored the angry abuse and the probable curses within. He spun, and sang, shaking like he was having a fit, smooth motion replaced by spasmodic jerking as his skin changed colour and something like smoke started floating on the surface of his clothes. Maybe it was steam.

'Ah Callum,' said Ron.

'Not now, Ron,' said Callum. He then spoke to the driver. 'What are you doing? Stop it!'

'Callum, look at his eyes.'

'What?'

'Look at his eyes.'

'I could if he'd slow down, but he's spinning like a bloody centrifuge. What's wrong with him? He's going to explode, isn't he?'

'It's possible,' said Ron

'Seriously?'

Ron nodded.

'Quick,' said Callum. 'Let's get outta here. I don't have time for this nonsense. I have to get to the hospital. I have to see Ande.'

Before Callum could leave, Ron grabbed his arm. 'You're going to leave me here to deal with this?'

'That's up to you,' said Callum, pulling out of Ron's grasp. 'I need to get to the hospital. Maybe this isn't your business either.'

'Um,' said Ron, as Callum watched his gaze leave Callum's face and focus over his shoulder. 'I think it could be.'

'Huh?'

Callum turned. The driver smashed into him, knocking him flat on his back. He hit his head, groaned, rolled over, and felt for blood. He looked up to see Ron grappling with the driver who was changing shape continually. Ron clutched his arm, but the arm morphed into a snake. He caught his shoulder, but it vaporized. He clenched his throat, tightening his grip immediately, but the driver's head popped off his remaining shoulder, buzzed around in the air like a balloon which had been pricked. The driver appeared solid, then gaseous. Dark, then light. Callum had never seen anything like it.

He pulled himself to his feet, stood and watched the battle. Ron was doing something weird with his eyes now. A new trick. His head was spinning, much like the driver had been prior to his attack on Callum. Soon, Callum couldn't tell the difference between the driver and Ron. All he saw was a cyclone of colour and various bits and pieces: an ear, an eye, a piece of cloth, whirling in a tight circle as though confined inside an invisible tube.

Suddenly it stopped. The show was over. Ron stood beside the driver who looked unnaturally sheepish. Head down, shoulders slumped, he appeared uninjured, apart from his pride. Ron was patting the guy on the back, comforting him as though he was a child who had fallen and scraped his knee. The driver was oblivious to everyone and everything except his embarrassment.

He climbed back behind the wheel of his cab – the engine was still running – muttering and mumbling.

'Time to go, Callum,' said Ron. 'And close your mouth. You're dribbling.'

Callum wiped his mouth instinctively, although there was no saliva to mop up. 'What the hell was that?'

'I'll explain it on the way. Let's go.'

'Are you all right, mate?' said Callum, getting back in the taxi.

'Uskudar Hospital?'

'Right.'

'Yes, sir.'

Soon they were on their way once more. The noise settled back into its regular rhythm, as they moved along briskly toward the other side.

'Okay,' said Callum to Ron. 'Start talking.'

'Pretty much ever since I was assigned to you, my kooky human friend—although of course, I was sent out in complete ignorance—I've had one spotty little puffed-up wannabe demon after another coming to take me out or take me down. I didn't know why, but suspected, because I'm a little full of myself sometimes, that these pests were simply wanting to challenge themselves against the best. Okay, not the best, even I'm not that conceited. Let's just say they wanted to test their skills against a highly rated opponent. To what end, I don't know, but I do know exactly how it ended for each and every one of them.

'These assailants provided varying levels of difficulty for me. Here and there, I was sorely tested, but I never worried about losing until we came here to Istanbul. There was this total sicko nut case in the airport.'

'Is it my imagination, Ron?' said Callum, interrupting. 'Or are you using much less formal language these days?'

'I'm still feeling for the juice.'

'I don't know what that means.'

'I'm still experimenting with it all to try and get the right mix. You know I get picked on quite a bit for the way I talk.'

'Poor thing,' said Callum, suppressing his laughter. Ron could be so childishly precious sometimes.

'Please continue your long-winded explanation of the weirdness back there.'

'This creature at the airport called herself Patricia and talked like she was the Queen of England or some such. She appeared quite friendly at first, although her appearance was unusual enough to keep me on edge. Most demons don't get into dress-ups. We'd rather just be ourselves, but Patricia was very serpentine. She looked like the offspring of an ill-conceived union between a snake and an octopus.'

'Wow, there's an image I'll find hard to shake.'

'The thing is, Callum,' said Ron, shifting his voice down an octave as though he had something significant to say but didn't want anyone else to hear it. 'Although she nearly killed me, as far as I could tell she was just lonely and desperate for company. She rabbited on about doing someone a favour, and not wanting to upset this someone, by letting them down, but all I heard and saw, was a sadistic maniac.'

'I've got to say, Ron,' said Callum. 'Coming from you, that is a truly heavy description. So, you fought her and she almost topped you.'

'She held me captive. I was a prisoner, and she was torturing me.'

'What a devil!' said Callum in mock outrage.

'Thanks for the sympathy.'

'You're welcome, Mr. Tangent.'

'Mr. Tangent?' said Ron. 'Oh. I got you. Anyway, that one back there was something new. It was a straightforward possession at first. I was trying to tell you that because it was such obviously abnormal behaviour that there couldn't have been any other explanation. I believe the intention of the demon was to delay you. I don't know why. But the over-the-top method, the theatrics of it, well…'

'Maybe just a show-off demon who likes to dance' suggested Callum.

'Liked,' said Ron.

'What?'

'Liked. As in past tense.'

'Right,' said Callum. He presumed dead demons went to Hell, back to Hell. He wanted to ask but didn't want to open up another can of worms. He was still finding his way through this new reality. It was enough for now to accept the presence of supernatural beings on earth, and by extension, the almost certain existence of God and Satan. As for the ultimate resting place of the departed? Callum felt quite reluctant.

'For sure,' said Ron, 'the demon was trying to stop you from getting to the hospital, but having succeeded spectacularly with that mission, it appeared hungry for more action. I don't know. I do know it ignored me until after you got out of the cab. That eye-wateringly fast spinning it created, and which I joined, was nothing more than an optical illusion. There was nothing speedy about it. We were wrestling inside it, at least from the outside looking in, at a normal pace. It was quite strong, but I think weakened by the possession, especially the ostentatious dancing.'

'Possessing someone is hard work, is it?'

'It depends,' said Ron. 'It's complicated and requires a lot of power and practice. You remember how well I did with Pitch on Flight 444?'

Callum laughed. 'You know we'd been talking about *Poltergeist* and horror movies. And then…'

'Here's Ronny.'

The taxi finally finished its journey across the First Bridge, then swung right, immediately plunging into a snarl of vehicles of all shapes and sizes. It was virtually impossible to get an unimpeded run to anywhere in this monster of a city. Ron had fallen into a strange silence after giving his best impression of crazy Jack Nicholson in *The Shining*. The driver remained subdued, even dialling down the cursing, fist shaking and steering wheel slamming. Callum took advantage of the lull. Thinking of Ande, lying wounded in hospital, he prayed for her, willing his words and his heart directly to her on the wings of angels.

Chapter Thirty-One

Uskudar Hospital rose from the corner like a stack of five huge fish tanks in a massive aquarium, its glass front glittering in the midday sun. An enormous Turkish flag was hung from the roof, reaching down to the top of the second-floor window. As the taxi approached Callum wondered how much of the surrounding building belonged to the hospital. The aquarium, complete with large circular windows on the edge of each floor, seemed too small to be a hospital, so he presumed an injection of capital from a generous benefactor, or perhaps the state, facilitated the design of a feature section of the otherwise nondescript and dilapidated edifice. No doubt, behind the façade was a labyrinth of treatment rooms and offices.

The taxi stopped out front of a modest-looking entry. The signage said Turk Hospital.

'Is this the right place mate?' Callum said to the driver.

The driver looked confused.

'Uskudar Hospital?'

'Uskudar,' said the driver with an unsettling tone of certainty. 'You pay now.'

Callum paid the driver, got out of the cab, and

walked to the front door. Now that he was closer, he could see 'Uskudar' in small type above the word hospital. It turned out to be a private hospital, which was troubling, because as far as Callum knew private hospitals didn't have emergency departments, at least not in Australia, they didn't. He walked to the counter, was greeted by an efficient-looking middle-aged woman wearing a lilac hijab. She studied Callum without expression.

'A friend of mine was brought here not long ago. I want to see her.'

Instead of answering, the woman stood and walked to the other end of the administration booth, spoke quietly into the ear of another woman, who left her seat and came to speak with Callum. 'Can I help you?' she said, smiling uncomfortably.

'My friend Ande was brought here in an ambulance. She was injured.'

The woman dropped her smile, began tapping the keyboard in front of her. Callum waited; bewildered and anxious to see Ande, he summoned patience.

'Your name?'

'My name?'

The woman nodded.

'Callum Steele.'

A clipboard appeared and was pushed toward him. Callum accepted it without question, as he did the pen which followed soon after. The instruction came next, but Callum didn't need it. After filling in the form, which was in English, fortunately, he handed the clipboard back to the woman, asking where he would he find Ande.

'Sit down, please.'

Callum obeyed, despite his rising exasperation, and was soon rewarded for his self-control by the arrival of an orderly who beckoned him to follow through an automatic door to the left of the reception counter. The orderly waved an electronic key at the door before marching through with Callum in tow. He followed the silent and fast-walking orderly, passing several treatment stations on the way, observing the patients. An elderly man with wires attached to his bare hairy chest nodded at Callum as he passed. He heard snippets of conversation but could make nothing of any of it. Doctor-patient stuff no doubt. Questions. The never ending and repetitive questions medical professionals asked. Patient, family member stuff. Words of comfort, words to distract everyone from the unpleasantness. Hospitals were pretty much the same all over the world albeit with varying degrees of cleanliness, technology and space. Callum wondered whether they had a universal healthcare system in Turkey, or whether it was like Thailand and many other developing countries where money talked louder than compassion or criticality.

The orderly stopped suddenly, so abruptly that Callum nearly crashed into his back.

'Callum!'

'Ande!' said Callum moving quickly to her side, wanting to touch her, reaching out in fact before pulling his hand back. 'Sorry,' he said. 'Are you okay? Stupid question. How do you feel?'

'Also, a stupid question.'

'Oh my God, Ande. I just don't know what to say.'

'You don't need to say anything,' she said. 'Just sit down and relax. You seem to be in a bit of a state.'

Callum looked at her, stared into the burning darkness of her eyes, felt tears welling in his own. He sat as directed, unable to avert his eyes from the sight of her bandage bound arms and face. 'I seem to be in a bit of state?' he said, emphasizing 'I' to make sure Ande caught the irony in her words.

Callum's phone rang, demanding his attention, but he couldn't bring himself to retrieve it from his pocket.

'It's okay,' said Ande. 'Take it.'

By the time he got hold of it, it stopped ringing, but he saw Pitch's name on the screen in the missed call notification. He called him back, excusing himself as he listened to the dial tone while walking out of the cubicle.

'How's things with you and Margie?'

'We're getting there,' said Pitch. 'She's talking to me now, but they aren't pleasant conversations, and they're very short.'

'Sure,' said Callum. 'It's going to take some time. Don't give up, will you?'

'Thanks. How're you guys? How's Ande?'

'Actually,' said Callum, walking back into Andes' cubicle. 'She's right here. I'll put you on speaker.'

Callum pulled the phone away from his ear, stared at the screen.

'You know how to do that, right?' said Ande.

It was comforting to know that Ande was not so badly injured, nor emotionally fragile that she couldn't give him a hard time. He smiled at her, before tapping the speaker button then laid the phone on the edge of the bed.

'How are you, Pitch? I miss you.'

'Hi Ande,' said Pitch. 'Two for the price of one. Lucky me. I'm doing okay. What's going on?'

'Just hanging out in the hospital.'

'I'm guessing neither of you is the patient.'

'Actually,' said Ande, raising her bandaged hand off the bed slightly even though Pitch obviously couldn't see it. 'I had a bit of an accident.'

'It was no accident,' said Callum, firmly. 'It was a bit of selfish stupidity on my part.'

'Callum,' said Ande, protesting.

'No. That's the truth. It was a dangerous situation and I put you right in the thick of it. Instead of protecting you, I nearly got you killed.'

'That's a bit of an exaggeration.'

'Would someone mind filling in the backstory for me?' said Pitch. 'Was it another swarm?'

'Yes,' said Callum, wondering how much detail would be appropriate at this time. He looked at Ande. She scratched the back of her right hand with her left. 'I'm pretty sure that's not a good idea, Ande.'

'Huh?'

'Don't scratch. You'll open up the cuts.'

'Cuts?'

'A shop front window exploded at the end of a swarm and Ande had her face pressed to the glass watching the Alpha beetle so it wouldn't disappear. Just until I could get inside and grab it. Ande, stop scratching.'

'It's itchy.'

'Obviously.' Callum turned, searching for a nurse. 'Excuse me,' he said, calling out with his hand raised. The object of his attention nodded and walked over to the bed.

'She's itchy.'

'Sorry, Pitch,' said Ande.

'No worries.'

'Itchy,' repeated Callum. The nurse seemed not to understand so he mimicked the action, then pointed at Ande who did likewise. 'I told you to stop scratching.'

'I can't help it, it's getting worse. There's something in there. Under the bandage.'

'What?'

A bubble formed on the back of Ande's hand… a vibrating bubble, then another. A beetle twisted its way from beneath the cloth dressing, followed by another. The nurse's mouth dropped open, but to her credit she didn't scream as more bugs emerged from inside the bandages. They were all over Ande's arms as well, turning the white cloth of the bandages to the awfully familiar kaleidoscope of beetle carapaces. Running up and down, falling from her arms onto the bed, then cascading to the floor, they kept coming, from beneath Ande's dressings, bursting forth like accelerated shoots.

'Callum?' said Ande, just before a bug flew straight into her mouth.

Momentarily paralysed, Callum watched his phone fall to the floor with scores of beetles riding on its back. Ande was fast disappearing inside the swarm. The nurse had fled. What was he to do? Instinct told him to run, but he couldn't leave Ande. Before he could decide what to do, she was buried under a truckload of bugs. It happened so fast. How could it happen so fast? Beetles were using her as a launching pad now, springing into the air looking for new victims, or desperately searching for something. For what?

'Callum?' said Ron. 'Are you going to do something?'

'Like what? What am I supposed to do with this?'

'Alpha beetle,' said Ron. 'Remember? Find the alpha beetle. I'll take care of Alix.'

'She's here?'

Ron was gone in a flash, a blur of movement, slashing through the cloud of beetles.

'Ron?'

Callum stared into the insectoid mass, straining to see through the chaos of tiny wings and legs. 'Barachiel,' he said. 'If you're around I could use a hand.'

Hot and frantic, Callum concentrated. For Ande's sake, he had to find the alpha beetle and kill it. He had to. Suddenly he saw it on the lump of bugs which covered Andes's face, somewhere near where her nose probably was. Was she still breathing in there? Could she?

The alpha beetle danced on the spot until it became aware of Callum glaring. It stopped and returned the look with a hostile expression on its tiny face. A face which was growing. The beetle itself was expanding, ballooning in front of Callum's eyes as though something was pumping it full of air. Callum leaned back. He moved away as the Alpha Beetle continued to grow, its limbs popping and extending, colourful bits of what looked like scales zigged and zagged away from the enlarging carapace. All the while, the beetle's face remained fixed on Callum's.

In the hate-filled space between them, the air was different, somehow repelling all the other bugs, their swarm boiling and swelling to fill the whole room, darkening it, blocking the lights, covering everything, but leaving Callum and the beast bug in a kind of bubble. In this space, this combat cage, Callum was soon facing a man. Or some hybrid of a man. What was he looking at?

When a huge tusk protruded from its forehead, Callum knew the answer. He was looking at the Sorcerer. As it stood on two barefooted human legs, Callum studied it, noting the insect appendages still present: an extra set of arms, two sets, but one was transforming into a human arm as he watched. A pair of silvery wings fluttered wildly behind it. This might have been what was clearing the space between them. Its face was unremarkable apart from the tusk beneath which large dark eyes suddenly blazed yellow.

As Callum watched the metamorphosis in horror, he steeled himself. Recalling Barachiel's word, he knew this was the moment he must abandon Ande to her fate and take on the Sorcerer. Alone. He trembled, shaking with rage and fear, which the Sorcerer seemed to enjoy. It might have smiled. It was hard to tell. Then it spoke.

'Callum Steele.'

Its voice was a terrifying mix of crunching gravel and high-pitched buzzing, but the words were clear. Spoken slowly, forced from a clenched jaw, the sound was less of an acknowledgment of Callum and more of a threat. How was he to fight this demon? Callum was too petrified to be afraid. This was a mortifying situation, and one from which he could not possibly hope to escape. Yet, he hoped. And he prayed, letting the pleading words dribble from his mouth, pushing them off his tongue, through his lips into the vacuum in which he and the Sorcerer stood. His prayers. Who was listening? Who would answer his cry for help? Barachiel? God himself? He was a man of faith now so his prayers must be answered.

The Sorcerer reached for Callum with both arms and beetle legs, shuffling forward on bare human feet. Callum didn't move. Couldn't move. But he must move. Must do something. Callum yelled at his body, commanding it to obey, ordering his hand to rise, form a fist and strike with all his might. What good would it do? He couldn't defeat this beast with physical strength, but he had to do something.

When the Sorcerer's Tusk was almost touching Callum's head, Callum finally felt a surge of power. A painful jolt of adrenaline generated a fist which he thrust into the Sorcerer's stomach. The Sorcerer appeared not to notice, its hands now with a firm grip on Callum who tried to shake free as the Sorcerer lowered his tusk towards the top of Callum's head. Callum prayed some more, felt more chemicals released, experienced more power. He struck again. And again. And again. Mighty blows infused with purposeful dynamism. He wasn't alone anymore.

Absorbing Callum's punches, despite their increasing violence, the Sorcerer uttered insults and ridicule, decrying Callum's efforts as pathetic and futile. His grip broken, then enforced. Tighter, more savage, then easing instantly in response to Callum's punches. Around and around they went in a masterfully choreographed dance of death.

Callum grasped the Sorcerer's hand, twisting it down and pulling the demon off balance. On his way down, the Sorcerer's tusk slashed Callum's chest. Callum felt the pain of that wound more keenly than anything else the Sorcerer had done to him, but he fought on, deflecting the strikes from the Sorcerer's hands and feet, while counterpunching as soon as the opportunity presented itself. Callum felt he could fight forever like this despite the pain. He appeared to be healing with supernatural alacrity. As fast as the Sorcerer could inflict a wound, Callum's body responded with light and warmth.

The Sorcerer's curses continued, flooding from his mouth in torrents of wickedness, as he battled Callum in the tiny personal arena. Callum hit and was hit. He wounded and was wounded. He bled and drew blood. And through it all there was no diminishing of his strength. The fight could have lasted indefinitely, but Callum had a sense that the end was near, and that it was his responsibility to bring the brawl to conclusion.

Somehow, as he battled with sustained aggression, his mind began to clear. It was as though he was setting his body on autopilot to allow his mind freedom to strategize. Not quite removed from the fight, he became aware of increasing distance. With his arms and feet on cruise control, running through alternating patterns of defence and offence, Callum saw the tusk, the mighty beetle's horn, and knew he had to break it. It needed to be snapped in two, but not without him first embracing its barbed sharpness. He saw it. Crystal clear in his mind's eye, Callum saw the decisive moment.

His body received several blows after he ceased fighting. The sorcerer was at first unaware of Callum's apparent surrender, and then unable or unwilling to accept it.

The two combatants stared at each other for a minute before the Sorcerer took hold of Callum's shoulders and with a fast and accurate downward thrust, pierced Callum's skin near his collarbone with its tusk. The Sorcerer pushed with all his might until the tusk ripped right through Callum, its point emerging from Callum's back. Unfazed, for he had foreseen what would happen, Callum acted without hesitation, grabbing the Sorcerer in a bear hug before folding his body in half. With his head falling to the left of the Sorcerer, Callum strove to reach the floor while keeping his feet firmly planted.

The crack was like a lightning strike, complete with the flash of brilliant white, as the tusk snapped off and the Sorcerer roared loud enough to shake the walls of Hell. Callum fell to the floor as the Sorcerer vanished, taking with him all the insects. Every single bug disappeared in that instant as Callum found himself on the floor in agony. The broken-off tusk was still embedded in him, and now that the fight was over, he felt the pain. Unbearable searing pain. Callum howled, writhing on the floor, as he felt the otherworldly power which had enable him to defeat the Sorcerer fading fast.

'Callum?'

He heard Ande's voice and felt someone's hand on him, but overwhelmed with the physical torture, Callum succumbed to darkness.

Chapter Thirty-Two

A warm, sunset-orange glow bathed the room as Callum wrestled his way through the fog of semi-consciousness. More difficult than waking from sleep, where the brain eventually kicks into gear with the aid of a solid dose of caffeine. Slower than being roused from the effects of anaesthesia after surgery. Something in between. Callum sensed light, but only intermittently. He could feel pain and pressure, but only sporadically. A part of him desperately wanted to stay locked in his private cocoon. Another part of him experienced an intense desire to escape the suffocating inertia.

'Callum?'

Who was speaking now? He discerned vibration in the air, humming in his ears, but muffled as though muted by earmuffs. He reached for recognizable sounds, for words, for meaning. He heard his name, but nothing else. Perhaps there was nothing else.

'Callum?'

Time passed with Callum fading in and out: at times on the verge of breaking free of the sluggishness. Each time he felt close to returning, his senses failed him and he slipped back into darkness. A flash of that beautiful auburn light, a whisper of heat on his skin, a stab of invisible knives. He might have lifted his hand, reaching for someone or something tangible, or he might have imagined it. He might have tried to speak, or perhaps the conversation was with his imprisoned self.

'Callum,' said the vaguely familiar voice. 'You're going to be okay.'

'Okay,' said Callum, although the voice sounded like someone else's. He tried again. 'I'm okay?'

'You'll be fine. Just try to relax.'

It was easier now, clearer, but he didn't recognize the voice. Moving his head very slowly, he opened his eyes, saw Ande smiling at him, her face bandage free. In fact there was no evidence of the wounds, no blood, no stitches, and no scars. She looked radiantly beautiful, the best version of herself.

'Ande?'

'It's okay, Callum.'

'What's wrong with…'

Callum plummeted once more into the soup of semi-consciousness. Cut off from his senses, he allowed his brain to concentrate on interpreting and processing what was happening to him. He had seen Ande, but she spoke to him in a strange voice, and she had miraculously recovered from her injuries. How could that be? Was he seeing a vision? Imagining something he wanted to see? Surely, his mind was playing tricks on him. Suddenly, he felt a breeze blowing on the side of his face. He turned to it, opened his eyes again and saw a white sand beach framing a sea of turquoise water. He smelled salt in the air, sniffed deeply.

'Callum?'

He ignored her this time, or him, or whoever, it was—not Ande. He didn't want to leave the beach, to forego the cool caress of the breeze. He felt life on that beach. It was real.

'Callum? Wake up!' the voice insisted, commanded.

'But I—'

'Wake up now!' barked the voice. 'Snap out of it, mate!'

'Pitch?'

The beach vanished, the vision slowly dissipating in the sunset glow. Callum closed his eyes, squeezed them tight. Sad and afraid, he tensed, trying to withdraw inside himself, away from the light and the voice.

'Callum. This is Barachiel. Can you hear me?'

Callum nodded. 'Barachiel?'

'The Sorcerer's Tusk is still inside you. It's poisoning you with dark magic. That's why you're feeling so weird, and why you can't wake up. Do you understand?'

'Why don't you just pull the damn thing out and heal him. You're an angel, right?'

'Ron?'

'Tell me you understand, Callum,' said Barachiel.

'Yes, I understand, but—'

'You need to concentrate,' said Barachiel. 'We will wait for one of your lucid moments. With your help I will remove the tusk, but we can only attempt to un-impale you when you are thinking straight. The key to removing it without hurting your further or killing you is timing. I can only pull it out when you are completely focused, and we might not be able to finish in one go.'

As Callum felt himself slipping away again, Barachiel's words become muffled and fractured. He tried to speak, but his tongue would not cooperate. There was a buzzing in his mouth, metallic tasting liquid bubbled and frothed. He coughed then blacked out again.

After some time, Callum moved back into the light slowly, like paddling to a distant shore with a broken oar. He persisted, willing his arms not to flag, not to fail.

'He's coming around,' said Ron.

'Callum,' said Barachiel. 'When you reach the beach—'

'What beach?' said Ron.

'Be quiet, Ron,' said Barachiel. 'You're not helping.' Then to Callum, he continued. 'When you reach the beach, get out of the boat and pull it onto the sand as quickly as you can. Okay? Are you with me?'

Callum nodded, wondering how Barachiel could see what he could see. 'Okay. What then?'

'Fill the boat with sand. Do it as fast as you can. You don't have much time. You're there, close enough. Jump out and pull the boat in. Quickly.'

Carrying out Barachiel's instructions, Callum began to scoop the soft, white sand into his hand and dump it in the boat.

'Use the spade, Callum,' said Barachiel.

'What spade?'

'Behind you.'

Working furiously, unaffected by fatigue, Callum grabbed the tool, shovelling sand like his life depended on it.

'Don't stop Callum,' said the angel. 'Your life depends on it.'

'My life?' said Callum. As he tossed a load of sand into the boat, the spade slipped from his grasp and flew into the air, landing a few metres on the other side of the boat. 'I dropped the spade, Barachiel. Now what do I do?'

Night descended quickly on the deserted beach, as though the daylight had lost its purpose and strength. Callum called to Barachiel but was powerless to stop himself sliding into the dark, foreboding sea. He floated aimlessly for an indefinite period of time, lolling and rolling with the current like seaweed.

'Callum?'

He opened his eyes, despite not having been aware they were shut. Barachiel's voice grew in clarity, extending into Callum's ears, tickling them with hope.

'Get to the shore and grab that spade.'

For a moment, Callum despaired at the thought of having to fill the boat again, until he found himself already on the shore, the soft sand welcoming his feet. He found the spade exactly where it had been before, and when he resumed his shovelling, was delighted to find the job half done. He again felt incredibly vigorous as though he would never tire of this or any other task, even that of Sisyphus. Was he cheating death as the founder and first king of Corinth had done? Inspired and bursting with power, he shovelled sand like a machine.

'That's great, Callum,' said Barachiel. 'Brilliant. Keep going. We're nearly there. It's nearly done.'

'Go Callum,' said Ron. 'You're killing it.'

'I told you to be quiet,' said Barachiel to Ron. 'Don't distract him.'

'I was trying to cheer him on,' said Ron. 'Encourage him, you know?'

'Shut up, Ron!'

Callum heard the exchange between Barachiel and Ron but was not at all diverted from the job at hand. Soon the boat seemed full, but to be sure he continued shovelling. Then suddenly, the spade was gone. The boat had also vanished, as had the beach, and the sea. Callum gasped and started on the floor of the hospital spasming as though shocked by electricity. A heavy hand fell on him.

Barachiel said, 'You made it, Callum. You did it.'

Scarcely able to believe what had happened, to extract the real from the imagined, Callum reached for his shoulder. At the point where the Sorcerer's tusk had pierced his flesh, he discovered his skin, his bone, and some gritty dust. There was no pain. 'What happened to the tusk?' He looked at Barachiel. 'You took it out.'

'We did it together.'

'I don't understand.'

'Join the club,' said Ron.

Callum turned to face his friend. 'Where were you before? During the swarm. Where were you?'

Ron had no time to answer because Callum remembered Ande. Scrambling to his feet—he'd seen the empty bed—he felt a rush of fear. 'Where's Ande?'

'I don't know,' answered Barachiel and Ron in unison.

'What do you mean? Where is she?'

He looked around quickly, searching for someone to ask. A nurse. An orderly. A doctor. Anyone. 'Where is she?'

'Calm down, Callum.'

Callum stared at Barachiel. 'What's there to be calm about? Where's Ande? She was here during the swarm, and I saw her when I was fighting the sorcerer or maybe after. I don't know, but I heard her voice. She was okay. Not hurt, but, but…help me find her. Please.'

Walking away from the treatment cubicle, Callum noticed the dead insects covering the floor. Alerted by the crunch of their lifeless bodies under his shoes, he was stunned and confused as though he'd just come out of a coma, which was not far from the truth. While he fought the Sorcerer, there was nothing outside the death-cage capsule of air in which they battled. After the fight, he didn't know what was happening as he wrestled against the death which stood behind unconsciousness.

He stopped and turned back to face Barachiel and Ron. 'So, you don't know where Ande is? Or if she's okay?'

Barachiel shook his head. Ron shrugged. Callum threw his hands in the air, exasperated. 'Now what?'

'Now Ron and I have some unfinished business,' said Alix.

'Where'd you spring from?' said Ron.

'From under the same rock as you, you pusillanimous pussball.'

Ron hopped over to Alix, getting right up in her smart-mouthed face, breathing what he hoped were noxious fumes all over her. 'How long did it take you to come up with the alliterative masterpiece?'

'Let's finish this Ron,' said Alix, holding her ground, seemingly unperturbed by halitosis. 'I'm sick of this ridiculous dance and I owe you for Twistix.'

Ron threw a punch which Alix blocked, then countered with her own. Ron dodged it with a neat feint to the right. He kicked at her knees, then quickly at her stomach. She pushed his foot down with both hands, stepped back and threw another punch at Ron's head. He ducked, stepped inside, hit her in the stomach a few times making her grunt. She retaliated with an extravagant spinning roundhouse kick which Ron evaded easily.

'I thought you said you didn't want to dance.'

Alix looked angry. Veins seemed to be popping and pulsing all over her body. Her skin had darkened to match her mood. Ron seemed relaxed, as chipper and cheeky as ever. He was playing with her.

'You know Alix,' said Ron. 'I liked you. I really did. From that first time I smashed you through the window at St. Mary's. I liked your style. I thought we had something.'

'You're an idiot.'

'So, now we're going for grade three insults? Is that what we're doing?' Ron moved away from Alix, keeping his eyes on her the whole time. He flexed his wings briefly, giving them a bit of air. 'Okay,' he said eventually. 'Let's do this, stick insect.'

On hearing that woeful excuse for a slur, Callum laughed out loud.

'Shut up in the gallery, thanks,' said Ron.

Taking advantage of the distraction, Alix launched herself at Ron, and this time she connected. It was only a glancing blow, but enough to knock him off his feet. He quickly scrambled upright and adopted his best, most menacing fighting pose. 'Okay, Alix,' he said. 'Enough playing around.'

Ron marched towards Alix, inviting a flurry of punches and kicks from her, all of which he defended, until at last when she tired, he moved in for the kill. It was the fastest punch Callum had even seen and shocking in its force. Alix flew backwards, crashing across desks, scattering stuff everywhere. Ron wasted no time with his pursuit, leaping on top of Alix as she shook off the effects of his mighty strike. Before she could recover properly, Ron was on top of her with his hands around her throat. She squirmed beneath him, but he was irresistible. Ron squeezed tighter and tighter, pressing his thumbs into her carotid, breaking the skin, causing her to scream, then she was gone.

Ron stood, chest heaving, wings extending and retracting slowly, like he was trying to cool his body down.

'That was impressive,' said Barachiel.

'You didn't think to throw your hand in?' said Ron.

'It was a private matter between you and Alix, right? It wasn't my place to get involved.'

'Not your place,' said Ron. 'You just bought yourself a front-row seat and enjoyed the show.'

'Something like that.'

Ron glared at Barachiel.

'Hey fellas,' said Callum. Caught up in the action, he'd forgotten Ande, but now in the calm, she rushed back in. He turned to Barachiel. 'Where is she? Where's Ande?'

'Let's have a look around. She can't have gone too far in her condition.'

'Unless someone took her,' said Callum.

'Who would've taken her,' said Ron. 'And where?'

Callum threw his hands in the air, raised his voice. 'I don't know but she's not here. That's what I know. She's gone.'

Chapter Thirty-Three

They searched the hospital for an hour, traipsing through a thick carpet of crushed bugs from corner to corner, floor to floor. Doctors, nurses, and police were everywhere: a new infestation, this time of emergency workers. Callum asked everyone he met, but even those few who understood what he was saying offered no hope. They didn't know Ande. Hadn't seen her. Couldn't be expected in the current circumstances to help look for one person. So sorry. For Callum, it was like a tragic game of charades repeating ad nauseum.

Finally, abandoning the quest, Callum sat on the flat roof of the hospital staring out across the city to the shimmering Bosphorus. Ron and Barachiel were with him, silently comforting.

'I don't get it,' said Callum.

A breeze kicked up, pushing some litter across the roof. Callum watched a cigarette carton rolling towards the edge. It hit the raised lip and came to a sudden stop. A metaphor for his life. Pushed along by circumstances, pulled in one direction then another, before being flipped. No control. No choices to be made. Nothing but resignation to malevolent, invisible powers. He'd tried to resist being sucked into the chaos which reigned outside his safe, predictable, and rational world. He tried.

Callum stood, walked over to the cigarette packet, and picked it up. The plain packaging, growing in favour around the world under legislative stricture, showed an image of bare feet. In focus, attached to an unseen corpse lying on a stainless-steel bed, the big toe of one foot was adorned by a medical tag with a date on it. Unnaturally coloured, the foot warned smokers of death. He flicked the packet over the edge, turned to face his patient companions. 'It's a filthy habit,' he said.

'Are you going to be okay, Callum?' said Ron.

'I don't know.'

'Callum,' said Barachiel in a voice smoked with fatherly concern. 'I'm leaving soon, but we need to talk before I go.'

'Of course, we do.'

'That,' said Ron, 'would be my cue to leave. And you're welcome.'

After Ron disappeared in a puff of resentful smoke, Barachiel said. 'You need to understand what happened when you fought the Sorcerer.'

Callum shook his head. 'I need to find Ande,' he said. 'My understanding can wait.'

'Be patient and be prepared.'

'I'm not in the mood for riddles, Barachiel.'

The angel stepped closer to Callum, reached out to touch his arm. Callum looked up at him, saw the boundless kindness illuminating his eyes. 'I don't care about any of this,' he said. 'I just want to know where Ande is.'

'We can't find her.'

'Thanks for stating the bloody obvious.'

'Let me tell you a story.'

'No! No stories. No riddles.'

Callum knew he was yelling at Barachiel, but he couldn't help it. It was unfair and futile, but his heart was breaking with anxiety about Ande. Already eroded by the fight with the Sorcerer, Callum's strength to stand against his own anger was flooding away, like water through the burst walls of a dam. 'Sorry,' he said.

Barachiel placed his hands on Callum's shoulders, infusing him with something warm and comforting. 'This is an old Turkish parable. A police officer sees a drunken man intently searching the ground near a lamppost and asks him the goal of his quest. The inebriate replies that he is looking for his car keys, and the officer helps for a few minutes without success. Then he asks whether the man is certain that he dropped the keys near the lamppost.

'*No*, replies the man. *I lost them somewhere across the street.*

'*Why are looking here then?* asks the surprised and irritated officer.

'*The light is much better here,* says the intoxicated man, beaming as though he's a genius.'

'I don't get it,' said Callum. 'I mean, I get the parable. It's looking in an obvious place or doing something easy even though you know doing it the hard way will give you better results. Or if you look where you actually lost something, you're more likely to find it.'

With an eternal patience, Barachiel watched

Callum, waiting for the penny to drop.

'She wasn't there. We looked everywhere. She wasn't on the bed, or under it. We looked. She wasn't anywhere around there. Not on that floor. Not—'

'You're missing the point, Callum.'

Callum glared at his huge angelic friend. 'Do you know what I think you should do with the point?'

'All right, Callum.' Barachiel held up his hands in mock surrender. 'There's no need to be rude. Let's talk about the Sorcerer.'

'Yes. Let's,' said Callum, knowing how churlish he sounded, detesting the petulance in voice.

'The obvious question to ask is did it really happen?' Barachiel paused, but Callum didn't want to encourage him. 'You first saw the alpha beetle which you recognized from the rug shop in the earlier swarm. When the alpha beetle here at the hospital transformed into the Sorcerer you remembered what I told you, and although at first taken off guard, you quickly recovered and fought him. And you fought well.'

Callum shrugged. Barachiel waited.

Callum caved in. 'The things I saw, the visions, as I kept switching between the hospital room and the island. Was that real?'

'The magic the Sorcerer used on you was hallucinogenic. It is not unusual for angels and demons as well to use these methods when fighting each other. The curse continued after he died because although you defeated him, he left a final poisonous and potentially fatal spike in your body. His broken-off tusk. That's when the magic intensified. There's always a physical battle, Callum, but this is only a small part of what is really going on in the world. The real fight is spiritual and it's all about choices. I couldn't directly intervene to save you unless you were prepared to stay in the fight. You had to choose to continue. You had to choose life.'

'But when I was in la-la land, I was on a beach, and I was safe.'

'You thought you were safe. You weren't even on the beach. You saw the beach, but you were in the sea.'

'I wasn't safe.'

Barachiel shook his head. 'You needed to get to the shore. That's why I kept encouraging you, kept giving you instructions and once you'd filled the boat with sand—'

'So that it couldn't be washed away by the incoming tide. It was too heavy.'

'It wouldn't have lasted for long, but long enough for us to finish the journey of healing.'

'And the point of it all?' said Callum. 'What does it mean?'

'It means there's no turning back for you now, Callum. Do you remember our conversation in your hotel room on the night of your awakening? When you first experienced something which was utterly impossible to deny, even for you? Do you remember all our subsequent conversations?'

'There was, there is so much to get my head around,' said Callum. 'Too much. I'm still trying to figure it all out, and what about the Sorcerer? Is he dead?'

'The tusk with which he tried to kill you was not

only the symbol of his cursed existence, but also its source. When you snapped it in half, you ended both the curse and his life.'

'What happens now?' said Callum. 'I don't know what to do or what I'm supposed to do. My mind is like an overflowing trash can.'

Barachiel smiled. 'Take your time, son of God. Take your time.'

The angel disappeared without another word, leaving Callum bemused but gratefully distracted, albeit temporarily. With Barachiel gone, fear rushed back in with an image of Ande, alone, hurt, and frightened, swirling in the dark centre of Callum's anxiety. Where was she? Was she okay?

When he hit the hospital lobby, the elevator doors slid open to present another level of mayhem. Callum could only see minor injuries among the wounded, but there were scores of medical staff flitting about, furiously triaging them. They buzzed like bees, an army of pollinators, landing on flowers, before flying off to others, as they assessed each patient, deciding the next step in their treatment. Dead insects, broken glass and other debris covered the floor. In the middle of the nurse and doctors, Callum noticed splashes of blood twirling on the blue and white dance floor of their uniforms.

Callum's phone rang. For a second, he forgot where it was. Still in his pocket and surprisingly still charged, he pulled it out, swiping up to answer.

'Everything all right, now?' Pitch's voice betrayed nothing. It was as though their previous conversation had not been suddenly put on hold for the last three hours. Three hours. No sign of Ande. As much as he couldn't stand the thought of it, Callum had to concede the obvious. What was obvious? She had been taken.

'Callum?' Pitch interrupted his thoughts. 'Are you there?'

'Yeah, sorry.'

'What's going on?'

Callum stepped out of the lift, finally free to move forward through the knot of distressed humans. 'It's a real mess here.'

'Another swarm?'

'Not just another swarm, mate. The mother of all swarms. All five floors of the hospital are wrecked and there are hundreds of wounded.' Callum weaved his way to the side of the lobby where he spotted a space against the wall. There were police at the door who were not allowing anyone to enter or leave, by the look of things.

'What about the alpha beetle?'

What about the alpha beetle? Who cared about the alpha beetle? Callum was so sick of the sight of bugs that he decided he would have to go to live in Antarctica or find a relatively safe volcano to call home. There was nowhere else on earth he could go to escape them. 'Dead.'

'Mate, you sound as flat as a tack. You nailed the alpha beetle. Where's the manly scream of victory? Are you okay?'

'I'm…' Callum couldn't finish his sentence. A few words came to mind, but none of them properly articulated what he was feeling. He felt numb and hopeless.

'You're what?'

'I'm a mess, really.' He pressed his back against the wall and slid down into an uncomfortable squat. 'This has been...' What? A nightmare? A catastrophe? 'This has been the most exhausting and confusing experience I've ever had, and I've had a few now. Ever since I met you on the flight to Thailand, my life has lurched from one earthquake to another.'

Pitch laughed. 'I've been accused of pride—especially by my wife of late—but if I were to accept responsibility for all the weird stuff that's gone on since we met, I'd be in danger of blasphemy.'

'I didn't say I blamed you,' said Callum, standing and shaking his legs in turn to expel the pins and needles.

'Take it easy,' said Pitch, struggling with a residual chuckle. 'It's all good. I reckon you just need a break. When are you coming home?'

'Next week.'

'Great.'

Callum studied the door, trying to figure out how the system was working. People in uniform with passes were being allowed in, but no one else. Callum could see a mob of journalists outside, heaving behind a police barricade.

Pitch continued, overriding the silence. 'There's no need to get into it straight away when you get back, but come April, you definitely want to check out the dragonflies in the Northern Territory.'

Seeing a path through the people, leading almost all the way to the front door, Callum decided to leave. He stepped carefully, over and around obstacles of limbs, bodies, and medical equipment. Checking out more bugs was the very last thing he wanted to do. He'd rather be locked in a room and forced to watch reality TV non-stop for a month. 'Pitch, I'm a bit over insects. You do know what's been going on here, right?'

'There's evidence of a coming plague.'

'Like I said, mate, I'm had enough bugs to last the rest of my life.' The mention of the word plague reminded Callum about the six plagues which were supposed to emanate from the Sorcerer's Tusk. The beetles were obviously the first, and thanks to Callum, also the last.

Undeterred by Callum's lack of enthusiasm or even interest, Pitch continued, 'Have you been to the Top End?'

'No.'

'There you go. You call yourself a hotel reviewer, aficionado, guru. You've prob—'

'No.'

'—you've probably been everywhere else, so—'

'No Pitch. I'm not in that game anymore and I'm done with bugs. I'm serious.'

At the door Callum explained who he was, why he was at the hospital, and gave assurances that he was not injured. The door was opened for him, and as he stepped through, the media glob, surged as one, like a pride of hungry lions with prey in their sights.

'Come on, Callum,' said Pitch. 'Come to Darwin with me. See this epic plague of dragonflies. It'll be incredible. The best experience of your life and the weather up there in the dry is perfect.'

'See you, Pitch. I'll give you a call when I get back Down Under.'

Callum hung up, shoved his phone back in his pocket, looked for a way through the scrum of microphones and camera. The mix of skin, bone, metal and plastic, and the sizzle of their energy made him shiver. They reminded him of insects. Once he got close to them, they mostly lost interest in him, but one female journalist beckoned him nearer.

Hoping she would grant him safe passage through if he answered her questions, Callum obliged.

'How are you? Are from America?'

Funny how all westerners overseas were assumed to be Americans. 'No,' said Callum. 'I'm from Australia. Can you let me through please?'

'Can you tell us what happened in there?'

'It was an insect swarm. Can I get through?'

'How many insects do you think?'

Callum smiled for the first time, he realized, in several hours, maybe longer. 'A lot.' He figured more inane questions were sure to follow, but he'd had enough. 'Let me through now,' he said to a policeman nearby. Stony-faced silence met him, so he repeated himself. 'I want to go, let me out of here.' He gestured. 'Let me go.'

'Were you hurt by the insects?' said the journalist in a typically stubborn display.

'They nearly killed me, lady.' He stared at her, as the policeman shifted the barricade slightly to allow passage. 'I almost died.'

The woman stared back, mouth open, as she was forced to shuffle backwards.

On the other side, Callum looked up and down the street, searching for a taxi to take him back to the hotel. Then he saw her. Ande. Her unmistakable afro crowned her knees, around which her still bandaged arms were wrapped. He ran to her.

'Ande!' he cried, falling to his knees beside her. 'Ande? Are you all right? I thought I'd lost you.'

Ande raised her head, just enough to turn it sideways. 'Take me home please, Callum.'

Grabbing her in an exuberant an awkward hug, Callum whispered in Ande's ear. 'I love you, Ande. Of course, I'll take you home.'

A Muddy Red River

Shane Archer is solid, dependable and reliable while his younger brother, Rob, is reckless, selfish and unpredictable. Never close during their formative years, and further divided by distance in adulthood, they live disconnected lives until the corkscrew of life pits them on a collision course. They love, they laugh, they lose and with broken hearts and messed up lives they find strength in the women they love and in their family. Could each be the agent of salvation for the other, or will they be torn apart forever? *A Muddy Red River* traces the course of the lives of broken people who discover power to overcome adversity.

Love Sick Love

Angus has battled an obsession with sex throughout his adult life. Although outwardly a model husband and father with a respectable life and a well-paying job, he has a shameful secret life which he has become highly skilled at hiding.

Cassy is married to Angus and has no idea about his secret life. In fact, with her own worries she has been pulling away from him, emotionally and physically which is making his behaviour worse. Although she does not know it, Cassy is fanning the flames of an inferno which threatens to destroy their marriage.

Lovesickness: the eternal bane of humanity, the inescapable affliction which we simultaneously crave and fear. For Angus and Cassy, already in the thirteenth year of their marriage, the painful journey to true happiness has only just begun.

Lovesick is a brutally honest and confronting story of love, sexual obsession and hope.

Scorpion's Breath

Hotel reviewer, Callum Steele travels to Mai Sai in the north of Thailand where he becomes unwillingly tangled in a centuries old demonic feud. As his world is turned upside down by a series of bizarre and inexplicable events, Callum finds support from his flirtatious colleague, his friend the entomologist, and a mischievous and smart mouth demon named Ron. Will Callum lose his mind or embrace his awakening? Is this the end of Callum Steele or just the beginning? And what the hell is that stuff coming out of the mouth of the giant scorpion?

Other books by D. A. Cairns

The Devil Wears a Dressing Gown

Satan. Lucifer, Beelzebub, Abaddon: whatever he is called, the Devil means different things to different people. For some he is real, for others, he is merely a personification of evil. Many people deny the existence of the devil even though they profess to believe in God. Some say he is the source of evil, while others think blaming the Devil for the evil deeds of men is just an excuse.

The devil has been caricaturized to such an extent in popular culture that he is no longer taken seriously. Featuring an eclectic collection of new and previously published stories, and inspired by C. S. Lewis' masterful work, *The Screwtape Letters*, *The Devil Wears a Dressing Gown* is a revelation of, and an examination of, the many faces of evil.

Ashmore Grief

The story of an illegal immigrant who arrives in Australia by boat and goes on to become the Prime

Minister. The story of a woman at the end of hope who is rescued from a smuggler's boat only to become enslaved. The story of a man who has lost his way, and needs a cause for which to fight, and a reason to live. These three lives collide in Ashmore Grief: an epic tale of struggle. The struggle to survive, the struggle to belong and the struggle for purpose.

Loathe Your Neighbor

David Lavender is a man with a talent for making bad decisions. In his fortieth year on planet Earth, a dangerous restlessness overwhelms him, and, as his marriage crumbles, and a dispute with his neighbour escalates, he responds to theses crises in his life with characteristic folly. Frozen out by his mysteriously indifferent wife, Lilijana. Baited by his cantankerous stepson, Tomo, and alternatively supported and rebuked by his two best mates, Matt and Chalkie, will David successfully negotiate the minefield which his own discontent constructed, or will he destroy himself and everyone around him?

Devolution

2112 AD. For the sixty years following the Intercontinental War, Asia has been ruled by a delicately balanced coalition representing three major tribes;

Newtonians, Deists and Adonites. The murders of two senators in separate incidents in Asia's capitol, Mumbay, now threatens the fragile peace that exists among them. Police Chief Inspector, Adrian Jacobssen; recently widowed, world weary and cynical with nothing left of value in his life except his job, sets out to find those responsible for the murders. His failure might result in another war. The key could be the mysterious disappearance of the eighteen-year-old children of the murdered senators. Unaware that Jacobssen is looking for them, 3-11-15 and Veena, together with a third friend Joshua, have left on a journey which will test the strength of their friendships by plunging them into a crucible of tribulation. They hold the fate of the world in their hands but don't even know it. Will Jacobssen find them in time to save them, solve the murders and prevent war? In Devolution, romance and friendship, fear and respect, faith and folly, truth and lies all confuse in a future world which no one would dare imagine.

I Used to be an Animal Lover

Why do some people love animals so much? Why don't some people love animals as much as you? Have you had both good and bad experiences with animals? Can you imagine a world without them?

Don't be fooled by the title. I Used to be an Animal Lover boldly goes where no book on animals has ever gone. From the bottom of the ocean to outer space, and deep into the human psyche. D.A. Cairns explains exactly why animals can be both our best friends and our worst enemies.

With a terrific collection of animal quotes and idioms, D.A. Cairns uses humour, imagination and personal experience to show you the very best of the animal kingdom in this superficial and unscientific zoological memoir. Will you ever look at animals the same way?